MW01688427

Goddess of Rain

Part 1 of The Lost Gods Series

By Jane Frkovich

Copyright 2022 Jane Frkovich

ISBN: # 978-0-9950630-5-1

ALL RIGHTS RESERVED. This book contains material protected under International and Federal Copyright Laws and Treaties. Any unauthorized reprint or use of this material is prohibited. No part of this book may be produced or transmitted in any form or by any means, electronic or mechanical, including photocopying, recording, or by any information storage and retrieval system without express written permission from the author/publisher

Chapter One

Today, the best thing that's happened to me all year took place when Colton Chase accidentally swiped my arm with his while we were in line together for frozen yogurt. No, that's not quite true. We weren't in line together. I was there in line by myself, whiling away the time thinking about him, as I often do, when I turned around and saw he was really there right behind me. I was so startled, I flung my arm up and hit his bicep while letting out an embarrassingly loud, "Oh my God!"

So, in actuality, I swiped him with my arm. But what happened afterwards was all on him. He didn't ignore me, he didn't stare at me with disgust, and he didn't laugh in my face. Instead, he looked at me with the gravest concern, brought his hand gently to my forearm, and said in his deep, calm voice, "Zoe, are you okay?"

That moment was everything. *Zoe. Concerned face. Are you okay. Hand on arm.* Colton Chase knew who I was and he was being nice to me.

In a reflexive moment, Colton Chase responded with kindness instead of being a jerk, and that is a surprisingly rare quality in humans, as anyone who takes public transit knows. Most importantly, when Colton touched my arm, a river of warm electricity ran through me. It filled my being with happiness and lightness.

I smiled and nodded my head insanely by way of reply. He smiled back and then returned to reading the yogurt menu board. But before he turned his gaze away, his eyes briefly met mine, and I could swear there was something there behind his eyes. They sparkled in a friendly way, but for a brief second there was something else that I can only describe as *a knowing.*

I'm sitting cross-legged in the park near my house sucking on my frozen yogurt spoon. It's a warm day so I threw on a pair of shorts and a sweatshirt. As I absorb the last remnants of raspberry cheesecake yogurt with blue chocolate M&Ms, I pull out my phone to check Colton's Instagram.

I do this three-times a day. No, that's not true, I do it six times a day. To be completely honest, that might not be right either because I check his feed first thing in the morning, throughout the day, and last thing before I go to sleep, sometimes checking several times until I fall asleep so that I wake up in the morning still clutching my phone.

I don't know why I lie about this, it's perfectly obvious that I am a full-on stalker of Colton Chase. Not the criminal kind, but the kind that everyone is when they are crushing hard on someone. No one likes to admit it, but we all do it, and chances are someone is doing it to you at any given time. Normal people can do this in a way that is harmless to the intended. That's what makes us not criminals.

Sometimes I wonder though, if I am normal. If my crush has gone from obsession to *Obsession* with a capital "O." I'm not worried I'll bring harm to Colton. I'm worried that I will bring harm to myself. Spending time thinking about someone is probably okay if you can indulge yourself in that for a while and then go back to living your own life. The thing is, I'm not sure that I have my own life. I'm kind of just there.

I don't feel tethered to the earth. I am one year out of high school and I'm working at a boring, pointless job. I have no boyfriend, my dad's been gone for a long time, and to top it all off, my mom fell off a cruise ship and died not long after I graduated from high school. She was on a trip with a man she had recently met on a dating app. I was fully encouraging her to take the trip and enjoy herself. I was all, "Go, it will be fun, what can happen on a cruise ship? There's 700 people there!" Of course, like all online daters, our main worry was being fooled with a really old profile picture.

Oh my God, Colton's posted a selfie of himself in line at the frozen yogurt store! You can see the back of my head! It's our first selfie together! What was he really thinking when he saw me in line, what did he really want to say?

"Honey, I'm so happy to see you."

I hear a voice break through my thoughts. I gasp in surprise and almost drop my phone. I look up and see the hem of a diaphanous blue maxi dress.

The fabric is so pretty and looks way too nice to be casually thrown on for a trip to the park. I let my eyes travel upwards to see who this person is who seems to know me, and when I get to her face, I stop and freeze. My mouth drops open and I can't find my voice. My breathing is coming in rapid, shallow breaths and I don't have enough air to get the words out. I close my eyes and focus on taking deep breaths. My breathing slows and I open my eyes. At last I am able to speak and I say in shock, "Mom?"

Suddenly I am in an embrace of filmy blue and the scent of citrus. There are kisses all over my face and long black hair brushing over my eyes so it's difficult to see. Finally, I say, "Is it really you?"

She grabs me and begins the whole kissing routine again. I feel her tears splash down my face and know that it is her. The hardness that I have held around myself for years like a shell begins to ripple in places and crack. There is enough flexibility that I can bend and soon I allow myself to melt into her embrace. I hug her back and feel a little bit of the heaven I must have felt when she used to hold me against her shoulder as a baby. I am secure and tethered with her on the ground.

"I have missed you so much," she says with a beaming smile. She blinks away the tears and her lashes look incredibly long and lush. Are those false eyelashes? Did my mom stop and get lash extensions before coming to find me?

I stare at her and she looks amazingly beautiful. My mom had always been a pretty woman but the person before me now is full-on vixen. She had been an anchorwoman before she had me and had kept her polished TV prettiness while I was growing up. She had worn her hair in her anchor bob, minus the regular maintenance and hairspray. Her style was middle-grade mom, just stylish enough not to be embarrassing, and nothing sexy so as not to mortify me. Mom 2.0 has thrown that rule book out the window.

The woman before me has raven black hair cascading in loose waves down her back; two side locks strategically framing her chest. Did Mom always have a chest like that? A subtle hint of cleavage peaks out of the top of her dress. The fabric skims her body so her small waist is accented, and a clear S-curve of a figure is there for all to see. What had she been doing with her time, daily Pilates and plastic surgery?

"What the hell, Mom?" I say, feeling a little cross. "You fell off a cruise ship! What are you doing here? What happened? And what did you do to your hair? Are those extensions?"

It is the part about the extensions that seems to irk her the most. "These aren't extensions," she replies while smoothing down a tousled wave. "I can grow *hair,"* she says with a touch of irritation.

I sigh and try again. "Mom, you were dead. You and Zeus DeMarco fell into the water. There was a huge storm and they never found your bodies. But there is no way that you could have survived that. How did you get here?"

My mom reaches for my hand and looks at me with thoughtful eyes. She seems to be taking a moment to compose her thoughts before answering.

"I didn't really fall off a cruise ship," she says in a slow, measured voice like she is dumbing something down for a toddler.

"I was…" She hesitates as she searches for the word. "I was sort of abducted. By Zeus."

I gasp and tightly clasp her hand. "He kidnapped you?!" I say with alarm. "Where is he? How did you get away?"

My mother furrows her brow as she looks at my distress. No Botox there. Yet somehow, she looks way younger than when I last saw her. She purses her lips and I can tell she is still trying to find the words to tell me something.

"It's not like that," she says quietly and slowly. "It's too complicated to go into right now and we really don't have much time. The world is not very healthy and I have to get you out of here. Trust me on this, okay? Let's go home and have a nap and then I can take you some place safe."

My mother is talking gibberish. I guess it is no surprise considering the trauma she has suffered. Kidnapped! I know she isn't making much sense, but I am concerned that Zeus is still out there looking for her.

"Mom," I say, "how did you get away? Are you still in danger?"

"No, sweetheart," she says, "Zeus is fine with this. He knows I'm coming to get you. But we really need to get home and get some sleep so we can get a move on. Are you still living in our house?"

My mother is tugging at my hand and trying to get me to walk in the direction of our house. If she trusts her kidnapper, she must have some kind of Stockholm Syndrome. Maybe he is using her to kidnap me too. This guy is sick; he is probably putting together a harem of mothers and daughters.

"Mom," I say, while trying to hide the panic in my voice, "I'm really glad you're home, but I think you need to see a doctor. Just to get checked out because you've been through a lot. After that, we can go home and sleep if you want to. Let's go now to the hospital."

My mom looks at me and shakes her head. She puts her arm around me and tries to guide me in the direction of our house. She is looking straight ahead with an expression of determination. I put my feet into the ground and I refuse to move. My mother pulls harder and I feel the panic rise in me. I want to run away from this crazy scenario, but at the same time I have intense fear that my mother will disappear and I will never see her again. I am overwhelmed with feelings and the panic inside me is threatening to explode.

"I don't feel comfortable going anywhere with you, Mom!" I say in a Minnie Mouse on speed voice. "Please let's go to the doctor! Please, let's go to the police!"

Mom stops her pushing and dragging and comes to stand in front of me. She reaches her hand out and softly strokes my cheek.

"Oh, honey," she says, "I didn't mean to scare you. It's so difficult to tell you everything. I was hoping we could just have a nap and then I could make it clear to you when we woke up. But I'll do my best now. Do you want to take an Ambien first to calm down? I brought some with me."

Of course, she has drugs with her. Zeus probably has her primed with drugs all the time to get her to do what he wants. I shake my head no and work hard to steady my breathing to give her a chance to talk.

"I was taken by Zeus," my mother says slowly, and then pauses. She looks at me expectantly.

"I know," I say, "you told me that."

"By Zeus," she says, and pauses again with a slow encouraging nod of her head. Her eyes are large and unblinking as she stares at me.

"I know, Mom," I say, "you told me that." She continues to be silent and stare into my eyes, like she is willing me to understand. Suddenly, it dawns on me what she is trying to say.

"Mom," I say mimicking the slow way she has been talking to me, "do you mean Zeus, like the Greek god? The god of fire and sky?"

My mother's face breaks into a smile, "Yes! Zeus!" she says with elation. "He's the god of the sky, not fire, but I can see your confusion because he uses thunderbolts. Thunderbolts and lightning go together, and lightning causes fire, so I can see how you would make that connection. Yes, I was pursued by a Greek god," she says with a little laugh.

My mother has completely lost touch with reality. When I was younger, I knew the day would come when our roles would reverse and I would have to take care of her. I didn't expect that day to come until both of us were sporting gray hair. Hopefully, with therapy she can get back to a place where she can deal with reality, but for now I think the kindest thing would be to go along with her delusion and get some helpful information from her. Maybe if we go home and have this nap she is hankering after, I can get her to go to the doctor with me. If her kidnapper Zeus should suddenly appear, I have my phone and I can call the police.

"Mom, let's go have a nap. A sleep is a good idea," I say. My mother smiles at me and we begin to amble along. I offer her my arm and she takes it. I want to be able to grab her quickly in case she should suddenly decide to bolt.

"Soooo," I say, while giving her a sidelong glance. "When Zeus first…took you…how did that happen? We thought you had drowned."

My mother is now humming and strolling along beside me like she is lost in a pleasant reverie. My question remains unanswered for a couple of beats, and then she seems to rouse herself to attention.

"His brother helped us get away," she says amiably, as we walk the short distance to our house.

His brother? More than one person was in on this?

"Who is his brother?" I ask, hoping to get a name I can use.

"You know," she says in her upbeat tone, "Poseidon."

Sigh. "You mean with the trident," I say, closing my eyes in exasperation.

"Yes, honey, Poseidon with the trident. Who else? Although he's okay with being called Neptune too. He made that big storm appear so we could disappear with no one noticing."

"Zeus is able to make people disappear?" I say, trying to sound casual.

"Sweetheart, Zeus is able to do a lot of things. Remember the story of Leda and the swan? How he turned into a swan?"

In the story, Leda sleeps with Zeus while he is disguised as a swan. No issue of consent there at all. Eyeroll. This guy has really done a number on her. I decide to test the waters and see how deep her affection for him goes.

"So, Mom, I'm confused about your relationship with Zeus. You said he sort of kidnapped you. What's going on between you two?"

My mom's happy reverie seems to break and her mouth narrows into a grim line. I feel bad for making the smile on her face disappear. She steals a look at me and then she seems to rally.

"You know, the Greek gods are not really gods, they are a species," she says, as she daintily lifts the hem of her skirt so she can walk better. Her legs have a slight sheen to them, like they have been freshly sprayed with coconut oil. "And they don't live here. They never have lived here permanently. Most of them anyway. They live on Olympus. It's a planet, not a mountain. They just like to visit Earth, and in ancient times they used to visit a lot because they like to…" My mother pauses and a pained look crosses her face. She shrugs her shoulders and continues, "They like to play with us. Kind of like cats and mice. We being the mice."

As she says this, my mother reminds me of her old self, the analytical reporter. If I didn't know any better, I would think she was speaking about well-researched fact. I remain silent in the hope that she will continue to talk to me in this way and give me some useful information.

"The Olympians have always looked to us for amusement. They like dating us too. They've been doing that since we could weave fabrics and sew clothes. Esthetics are important to them," my mother says. "Looked at one way, my story could be called a love story. You know, he saw me long ago, on the airwaves when I was still an anchor. They get them there. They monitor our electronics. He says he fell in love with me then." My mother looks wistful and a little sad.

"Then years later," she continues, "he saw me on Tinder and he wanted to meet me."

"They use our dating sites?" I say incredulously.

My mother looks over at me with a small smile. "Zoe, our whole planet is a dating site for them." We have arrived at the door to our home.

"Let's go inside and have that nap now," she says with a renewed cheerfulness. "Now might be a good time to take that Ambien."

She is right about that. I could use an Ambien. And a Tylenol, and a glass of wine, and a surgical grade sedative. The calm way my mother speaks about her utterly crazy situation is making me feel unbearably anxious. My chest is constricted and I feel I could throw-up my frozen yogurt at any moment. I wordlessly take the Ambien she offers and slip it under my tongue as we go inside.

Before the drug can take hold of my body and relax me into sleep, I feel compelled to say something to her.

"Mom," I begin, "can you just tell me, should we be worried about Zeus? Are you trying to escape him?"

My mother looks at me with a puzzled expression as she pulls back the covers to my bed. "No, honey, I'm not trying to escape him. We're on our way to meet him." She has a happy, expectant, and completely content expression on her face as she lies back on the bed and her mane of hair fans out prettily across the pillow.

"He's got a spaceship," she continues. "He's giving us a ride out of here. Earth doesn't have much time left."

Chapter Two

My mom is in a relationship with her boyfriend-turned-kidnapper and thinks he drives a spaceship. I have an elaborate fantasy life with my non-boyfriend and fellow frozen yogurt aficionado, who in my imagination drives a Ferrari with the top down so I can sit beside him with my hair blowing in the wind. I'm in no position to judge her.

In realty, I'm not sure what kind of car Colton Chase drives because I usually only see him out walking. Once, I saw him getting onto a bicycle. He's someone I spot in glimpses here and there and I've had to fill in the blanks on who he really is with a mixture of stealth observation, rumor, and totally unfounded beliefs.

He came into my life a few months after my mom fell off the cruise ship when he suddenly appeared in my neighborhood. He has been a fixture ever since. When I say "came into my life," I should clarify — this has been completely one-sided up until now, and I am in no way part of his life.

But, he does somehow know my name. Maybe he saw it on my cup when I collected my coffee at Starbucks. Because of course, I first saw him at Starbucks. Let's just call Starbucks what it is — a human zoo for checking out hot people while they are freely interacting with the everyday folk. Hot people go out for coffee regularly and will even stand in line for it. Starbucks figured this out and built an empire around it.

I was sipping my green tea skinny latte, which looks like pureed kale with a skim of sea scum bubbles on top. It's a sad drink. I was in a sad place, having just lost my mom. I was alternately biting my nail and chewing on the string of my hoodie like the head case I was. The door pulled open, and I looked up out of social instinct to see the latest entrant to the zoo enclosure. I was met with the vision of Colton Chase, a man so gorgeous that my nihilism took a step back and a space opened in my heart and mind for him to reside. In that moment, he glanced in my general direction and I spit my hoodie string out in horror. I wanted to unzip my hoodie and show that yes, I am a girl, and there is a body under here. But I had thrown it on over my bra and wasn't even wearing a shirt underneath. I vowed then and there to at least wear a top when I left the house.

I seemed to see him a lot after that on my limited forays from home. He would be turning a corner as I was walking down the street. Or he would be casually chatting with other good-looking, well-dressed people in a corner of Starbucks. It appeared he was having business meetings with these people. I learned enough about Colton Chase through a Google search to know that he was some kind of wealthy tech entrepreneur and pretty famous in the tech community.

Apparently, he had sold his first company for a lot of money and was now working on plans to launch another enterprise. In my experience, twenty-something tech entrepreneurs are not generally the nerdy, socially awkward types people talk about in the media. The run of the mill tech entrepreneur looks like the run of the mill star in general, more Winklevoss than Zuckerberg. They are the kind of people that get to do all kinds of fun stuff. Rumor has it that Colton Chase was a DJ in Europe for six months and dated Taylor Swift. I knew he was trouble when he walked in. Maybe she wrote that for him.

I don't know what kind of company Colton Chase is launching but I think it is some kind of save-the-world technology. I've heard him say something like that when I've eavesdropped on his conversations at Starbucks. I know most tech entrepreneurs sell their concept by saying they are going to change the world, but I think Colton Chase is really trying to do something different.

I also think he may have a rescue dog because sometimes he walks down the street with a dog. But a genuine rescue dog, not the kind that happened to be born in the pound but was still a cute, utterly adorable and adoptable puppy when you got it. His dog has the look of a pup that has had a hard life with scars visible through its short fur, swelling on his shoulder blades that spoke of some kind of injury, and a Velcro-like attachment to his rescuer-owner.

Colton Chase is the kind of smart, handsome, sophisticated, rich man that my mother probably hoped I would end up with. She always said that those things are icing on the cake, but that the cake itself had to be made of kindness, compatibility, and unbridled love. I look at my mother peacefully resting on the bed and I wonder how she managed to go so far astray from her own ideals.

"You look like a mermaid, Mom," I say, as I climb into bed next to her.

"Mermaids are actually vile creatures," Mom says, without opening her eyes. "On Olympus they're called Sirens. They look all beautiful and enticing until they lure sailors to their death. Once that happens, the façade drops and they become old crones. But thank you, I know you meant it as a compliment."

"My mom is the object of affection of an actual god and I don't have even a regular boyfriend," I muse. My mom may be living in a fantasy world, but I do admire the way she has cast herself.

"You must have plenty of men asking you out," she says, as she opens her eyes and turns her head to me.

"Mom, I really don't. I was going to go to the animal shelter today to pick out some cats. Not just one, at least two or even three. I figured it was time to go full-on cat lady."

My mom sits up in bed and turns to look at me. She arches a perfectly groomed brow and gives me a head to toe scan with her eyes. Weren't her brows more on the skimpy side? Did she try microblading? After a moment, she says, "Have you tried a push-up bra?"

I laugh and say, "Mom, underwire is not going to transform me. I've just never been a siren."

"What did I tell you about Sirens?" she says, "They're all a façade, which is the same as attitude and good presentation. You are beautiful and always have been, you've just lacked the confidence. Remember what you said about every popular girl, ever?"

"She's not really that pretty?" I volunteer in a small voice. I suddenly feel very catty.

"That's right. Every popular girl has just mastered the skill of believing in herself and getting others to believe in her too. I don't really know how some girls have that figured out from an early age. I didn't have that kind of confidence until I started doing well at my job. That got lost for a while, but if there is one thing I can say about Zeus, it's that he completely believes in who I am."

I am pretty sure that Mom is in an abusive relationship, and this was all part of negging by Zeus, but I remain quiet. I feel the Ambien begin to take effect and cuddle into my mother.

"When we sleep, we are going to lucidly dream," she says, "Do you remember how I taught you to do that?"

"Of course," I say, "I do it all the time. Sometimes I don't like what I'm wearing in a dream and I change it."

"That reminds me," Mom says, "Could you change into something that makes you feel good, like a dress and a pair of nice shoes?"

"For sleeping?" I say, "What's wrong with what I'm wearing?" I am wearing a pair of gym shorts and an over-sized T-shirt.

"It's psychological," Mom says, "to help you feel confident in yourself. Go to sleep feeling glamorous and you'll wake up feeling that way. And put on a push-up bra."

I don't want to argue with her, and it seems a small thing to do to make her happy. It feels good to have a mother again to offer me advice, good or bad. I get up, put on a maxi dress, heels, and a ridiculous push-up bra and go back to bed. I nestle my head into my mother's shoulder and she reaches for my hand.

"Now when we dream," she says, "I want you to do as I tell you. We're going to have a flying dream. Just follow my instructions and you'll be fine."

"How can we have the same dream?" I say sleepily.

"We share a consciousness, all people do, at least those who have the same stardust as their base element. Have you heard of Carl Sagan?" she says.

"Sure, I have," I reply.

"Then maybe you remember him saying that when a star dies, its elements fall to Earth. We are all made of those elements, so we are all made of stardust. The catch is that not everyone has the same stardust in them. But when they do, they are inextricably linked and we share a consciousness. I've been doing a lot of training in this. When we dream if we think of each other, we will share consciousness in our dream, and then we can affect each other."

"Did you learn this in yoga?" I say.

"In a type of Olympian yoga, yes," she says.

"It shows," I say with a yawn. "I thought it was Pilates."

"Now, when we dream it's very important that you hold my hand, especially when we fly. We won't be able to get into the spaceship together if we aren't holding hands."

"The spaceship is picking us up while we dream?" I say, and that is all I remember before I drift into sleep.

I'm in a dark landscape of soaring fir trees. I'm running so fast that the trees become a blur of green. My mom is beside me, and she looks like a goddess herself with her dark hair flowing behind her, her liquid blue dress catching the wind and soaring outward like a cape. She turns to me with a beatific smile and outstretches her hand to me. My fingertips touch hers, and then our hands clasp. We are running as fast as we can under the night sky.

"Are you ready to fly?" Mom says.

"Yes," I say, "but I will need my hands so I can flap my arms."

"Don't do it that way," she says, "take big leaps with me and jump. We go higher and higher, until we are eventually flying. Okay, hold on tight so we can start."

I hold on tight to her hand and prepare to jump, when off to the side I see someone running alongside me. It's my friend from work, Brandon. With his long legs and cheerful demeanor, he has a puppy doggish quality as he trots along. I look at his cute face and I feel the way I always feel when I see Brandon — I feel happy. My mother turns to look at me and spots Brandon beside me.

"Who's that?" she says curiously.

"That's Brandon. Remember we used to play together when we were little?" I answer.

"Of course," she replies, "how is his mother? She was such a nice woman. She had the best recipe for chocolate tiger brownies."

"She's fine," I say, "still baking. Anyway, I hadn't talked to him in years, and then he and I got to know each other and became friends over the summer. He's home from university for the summer, and he has a summer job at the grocery store I work at."

"Is that your summer job too? What do you do there?" she asks.

"It's my *job*-job," I answer. "I don't go to university."

"WHAT?" My mother stumbles and then screeches to a halt. I theatrically get flung forward while still clutching her hand, my arm rippling back and forth like a strand of spaghetti.

"Why don't you go to university?" Mom says in dismay. The spaghetti arm slowly recoils and returns to normal. "I left money for your education. What happened?" she exclaims.

"Well, Mom, a lot of things happened. You fell off a cruise ship and died, for one! Except you didn't. It turns out you were traipsing around the universe with a retired Greek god. And getting what looks like some pretty major enhancements.

My mom looks at me with big, sad eyes. For a moment she morphs into an actual anime.

"Mom, can we maybe talk about this when we're not dreaming? I'm afraid you are going to change into a monster or a witch or something," I say.

"Yes, I know what you mean," she says. "For a moment when we stopped running, you started to turn into a ten-month-old infant."

My mother reaches for my hand and she looks like herself again. The new and improved version of her, not the one I grew up with.

"We don't need to talk about this now," she says, "but everything you see of me is what's always been there. It was just hidden for a really long time."

At that moment, Brandon comes walking up to us. "Hey," he says, with a nod at my mother and me.

"Hi, Brandon," I say back. My mother just stares at him.

"Don't talk to him," Mom says, "then he should go away."

"Yeah, the thing is, Mom, I don't want to be rude to him. He's a really nice guy."

"Honey, he isn't even there," she says, "this is your imagination. Just ignore him and he'll disappear and we can be on our way."

Brandon has gone over by a tree and appears to be kicking a small stone between his feet like a soccer ball. His head is down, but slightly cocked. I get the sense that he's listening in to our conversation unobtrusively.

"Mom, I hope you understand, but I feel guilty making him disappear like that. I've been dreaming about him a lot lately, and I think it's because we were friends when we were little, and it brings me back to that innocent time. When I hang out with him in my dreams, I wake up feeling happy. Just so you know, most days I do not wake up feeling happy. It's not right to just get rid of him like that because it's not convenient."

My mom looks at me with her sad eyes again. “Do you see a black cloud over my head that contains the words ‘mom guilt’?” Mom says.

“Yes, now that you say that, I do,” I say.

“Okay,” Mom says with a sigh, “what would you like to do with him?”

“Can he come with us?” I say, “Can I hold his hand and he can come flying with us?”

“Sure,” Mom shrugs, “it won’t make any difference when we get there. He’s not really there, so he won’t be going into the spaceship with us.”

I can’t figure out how my mom thinks this shared dream is going to lead to us going on a spaceship together. I hope she won’t be too disappointed when we wake up on my bed in high heels and dresses.

“Yo, Brandon!” I call, and Brandon comes trotting over.

“Do you want to come flying with us?” I say.

“I want to stand with you on a mountain,” Brandon sings at me. We don’t normally sing at each other but this is a dream.

“I want to bathe with you in the sea,” I join in singing with him.

I look over at my mother and she has morphed into a question mark.

“Truly Madly Deeply by Savage Garden,” I say to my mother. “We like the nineties together.”

She has changed back into herself, but continues to look at me with puzzlement.

Take my hand, Brandon, we’re going to go flying. The jumping kind,” I say. Brandon takes my hand and I take my mom’s hand. We start to run again as fast as we can. I’m the first to take a leap, my legs taking a few steps in the air before I land again.

Brandon and my mom glide along behind me. We take a few more steps and this time take a leap together. We are plunged powerfully into the sky, our airborne strides lengthening and keeping us afloat.

We touch briefly on the ground and then bounce into the air again, now so high that we are over the treetops. Like expert aviators, we catch a wind under our feet and begin to sail higher. We all adjust ourselves so we are lying flat and floating on air, our connected arms outstretched in one continuous wing. We find the wind and soar left and right, always synchronized in our movements. We are far above the trees now, the landscape looking like rolling hills of green with intermittent patches of light from the cities.

We go higher and higher until the air begins to thin and I find it difficult to catch my breath. I look over at Brandon and I can see from his slightly nervous expression that he is having the same difficulty. I look over at my mother and she doesn't look at all nervous. Her dark eyes have narrowed into a look of triumph and with her free hand, she seems to be reaching forward for something.

Then all at once, there is a clap of thunder in the sky that goes not just around me, but also through me. I feel like every molecule in me has exploded into a million little pieces, and then within a millisecond they come back together again. When I am once more in one piece, there is no air below me, but instead I feel a cold, hard surface beneath my outstretched body.

I flutter my eyes open, expecting to find that I have fallen off my bed onto the floor. Instead, I find myself alone in a cavernous room that is only partially lit. I take a deep breath and for a moment the air has a slightly acrid smell, like the smell after a summer forest fire. I shake my head and look confusedly at the dark around me. A low electric buzz can be heard in the air. The buzz is suddenly punctuated by a clamorous burst of metal sliding away from metal. I realize it's the sound of a door opening.

I am not alone anymore. Out of the shadows comes a beautiful young man of about my age. He has something in his hand and he seems to be pointing it at me. It's hard to tell what it is because it's dark in here and he's still far away.

Is it a gun, or maybe a knife? Is he going to hurt me? He gets closer and closer until I can make out the crystalline blue of his eyes. They crinkle into a smile and I can now see what he is holding. He's not pointing it at me; he's offering it to me. It's a golden, bejeweled chalice and he's holding it proudly like it's the Holy Grail.

Chapter Three

"Sit up and have a drink of this," the handsome man says, as he kneels down beside me. He smells of cinnamon buns. This is a sensory-rich dream. It must be the smell of the toaster strudel I made this morning and it wafted into my dream. It's like how I always dream of crashing waves when I need to pee.

"Do you wake up thirsty?" he says. "I always do. Combine that with air travel and you must be parched. Have a sip."

He's expecting me to drink out of this ornate cup that would look more at home in the Vatican. I take the cup because he is insistent, but hold it in my hand without drinking. The muscles in my thighs and glutes tense as I ready myself to kick him in the throat with my stiletto healed sandal if he should lunge at me. My sport was cheerleading and it gave me strong legs and a high kick. I was also raised by a single mother who thought it important that I know how to fight off an attacker. My muscle memory is itching to spring into action and stab at his vulnerable instep.

Before I make a move on his eyes I can't take back, I take another look at him. He is smiling at me and giving me little nods of encouragement. What is wrong with him? Does he really think I'm going to take a drink from a stranger? His smile turns into a slightly puzzled frown. I put the cup down beside me and absent-mindedly push it away from me. Now he looks affronted. He stands up and away from me.

"You don't feel like drinking?" he says in a haughty tone, as he arches his eyebrow. He snatches back the cup and starts inspecting it for damage. This guy is unbelievable. He's way too invested in his cup and he's a stranger trying to push strange drinks on me, and I'm the one who is inappropriate? He's also wearing no shirt and is dressed in some kind of man-skirt that reaches a few inches above his knees. Golden, shoulder-length hair frames his perfectly chiseled features, a light dusting of scruff covering his face. If he was handsome when he was smiling, annoyed he is smoldering.

I like dreaming about good-looking men, but this one is not being cooperative. I decide to take lucid control of the dream. Maybe I can change him into Colton Chase.

Nope, he's still the same mini-skirted, perturbed man. I flutter my eyelashes and twirl my hair flirtatiously. He gives me a slight sneer. My own subconscious is disgusted with me.

"This is ridiculous!" I say to myself. "Wake-up! Wake-up! Time to end this dream." Nothing changes.

"How long are you going to stay on the floor?" The man drawls. "Perhaps you'll let me help you up?" he says, while offering me his hand.

I take his hand and it feels incredibly warm and strong. I feel stiff and a little bruised on my bottom, which would make sense as I fell seemingly from the sky onto a concrete floor. But that happened in my dream, so I really shouldn't feel anything. Why aren't I waking up? What is happening?

The handsome man's expression softens. "Are you okay?" he says, "You look confused. Let me properly introduce myself. I'm Ganymede. You look like you could use some freshening up, so why don't I call a few of the girls to help you? Astrape! Bronte! Someone needs some hair and make-up over here."

Ganymede. That name has a familiarity to it. It triggers memories of my seventh-grade class with Mr. Fisher.

He loved to teach us about algebra, and grammar and — Greek mythology! Ganymede was from Greek mythology! He was sort of a servant to Zeus, a kidnapped Trojan whom he made his cupbearer. I suddenly feel sick to my stomach. I clap my hand over my mouth and realize I could be sick all over the floor because maybe I actually wasn't dreaming at all.

Ganymede comes running over and wraps his arm around my body to prevent me from falling. I lean into his shoulder and allow myself to breath in his warm, male animal scent. I reach my hand up and caress the shiny, golden bristles on his face. Then I snap my hand back because I realize this isn't a dream, and I'm the one acting like a creep.

"Greek mythology is real?" I say, lifting my head up from his chest to look into his crystal-blue eyes. "What am I doing here? Is this Olympus?"

"Shhh," Ganymede says, as he lightly strokes my hair. "They're saving you. You'll be alright. Just a tip, though. Don't use the "M" word around the gods. It's a really bad word to them." He looks at my confused face and mouths the word "mythology," then puts his finger to his lips and shhhs me.

I push away from his chest and look for something to throw up into. Ganymede grabs me by the wrist before I can scurry away and offers me a peacock-blue silk scarf. I manage to stifle my gags but feel myself breaking out into a sweat. I use the scarf to dab at my forehead in frantic little pats with shaking hands.

"Astrape! Bronte! Could you please get over here and help me? Marcella's daughter is freaking out!" Ganymede says, as he leads me over to what looks like a sitting area in a fancy doctor's waiting room. It has couches and chairs upholstered in a taut gray fabric. Very dimmed lights hang suspended over the area but I can't see any wires. I can see that the area has a wall behind it, and that off to both sides are doorways. It looks like there are paintings on the walls, but the room is still darkened and it is difficult to make out any kind of detail.

Two beautiful girls emerge from one of the doorways trailing small sparkly suitcases behind them on wheels. One of them is dark and exotic with a stormy expression. She would be a perfect runway model with her fierce look.

The other has pale, translucent skin and short silvery hair that is standing straight up. She is dressed in a white leather-looking strappy dress and thigh-high white boots. If this is heaven, Jean-Paul Gaultier is dressing the angels.

"This is what happens when you skip the transition protocol," the silver-haired one says, "Do you want an Ambien?" she says, getting some pills out of her suitcase.

"No!" I yell, while taking shelter in the corner of a couch. The three of them look at each other with a "whatever" look. Then from the same doorway the two women came through, my mother walks out wearing a new sequin-embossed blue dress.

"Honey, are you okay?" Mom says.

"I think I may have bruised my tailbone landing on the concrete," I say. I can't decide if she's crazy or I am.

"There's a way to soften your landing if we travel like that again. It helps if you throw in a back-tuck before you land. You know, like in gymnastics," Mom says.

"You know how to do a back-tuck?" I say incredulously. Who is this woman? I have done gymnastics and cheerleading for years, but my mother has never done it. The stunts we did seemed to terrify her, and my lasting memory from competing was looking out to the crowd and seeing my mother's worried face.

"Knowing gymnastics on Olympus is kind of like knowing how to play baseball back home. It's something everyone does when they are a kid, so I thought it was culturally sensitive of me to learn," Mom says.

"I'm sorry I wasn't here when you landed," she continues. "They insisted I change," she says, while side-eyeing Astrape and Bronte.

"Sorry, Marcella, we should have listened to you. Let me introduce ourselves to your daughter. I'm Astrape, and this is Bronte," says the dark, stormy one. "You are so beautiful, just like your mother. Except your coloring is the opposite! Now how about a little eye shadow? I've got a beautiful taupe that would be perfect for you," she says, while fishing around in her bag.

"And look at those blond curls," says Bronte, "So pretty! Let me just fluff it up a little bit."

I stare at the two of them as they stand before me, their hands full of brushes and powders. I will myself to stay calm so that I don't have a full-on panic attack. Who knows what their attitude is to hysterical women in this place? They give out Ambien like candy and are way too interested in my grooming so I can guess they like their women pretty and drugged into submission.

I turn to look at my mother and she smiles at me encouragingly. My eyes travel to her hair. Was there a new sparkly blue braid in her hair that matched her dress? And did she have blue sparkly glitter at the tips of her impossibly long lashes? That is when I lost it.

"What the hell, Mom?" I cry. "What is this place? You've been living here with Greek gods, and …and…Ganymede? You live here with Ganymede?"

My mom looks at me blankly and then glances over at Ganymede. He shrugs his shoulders and shakes his head at her with a raised eyebrow. She turns back to look at me.

"Well, Ganymede lives here," she says slowly, as if she is talking to a crazy person. Which at this point, she sort of is.

"He works for Zeus," she says, "and he lives in, so I guess we live together in a way, if that is what you mean," she says, while looking at me in complete befuddlement.

"He's GANYMEDE!" I yell. "He was kidnapped from the Trojans and made cupbearer to Zeus! Thousands of years ago! You poor thing," I say, addressing Ganymede, "you've spent thousands of years here!"

At this point, Ganymede and my mother burst into laughter. Astrape pauses in her blending of my foundation and gives a little giggle.

"It's not funny!" I say, "Kidnapping is not an acceptable way to get girlfriends or employees!"

"Honey," Mom says, "We're not laughing about that. We're laughing that you think Ganymede is thousands of years old. This isn't the original Ganymede. Ganymede was Trojan and human. A human always fills that position. Ganymede is just what they call the person who fills the job. He wasn't kidnapped."

"I was recruited when I was a Chippendale dancer on a cruise ship," Ganymede says.

"Olympus has a headhunter contract with a cruise-ship line in Bermuda," Mom says, "Poseidon manages that one."

"Is headhunting what you call kidnapping?" I say, "Is this the same cruise ship where you were kidnapped? And I'm sorry, but they couldn't have provided him with underwear?"

I pause for a moment and turn to address Ganymede.

"Sorry, Ganymede, it was just a quick glimpse when you knelt down," I say. Ganymede looks the opposite of embarrassed and gives me a wink. I shake my head and turn back to finish yelling at my mother.

"Mom, you're living with a kidnapper! You've helped Zeus kidnap me!" I cry.

"Oh, no, no, honey," she says, rushing to my side, "It's not like that at all. You don't have to be here. This wasn't Zeus's idea. I insisted that we go get you. We monitor the earth and it's really not doing well. All the storms, droughts, hurricanes, and floods you see, they are getting worse very quickly. Climate change, or Hephaestus's Curse as we call it here, is progressing much more quickly than people think. The earth only has a short time before it's done."

"Five to ten years, tops," Ganymede says, "I would have come here for the trip anyway, but I've seen the data. Our swirly blue planet is toast."

"It's...it's going to... die?" I say, aghast.

"Death or life support," Bronte says, as she teases at my roots with a comb. "Would you like some hairspray?"

"No, I don't want some hairspray," I say, pushing it away in disgust. "Isn't that what destroyed our Ozone and got us into this mess in the first place? Mom, is this true? Is this the end of the earth?"

My mom nods her head yes and pats my hand. I look at her and feel such sadness for everything I am leaving behind. All those people! What is going to happen to them all?

"Mom," I say, "Is there anything we can do for all those people? Can Zeus help? He is a Greek god after all. Can't they perform miracles?"

Mom shakes her head no. "Miracles aren't really their thing," she says with a shrug.

Instinctively, I hug myself and start to rock back and forth. As I clutch my arm, I think back to earlier in the day when I thought I had reached the pinnacle of happiness because Colton Chase had brushed me with his forearm.

Poor Colton! And selfishly, I think, poor me because I am losing him from my life. I have spent countless hours thinking about him, yearning for him, and today I felt a shiver of excitement from that transient touch of our arms. It made real all those feelings I have been entertaining in my head. Even though I never really had a shot with Colton and he was out of my reach, there was a part of me that could hope that it would happen. Now, the separation of space had given my crush the full power of unrequited love.

"Mom," I say with tears in my eyes, "we can't just leave them to die."

"They probably won't all die," Mom says, "but the destruction of their habitat means they'll have to live differently. They'll go into a kind of Stone Age or dark ages. They may have to live underground or in cities that are fortressed from the elements until they can fix things. *If they can fix things*. Cultural activities, sports, leisure, all the things you do for fun, will fall by the wayside as they just concentrate on survival. I couldn't leave you to that."

That sounds like every zombie apocalypse movie ever made. "Let's get more people up here, then," I say, "Let's dream them up here."

"It doesn't work like that," Mom says. "We were able to do that because Zeus's ship was in the earth's atmosphere and Zeus has a part of me that we could connect with so our consciousness could connect. We could travel on our shared consciousness to his ship."

"A part of you?" I say. I look at my mother in her long, sparkly gown. Were there parts of her missing under that fabric? Did he cut her? "What part of you did he take?" I say warily.

"My heart," Mom says simply.

That momentarily stops me in my tracks. I don't like the thought of my mother in the thrall of this sketchy dude. Most of the stories I remember about Zeus were mythological variations of guy goes into a bar and roofies a girl. We will have to talk about that later, but for now, what she says gives me an idea.

"Mom, if someone has a piece of my heart, doesn't that mean I can bring them up here? If I'm in love with somebody, can I save them?"

"Sweetie, I thought you weren't dating anyone?" she says. I look down at my hands, embarrassed.

My mom gets a clue and says, "I wish you could do it that way, but the person must want to join you. They have to be part of the process. We just had so little time. I couldn't set things in place so we could bring more people with us. Zeus can't keep his ship for long in the area."

My mom has a guilty look on her face. It suddenly hits me why Zeus couldn't hang around Earth. If he had done half the things he was purported to have done in Greek mythology, he was probably on some intergalactic sex offender registry.

"Mom," I say, "how did you get down there? Was there someone on Earth whom you could share consciousness with and willingly connect with?"

"No," she says, "I arrived in a transporter pod. It's a protective sheath that burns off as you enter the atmosphere. They are like individually wrapped packages for people. They are so small and unobtrusive that they aren't picked up by any of Earth's monitors. You have to land in the water. It comes with a little raft that opens when you land. I still got pretty wet, though."

I remember how beautiful my mom's hair looked when she arrived. "You didn't look wet when I saw you," I say. "Did you stop and get your hair done?"

"I didn't want to frighten you by showing up all wet. The last you knew of me, I had fallen off a cruise ship into the ocean. I didn't want you to think I was a ghost," she says.

"What about your eyelashes?" I say. "They look made out of mink."

My mom bites her lips and looks away. After a long pause, she finally says, "Esthetics are a big thing here. And you know, it's not really that bad a thing. Look at what Astrape and Bronte have done," she says, as she holds out a mirror for me. My curly blond hair is flowing in gently tousled waves around my shoulders, my skin is lightly bronzed, and my eyes have been finished off with iridescent purple eye shadow and a dramatic cat eye.

"Wow," I say, "look what five minutes can do."

"Exactly," Mom says.

"It's like having your own personal Sephora on the ship," I say.

"Oh, we have a Sephora on the ship," Mom says, "they're everywhere."

It's good to have her back. If I have to give up all I know of life on Earth, at least I get my mom back again.

The year she was gone was very dark. Time played tricks on me. The days passed slowly and felt long and empty, but then sometimes I would shake myself and realize that three weeks had passed without me noticing it. I would get up in the morning and count the hours until I could reasonably have a nap. I'd sleep at mid-morning like a toddler, then wake for lunch and sleep another two hours. There would follow a long afternoon of TV-watching or playing on the internet until I could eat dinner. Then more internet until I fell asleep on the couch and the whole thing would start again. This went on for so long I didn't notice that university had started and I had missed it.

Eventually I would have to go out to get food, so I would go to the grocery store every few days to pick up something to eat. After a few months of this, I noticed a help wanted sign in the store's window.

So, I started working there, and my daily visit to the grocery store for an hour stretched to eight hours ringing up groceries. I would go home afterwards and pick up where I had left off with my internet and falling asleep on the couch routine. For a treat sometimes, I would walk down to Starbucks for a sad latte and a glimpse of Colton.

Months passed in this listless state when Brandon started working at the grocery store for the summer. We hadn't talked in years, but he and I went way back because we had gone to preschool together.

My earliest memory of him was being at the park with our preschool friends and our mothers on a sunny afternoon. It was a hot day, and our mothers had decided a good way to cool us off was to have their own tiny-tot Hunger Games and outfit us with water guns so we could shoot each other. The boys took to it like, well like a duck to water, and immediately began chasing each other and spraying to kill. The girls stared at their mayhem for a while, looked at their guns, and then decided to abandon the whole enterprise for a tea party in the sandbox. But not me — I wanted to chase and shoot some boys.

I grabbed my gun and one of the guns abandoned by the girls and ran, double-barreling, it toward the boys. They were ricocheting randomly around a big field, every boy in it for themselves. As I came charging in, I let out my own personal victory cry and all the little boy heads turned to look at me. They stopped shooting at each other and stared at me. Then without saying anything to each other, by some telepathic means of communication, they all made the decision that they would organize and it would be the boys against the girls. Or girl singular, since I was the only one. They came charging at me. Seeing this mass of mini testosterone baring down on me, I turned and ran. But I would not give up the fight, and would twist around and shoot at them as I ran. Make no mistake, this was fun, and I shrieked with laughter.

The mothers were roused from their contented lolling on their picnic blankets by the noise of battle. Seeing me take on the crowd of boys touched some deep chord of female empowerment inside them and they rose from their feet to cheer me on. "Go, Zoe, go!" they yelled. They were even cheering against their own sons.

I was fast but they were gaining on me. I should have kept running straight ahead, but I couldn't resist taking shots at them and kept turning around to spray them. I wasn't much of a strategist and ended up taking them in circles, the circles getting ever tighter.

Eventually the boys had me surrounded. They were moving closer with their water guns, their telepathic planning in effect as they moved in position to douse me all together. I stood with both guns poised, ready to go down by soaking them as well. Their eyes became intense, they raised their guns, I raised mine, and then suddenly, Brandon jumped from the pack and came to join me in the middle. He put his back to mine and whispered, "Let's get them, Zoe."

Well, we all got wet. Then we took the water that was left in our guns over to the sandbox and sprayed the sand to help the girls with their sand pies. But I will never forget the feeling of being utterly overcome and then Brandon literally having my back. For the rest of that summer when our playgroup met at the park, Brandon was my best friend. The thing about being friends in preschool, and later meeting up as adults, is there is always a part of you that relates to that person on a preschool level.

When Brandon began working at the supermarket and we began reconnecting, our casual greetings of "hey" or "how's it going", quickly became accompanied by some kind of pantomime or dance move. He'd meet my eye while he was stocking fruit and I was at the checkout stand, and he would do something stupid with the fruit. There are a lot of stupid things you can do with fruit. I felt I had to reciprocate but I didn't have access to such great props, so the very least I could do was laugh. I laughed all day at the stupid things he said and did, and he laughed because I was laughing.

Sometimes he would invite me out after work with his friends, and we would laugh at the goofy things we laughed at all day. After a while, laughing became normal for me again, and I could laugh at other things as well. At night he started to invade my dreams and that was great, because although I slept a lot, my sleep had been fractured and I never woke up feeling rested. When I dreamt about Brandon, I would have sweet dreams about running in fields with him, sometimes shooting water guns. I would wake up happy. That was a feeling I hadn't had since my mother died.

When you stop having that happy feeling it's odd because you would think you could go through the files of your brain and access a memory file that you could push like a button and remember that emotion. But I couldn't do that, it's like it was password-protected. When Brandon came back, it's as if he had the password, and there it was, all the happiness files could open.

I should have Brandon's back. I know he would do the same for me. "Mom," I say, "I wish when we were dreaming that Brandon had been real. I wish he was here."

In the depths of that big, cavernous room, I can see something moving in the shadows. Ganymede, Astrape, and Bronte stop what they are doing and look curiously in the direction of the movement. The room grows silent and I become aware of my own breathing. The movement morphs into a figure, and out of the shadows I can see a man walking towards us. His footsteps can be heard on the concrete, but he is still coming from too dark a place for us to see him clearly. Then suddenly, he comes into the light.

It's Brandon.

"Hey, Zoe," he says with a smile. "You got your wish."

Chapter Four

I leap off the couch, bound across a coffee table, and run to Brandon. On the way, I knock over Bronte's suitcase and hip-check Ganymede but I don't care. If you think you are essentially one of the last people on Earth and then someone you know shows up, someone whom you shared your life with, then the only possible reaction is to run to them and grab hold of them with all your might.

Which is what I do. I run into Brandon's open arms and throw my arms around his neck. He wraps his arms around me and hugs me tightly. I am so happy to see him I am laughing and smiling and kissing him. Yes, kissing him.

I kiss him first just on the cheek, his bristly cheek, and then the other cheek, and then back and forth until I finally land on his lips. Brandon is holding me in his arms and he full-on kisses me back.

I think the space travel is playing tricks with my mind because as I kiss him I feel that time has stopped and I am aware of everything that is him — his hand on my waist, his soft lips, the warm taste of his mouth. Then we stop kissing and I start smiling because I'm so happy. I grab his hand while still keeping one arm around his neck. I turn to look at my mother with a delighted grin.

"We saved him!" I say and beam back and forth between Brandon and my mother.

My mother is standing stone still and staring at the two of us. Finally, she says in a measured way, "Yes, I'm glad to see you, Brandon. You've grown up a lot since I last saw you. How are you?"

"Good, Marcella. School has been going well and I've been having a good summer, and it's been great getting to know Zoe again," Brandon says. He looks down at me and smiles.

I smile back and start to laugh again. Not because anything is funny but because I am so happy to see him alive that a smile alone is not enough. Laughing is simply my smile amplified. I stare at him in wonder because it seems like some kind of miracle that he is here. Also — that kiss was a wonder.

Is this what kissing is always like? I haven't a clue. This is my first kiss. I never had the chance before because no one in my school has ever asked me out on a date. I used to agonize about when I would finally get a first kiss but this last year I let that go while I was having a close relationship with my couch. My mom always said it would happen in its own time and when I least expected it and she was right. I should let her know she has witnessed a milestone. I turn to look at her.

My mom's face looks stern and she glances back and forth between Brandon and me. She takes a long pause and straightens her spine. Goddamn, my mom looks regal! Being the consort of the king of the gods has worn off on her.

"And you are okay with the news that Earth is going to die and everything you have known is going to be gone?" Mom says.

Brandon's face falls and he lets go of my hand. His shoulders visibly drop and he says in a low whisper, "No, I'm not okay with that."

I run over to my mom and say quietly yet urgently into her ear, "Oh my God, Mom, why are you being so mean to Brandon? He was probably sleeping peacefully in his bed when he got sucked up here and he had no idea the planet was going to go. His family is back there. This is upsetting for him. Can we be a little gentle with him please?"

"I'm trying to figure him out, Zoe," Mom says, giving Brandon a suspicious look. "I don't understand what he's doing here."

"You have to stop this, Mom. If anything, we owe him an apology. We brought him here against his will. We essentially kidnapped him," I say.

"We saved his life," she says.

"Mom, you have got to quit being an apologist for kidnapping," I say. "You weren't like this when I was growing up. It was always 'be careful crossing the street, wash your hands, don't get kidnapped'."

My mom purses her lips and seems to think about this. After a moment she throws up her hands and says, "You're right. Brandon, I'm sorry I was being blunt with you. It's just that it is unusual that you are here."

"Marcella, I think it's unusual I'm here too," says Brandon. "I don't know why I'm here. I'm very confused about everything."

Bronte has come to stand beside us. She looks like she is studying her aqua blue manicure but I can tell that what she really is doing is listening in to our conversation. Suddenly, she stops flicking at her nails and it looks like an idea has occurred to her.

"Maybe he's here for the Ganymede job," Bronte says to no one in particular while tilting her head and smiling at Brandon. "He's pretty cute."

I'm not too comfortable with how Bronte is looking at Brandon. Astrape is also looking at him with interest. She is twirling one of her long locks around her fingers while staring at him with long-lashed gleaming eyes. It's a look I recognize from many of the girls who used to visit the supermarket where we worked. They were noticing his tall, lean, yet muscular build, his luscious dark wavy hair, his sweetly handsome face.

I had noticed it too but I already had one unobtainable man to obsess over in Colton Chase and didn't need another one. I had seen the girls that would sometimes wait for Brandon after work, pretty and perfect in their short skirts and vampy shoes. My work ponytail and running shoes were a contrast in frump. He would go over to them, put his arm around them, and give them a quick kiss hello. He would then turn to give me a "later, Zoe", as I closed out my cash register. I had clearly been friend-zoned. I was certain he didn't juggle oranges in front of these girls.

Ganymede is glaring at Brandon. I think Ganymede must have been unaware that his job has been posted and they are flying in candidates. Ganymede tenses his jaw, squares his shoulders, and turns his back away from Brandon and me to address my mother.

"I will let Zeus know you are here," Ganymede says as he strides through one of the doorways in a huff.

At the mention of Zeus my mom seems to forget about Brandon and me and picks up a mirror and begins primping. She looks nervous as she arranges her hair and adjusts her dress. I'm not sure if she is nervous because she's scared to see him or because she really wants to see him.

I have spent the last year hating Zeus because I blamed him for my mother's death. They had both gone missing in the cruise ship accident but I always had a feeling that he had played a part in it. Wasn't falling off a cruise ship up there with tumbling off a cliff while hiking or tipping over in a row boat if you want to get rid of someone and make it look like an accident? It made no sense, of course, because there was nothing to be gained from killing my mother.

On another level, I wondered why he couldn't have protected her. Why were they out on the deck at all when they were in the middle of a storm? Over the past year, unfairly or not, my anger over the untimely demise of my mother had come to be focused on Zeus. I thought if he had just left her alone and not searched her out on Tinder, my mother would still be here.

When Zeus had first entered our lives, I believed he was going to be good for my mother. She had put off dating for many years after my father left because she wanted to be there for me. She had quit working as an anchor when she had me and by the time she became a single mother it was too late for her to try to get on TV again. She started a home-based video-editing business which allowed her to be around for me, but it did zero for her social life. She seldom met anyone new.

Over the years I had noticed newly divorced dads in our neighborhood would seek her out, but my mother always turned them down. I asked her why one day and she said, "I know their ex-wives, Zoe," as if this should be obvious to me. I don't know if this was some kind of girl-code for mothers or if she simply knew too much about the guys from their wives.

When I got into my teens and was old enough to be left alone, my mother gave online dating a try. She usually didn't make it beyond the first date. One of her last first dates before meeting Zeus was typical of her online dating adventures.

My mom met the guy at a restaurant for dinner. This alone gave her hope because usually the guys wanted to meet her for coffee on the first date, which she insisted to me was not a date at all, and they got screened out at that point. She said the guy was handsome (plus!), looked pleased to see her (plus, plus!), and pulled her chair out when she sat down (the trifecta!).

Things quickly took a turn, however, when he skipped over any small talk and told her the sorry story of how he came to be divorced, complete with a villainous ex-wife and his bitter take on humanity. The wooing was nil and the free therapy was very high. It was like the guy had never heard of trying to impress a woman on the first date. She had bought a new dress for the date and he didn't even tell her how pretty she looked.

A lot of her dates went like this, and I didn't blame her for not wanting to see them again. She must have done something that they liked, however, because they usually wanted to keep seeing her. Then she would have to turn them down, which made her feel badly. Afterwards, she would be so discouraged that it would take her another six months before she would go online again.

But Zeus was different. He seemed to have the finicky creature that is my mother figured out. I can't say for certain what went on during their first date because my mom and I have boundaries. All I know is she came home from that first date with an effervescent glow. "I like him," she said happily. As she leaned over my bed to kiss me good night that evening, I saw the worry line between her brows had softened and her eyes had a gentle shine. There was something bouncy yet calm about her step at the same time. It was like she had finally arrived at a tropical paradise at the end of a long journey.

Were there any hints that Mom was dating the king of the sky and ruler of men? He did say he had a doctorate in meteorology and worked for the government, does that count? The truth is, I hardly met the guy before he flew away in a spaceship with my mother. They were only dating six weeks when they went on the cruise together. It was way too early for him to be hanging out on the couch watching Netflix with the two of us.

But if I didn't get to see him, his presence was there. He texted my mom day and night with funny, charming messages that let her know he was thinking of her.

Once, when she had a late-night edit and couldn't go on their date, he left a home-cooked meal on her doorstep. Another time we came home to find our grass had been cut. He called later to say he came by with a mower because he had noticed it needed cutting. In retrospect he probably sent the goddess of agriculture, Demeter, by with her magic scythe.

Then there were the flowers. He sent them after the first date, and every time he wanted to remind her that she was special, which was pretty often. I'd catch my mom looking at the bouquets he sent her with a look of sweet happiness. She was hooked. Zeus knew how to get a woman after his actual eons of practice. It's really so simple to get a woman and I could write a very short book on how to do it using a series of tweets. *Bring her something. Pay lots of attention to her. Listen to her. Tell her she's beautiful. Boom! You're done. She's yours.*

I look over at my mom now as she gets ready to see Zeus. She tosses her hair and appears to have put on fresh lip-gloss. Oh my God, Mom, get a grip. This guy is the player of the universe; he's used all his moves on you. Bronte and Astrape arrange the folds of her dress and then disappear into one of the doorways. They re-emerge a few moments later pushing some kind of machine on wheels.

Bronte flicks a switch on the machine and aims it at my mother. I think it's some kind of portable hair dryer but it could be a wind machine. Her hair blows back and she looks like she's stepped out of a Beyoncé video. My mom's hair newly fluffed, Bronte turns off the machine while Astrape gives her a dose of hairspray. My mom looks so comfortable with all of this that I am sure it's an every-day occurrence.

"Zoe, it's late, why don't you have a sleep on the couches down here? Bronte can get you blankets and pillows. Everyone can meet fresh in the morning." Mom says. "I want him to let Zeus know about Brandon first before introducing you because we weren't expecting him." My mother gives me a kiss on the cheek then quickly turns around so that her dress flies out behind her dramatically.

Bronte walks by me as she is rolling her wind machine away. "I put blankets out for you," she says. "I think she missed him." This makes me want to vomit. She sashays away with the machine and out the door. Astrape follows, pulling a sparkly suitcase in each hand.

There's nothing to do but roll my eyes and wait for the arrival of supreme god Zeus. I look up at Brandon and he is staring at the door my mom went through.

"She loves him," he says simply. I feel a sea of protest swell up inside of me and I am about to argue with him, but I suddenly realize how tired I am. It would be just to sleep. Real sleep, not space travel sleep.

"Come on," Brandon says. He takes me by the hand and leads me over to one of the couches. Brandon lays down first, and then with a gentle tug from him, I follow and we spoon together on the couch. He's been such a regular visitor to my dreams that it seems natural to share sleep with him now.

"I could stay awake, just to hear you breathing," Brandon softly sings the first line from Aerosmith's "I Don't Want to Miss a Thing" into my ear like a lullaby. Nineties power-ballads can be so soothing. I smile and relax into his arms.

As I'm about to drift into sleep, there's a flashing vision in my mind of a man riding in a chariot pulled by four enormous black stallions. He has a black cape that fans out behind him as he comes charging towards me with the horses in full fury. Red flames shoot out from beside the wheels of the chariot and the horses leap over them.

On his head the man wears an etched bronze helmet that completely covers his face. I can't see who he is but there is something familiar about the man, like this has been a reoccurring nightmare I've forgotten. It fills me with a feeling of dread.

I reflexively hold up my hands but Brandon takes them and gently puts them down again. He holds me tighter and I can feel the steady beating of his heart. The chariot, which had been almost upon me, disappears in a burst of flame. The bad dream is gone. I relax and almost feel safe.

Almost.

Chapter Five

I awake to feel someone tickling my feet. Is that a feather? I want to find out who's doing it but I don't want to get up yet. My body is heavy with fatigue and I crave more sleep. I shut my eyes again and move my foot away from the irritant. The feather moves over to my other foot. I try to brush it away but it keeps tickling my toes.

"Stop it," I say, "that's annoying." I hear Brandon stir and he kicks his leg back. This seems to perturb the feather tickler.

"Hey, no kicking!" a buoyant voice says. "Come on kids, time to get up!" Well, now I'm awake, so I open my eyes and sit up to see who is disturbing us. Brandon reluctantly opens his eyes and props himself on his elbow. Standing before us is a man in his early twenties wearing shorts and a t-shirt. He has long, floppy hair that he keeps flipping back so it won't fall into his eyes. On his feet he's wearing sandals. I do a double take on the sandals when I notice two silver, feathery wings attached to each side of the shoes.

"Oh, gross!" I say, "Did you tickle us awake with your feet!?"

The man smiles and nods in answer then begins to twist his hair into a man-bun. He secures his hair and then claps his hands at us.

"Time to go, sleeping beauties," he says.

The man has the enthusiasm of a camp counselor waking his charges for breakfast and a morning swim. His casualness and lack of glitter is the exact opposite of the rest of Zeus's staff.

"Excuse me, but who are you?" I say.

"Come on, you know who I am," he says. "Feathers on the feet, prince of thieves, messenger of the gods, tour guide for the dead…."

"Are you Hermes?" I say, astounded.

"You got it!" Hermes says. "And also, I do a lot of work for my dad and he needs you to get up. So, don't worry about your hair, we'll take care of that later. Let's go!"

Brandon is sitting up now and is staring with his full attention at Hermes.

"You're on YouTube," Brandon says, "Aren't you Kristof Nylund? I've watched your Minecraft live feeds." Is Brandon ten years old? Brandon looks over at me and adds sheepishly, "We play it in our dorm. It helps for relaxing during exam time."

"Hey, yeah, good to meet you," Hermes says, "always good to meet one of the fans. Have you seen my YouTube apology reviews? I'll get a selfie with you after we get going. You can post it to where ever you want. But Dad's business comes first. So, come on, get up."

Hermes takes both of us by the hand and with one quick tug we are both standing on our feet and placed a good four feet away from the couch. I am reminded that the bouncy man standing before me is actually a god with powers and boundless strength.

I'm a little delighted to meet Hermes. He was always the most mischievous of the gods. He was a born scamp. When he was just a baby, a few hours old, he made off with his big brother Apollo's prized herd of cows. When Apollo caught him, they went to the old man Zeus to decide whether Hermes was guilty or not. Dad Zeus knew baby Hermes was guilty but he admired his lying bravado and made Apollo forgive the little guy. Zeus gifted Hermes with a magical winged staff that turned hate into love and to make it a matching set, he gave Hermes winged sandals. Hermes came up with a new musical instrument to give Apollo so it was all good. Only nine hours old and Hermes had everyone wrapped around his little baby god-ling finger.

Above all, Hermes was Zeus's son and the thunder god could always depend on his boy to do his dirty work. Way back when the original Ganymede was stolen by Zeus, Hermes was sent to smooth things over with the Trojan's family by gifting them with a pair of horses. Ganymede may or may not have become Zeus's lover. I'm going with may, since Zeus has sex with someone in basically every story ever told about him. Whatever the true job description of cup-bearer, it also meant Ganymede's parents would never see him again. You would think a pair of horses would not compensate for their loss, but when smooth talker Hermes delivered the news the parents were chill with it. He is probably going to scam me, but I am kind of looking forward to being scammed by a master.

"I just don't get why Kristof Nylund is here," Brandon whispers to me. "How can a guy who livestreams himself playing with blocks be a god?" Hermes apparently has the hearing of a god because he heard this.

"You're Brandon, right?" Hermes says. "Let me tell you something B-boy. Can I call you B-boy?"

"Definitely not," Brandon says.

"Okay," says Hermes, "then how about Bran the Man or Branny or Bran Stoker's Bracula and we shorten it to Stoke?"

"Nope," Brandon says with one firm shake of his head. Brandon crosses his arms and rocks back on his heels. He looks like he wants to hit Hermes.

"No?" says Hermes, "Okay, we'll figure that out later. So, anyway, Brandon, I've been in the communications biz for many a millennium and here's something important to know. Don't underestimate the power of a popular medium. Online games and YouTube are where kids hang out. I can get important messages to them that way. The earth is going down the tubes, in case you haven't noticed, and we've been trying to get that message to them before it's too late. It may seem like a lost cause, I know, but I keep trying."

"Sorry, dude, I meant no offense," Brandon says and he noticeably deflates. He uncrosses his arms and turns back into the amiable Brandon whom I used to build celery-based Jenga towers with at work. I guess this was just some kind of bro-off and they were setting their boundaries.

"I love your stuff," Brandon says. "I didn't realize you were trying to get a message out there."

Hermes reaches out and gives Brandon a good-natured pat on the back.

"No worries, Brandon. That's how you get a human to do something for you. Entertain them," Hermes says. "It's so dark in here. Let's bring up the lights."

Hermes takes an iPhone out of his pocket.

"There's an app for this," he says, as he swipes at the phone. Suddenly, lights come on and the whole room is illuminated. I can see for the first time that it's actually some kind of landing station for smaller vessels that travel to and from the ship. A long hallway separates us from a larger area where I can see at least three smaller spaceships parked. We have been hanging out in their version of an airport lounge.

"You two go ahead and get on the transporter," Hermes says to Brandon and me. "I have to finish packing up and then I'll join you. It's the first one on the left."

Brandon and I exchange a look. Did we have any choice but to do what Hermes said? He was a god, after all, despite the fact that I suspected his highlights were from the salon and not natural god adornments.

Brandon looks towards Hermes who is busy packing his gear. Then Brandon shifts his gaze towards the row of ships and gives them an appraising stare.

"I don't know about going on one of those ships with him, Zoe," Brandon says in a low whisper to me.

"I know," I say. "The first rule of being kidnapped is never go to a second location with the kidnapper."

"I don't know if we are being kidnapped so much as rescued," Brandon says. "The world is really falling apart. My grandparents always told me stories about walking through ten feet of snow to school. No one walks through ten-foot snow drifts to school anymore with climate change."

I am about to interject to tell him grandparents exaggerate about that stuff because it is literally impossible to walk through ten feet of snow without snow shoes. But then I realize he's right — our Earth is sick. We don't need anyone to tell us that.

"Is escaping the right thing to do?" Brandon says. "We get away, but then everyone else on Earth dies or lives through an apocalypse. I don't know if Hermes and Zeus and everyone else here are really who they say they are and they have magical powers. But they have technology. They might be able to help the Earth. I don't think I can just leave without at least trying to help save other people."

That's the thing about Brandon. He's a rescuer. That's probably why he spent any time with me trying to get me to laugh with creative uses for fruit. He couldn't just leave me in my sad sack state. I'm about to tell him what my mom said about shared consciousness and space travel, when from behind us there is the sound of a commotion. Someone is yelling and Astrape and Bronte start shrieking.

We turn to see Ganymede standing holding a giant silver cylindrical object that pulsates with power. It is as long as Ganymede and clearly heavy because the veins in his biceps pop as he holds it in his grip. Judging by the way Astrape and Bronte are cowering in its wake, it is also a weapon.

"Ganymede, be careful with Zeus's thunderbolt," says Hermes. "That thing could blow up this whole station. Please bring it over here and I'll wrap it up. I think I have some isotopic bubble wrap."

Ganymede ignores Hermes and takes the thunderbolt and twists it around so that it is pointing straight at Brandon and me. The end of the thunderbolt is open to reveal a yawning maw of an interior. Gases and smoke emanate from the inside, punctuated by flashes of light. The murderous depths of the thunderbolt are matched by the rage on Ganymede's face.

"What do I care if I blow us up," Ganymede says, "The earth is dying and I'm dying too because you're tossing me back there so you can hire this new cupbearer for Zeus. Do you think he'll know to check the claws to make sure the jewels aren't coming loose? No one cares how much I do. So now I don't care. We can all crash onto the Earth together and help speed things up."

Ganymede struggles to lift the thunderbolt onto his shoulder for the launch position. It's a tool made for a god and Ganymede lacks the god strength to easily pick it up.

It's true what they say. When you are staring death in the face your life flashes before your eyes. I see Brandon and I taking on the kids at preschool with our water-guns and I press pause on the scene. Our innate instinct to work as a team is still there. I don't even have to turn my head to look at Brandon to know that he is thinking the same thing.

In the seconds it takes for Ganymede to lift and balance the weapon on his shoulders, Brandon and I see our chance. I hit the floor with a yell and roll under a table and behind a chair. Ganymede is now distracted by my movement and takes his eye off of everyone else.

He doesn't see Brandon drop down and charge him. Brandon hits Ganymede at the knees and the cupbearer goes down. Hermes comes up the other side and grabs the thunderbolt from Ganymede before it can hit the ground. Brandon gets behind Ganymede on the ground and puts him in a choke hold. Hermes sprints away with the thunderbolt and returns a few seconds later with a long, polished staff with wings on it.

"Clear your arm from his chest, Brandon, I'm going to zap him with my staff." Ganymede is turning blue as Brandon grits his teeth and holds him tightly in the chokehold. With some hesitation, Brandon lifts the arm he has been using to restrain Ganymede's chest and holds it in the air while still maintaining a tight hold on his neck. Hermes springs forward and jabs the staff into Ganymede's chest. Ganymede stops struggling and his body relaxes.

"He's stopped breathing," I say. "Let go, Brandon. You've choked him out." Brandon instantly loosens his grip on Ganymede's neck.

"No," says Hermes, "that's not what happened. This magic staff turns hate into love. Ganymede, are you feeling better, buddy?"

Ganymede is coughing and rubbing his throat. He turns to Brandon and says, "Sorry about that, you'll do great at the job."

Brandon looks up at me in amazement. "It's fine," he says after a moment. "I'm really not after your job. I'm just here for Zoe."

Ganymede gets a dreamy look on his face. "Love," he says, "it's a magical thing. You and Zoe hold onto each other."

Brandon and I both look at each other and blush. Before we can give this too much thought, Hermes comes along and puts his arm around Ganymede.

"You're under a lot of pressure," he says to Ganymede. "No one is after your job. You can stay here as long as you like. There will never be another cupbearer like you. I know you are pretty good with a coaster too." Ganymede gives everyone a big smile. Astrape and Bronte each take one of his arms and they lead him towards one of the doorways. As they disappear together through the door, Ganymede can be heard saying, "You're so pretty, Bronte."

Hermes turns away from them and gives his head a shake as he looks at us. "Nice work, kid," he says to Brandon under his breath. Hermes then claps his hands and motions with his head towards the row of ships.

"Sorry for the rush," Hermes says. "I have to get you out of here because Hera is coming and she's not going to like Zeus's girlfriend's spawn and friend of spawn. Zeus got a text from Athena letting us know that she's put a block in Earth's space monitoring channels so that Hera can fly out here undetected. Athena has a legit government job working as a software engineer at NASA but she's also a hacker. She's competing with me for most jobs in the family. Anyway, the channels can't be blocked for long without detection so Hera will be on her way. We've got to go! Now!"

When he says Hera, I feel a chill go through me. Hera is the goddess I found to be the scariest in Greek mythology. She was the goddess of marriage, which is ironic because she had an awful marriage. She very wisely never wanted to marry Zeus in the first place but he was determined to have her and eventually wore her down. Once they were married, he cheated on her constantly and Hera was not one to look the other way. None of this good wife, political partner stuff for her: Hera got her revenge on every transgression she found out about. If Zeus so much as looked at another woman, even if the woman was innocent and rejected Zeus, Hera would stalk her and make her life miserable.

Zeus was afraid of her too. He once turned a girlfriend into a cow to protect her from Hera but Hera took the poor cow and had her guarded by a hundred-eyed monster. Hera really had no concept of justice when it came to her jealousy and anger. She turned the nymph Callisto into a bear because Zeus fell in love with her. Callisto wasn't even into him!

As a stepmother she was the worst. Zeus had baby Hercules with a beautiful Greek woman named Alcmene. Hera sent a bunch of venomous snakes into his crib as a baby present. Baby Hercules strangled each of the snakes one by one. You would think that might garner Hera's respect and she'd leave him alone. But no, she made it her mission to make the rest of his life as horrible as possible.

When Hercules grew up, Hera sent a fit of madness to him so that he murdered his wife and children. When he came to his senses, the grief-stricken Hercules asked the god Apollo for absolution. Apollo commanded that he perform ten labors to purify himself and serve a really mean king named Eurystheus for twelve years while he performed the labors. The labors got increased to twelve because Eurystheus was one of those employers who keep changing the goal post in a project and make you do extra work.

Hercules had to kill a lion with hide so tough no arrow could pierce it. Hercules used the skill he learned in his crib and strangled it. He captured a whole lot of dangerous and magical animals including the three-headed guard dog of the Underworld Cerberus. Most disgusting of all, he had to clean a stable for a thousand cows that hadn't been cleaned in thirty years. I would really like to know if anyone was even going in there to milk those cows. He gained immortality and fame for those labors because he epitomized the Greek ideal of *pathos*, the experience of virtuous struggle leading to fame. The Ancient Greeks thought you should have to work hard to gain fame. They would have hated Reality TV and social media.

Hera only let up on Hercules when he was burning alive on a pyre. Zeus looked over at Hera and said, "Honey, do you think he's had enough now?" She magnanimously agreed (this is sarcasm), and Zeus sent Athena in her chariot to take Hercules to Olympus. I'm sure their family dinners are not at all tense.

Now Hera, this vengeful goddess, is coming here. Do I have any relationship to Zeus by marriage? Am I his stepdaughter? I have no idea if this weird relationship between Zeus and my mother includes marriage.

But even so, does Hera care about children from another marriage who have nothing to do with Zeus? She's suspicious of any woman connected to Zeus so I might be in danger by proximity alone. My head is spinning and I have to ask my mother what she thinks. My mother — oh my God, my mother! My stomach drops at the thought of what Hera would do to my mother.

"Where's my mom?" I say with rising panic in my voice.

Hermes is bending over a table with Bronte packing a bag. He is trying to close it when she pushes some nail polish at him to pack. He waves her off and throws the bag onto his shoulders. I notice it's embroidered with a pair of little silver wings that match the wings on his shoes.

"Don't worry about your mom," Hermes says as he leans over to pick up another bag Astrape is handing him. "Does anyone tell you, you look a lot like her but the opposite, you know? She's black-haired, you're blond. Your hair reminds me of my Aunt Demeter's hair. She's a real Earth mother type with the blond flowing hair. She likes to wear flowers in her hair. You would look good with that. She would look great, wouldn't she, Astrape?"

"Demeter is an Earth mother, Hermes," Astrape says with a giggle as she bats her eyes at Hermes. "She's *the* Earth mother," she says beaming at her own joke.

"Haha, that's funny, Astrape," Hermes says, flashing her a smile. "Gorgeous and witty. I wish you were coming with us. I'll make it back here soon, I promise."

Hermes comes closer to Brandon and me and says in a low whisper, "Grammy Gaia, the actual mother earth, might not like that joke but the girl is cute. Come on, you two, let's get going, the ship awaits."

"Wait!" I say, "What do you mean don't worry about my mom? Where is my mother?"

"She's gone," Hermes says. "She and Zeus have flown out of here. She's sorry she didn't have time to talk to you. She really had to go. If Hera sees her with Zeus she's lucky if she's only turned into a cow or a bear. Zeus told me to look after you. We really don't have time to spare."

Hermes tries to put his hand on my back to guide me along but I escape his touch by all at once falling to the ground on my knees with my head in my hands. I had been holding my breath since the second Hermes said she was gone and now as I exhale I start crying uncontrollably.

Brandon drops the bags Hermes has handed him and runs to kneel beside me. He brings his concerned face close to mine and hugs me. "Zoe, it's okay," Brandon says, "Your mother will be okay. Zeus is with her."

But it's not okay. My mother is gone and she left without saying good-bye, just like the last time. I feel overpowering sadness hit me, my body clenched in pain. The grief is flowing through me and taking up residence in every cell. I am dizzy, and despite being on the ground with my head on my knees, I feel I'm going to faint. The blackness spreads across my vision like the ink from an octopus. It is almost black and then all at once there is a crack, like a whip, and the sound of clanging metal. The last thing I see is a carved bronze mask closing in on my face. Then it is dark.

Chapter Six

I am sitting in my local Starbucks drinking a Coconut Milk Mocha Macchiato. The caramel drizzle on top of the drink instead of tasteless green foam tells me that I am having a dream. That, and the fact that I have suddenly just appeared in the Starbucks and I don't remember how I got here. Strangely, I am still wearing the dress I put on when I went sleep-flying. I lift a lock of hair between my fingers and see that it has the same full, smooth curl brushed into place by Bronte.

The Starbucks is half-full with the usual mix of people bent over their coffees in conversation with one another. I am feeling oddly numb. I am content to just stare around me at the other people, sip my drink, and zone out. The buzz of conversation takes on a low, melodious hum, and I think it might be nice to stay here in this peaceful dream. Something bad has happened, but I don't want to think about it because then this would turn into a nightmare. I need a dream where everyone I know is alive and someone I love can be here.

My eyes drift to the doorway and I wait. I know he will be here soon. I take my spoon out and scoop a little bit of whipped cream onto my tongue. I taste the rich coolness of the cream and follow it with a sip of macchiato. Before I can bring my cup back down to the table, the door has opened. He has arrived. Colton Chase.

He does his usual quick glance around to look for the person he is meeting. It's like tech entrepreneurs have not heard of boardrooms because they all meet at Starbucks. He does a scan around the room. I would normally duck my head a little when he reaches my area so as to avoid accidentally making eye contact. But not this time. This is a dream and I can be who I want to be. I am beautiful and confident. I can talk to a guy like Colton Chase.

His eyes sweep the shop, and then like a magnet, they are drawn to the girl looking purposefully in his direction. Me. He stops and we lock eyes. He gives me a look that I feel down to my very soul. His eyes are deep and dark and mesmerizing. I look down at my coffee and then look back up again. He is still looking at me. Abruptly, he breaks eye contact with a shake of his black locks. Then he nods at someone in the corner and heads off to buy his coffee.

I watch as he has his back to me and stirs his coffee at the barista stand. I can see the tension of his back muscles through his slightly worn-looking leather jacket. He shifts back and forth a few times on his feet like he is considering something. He looks up at his friends in the corner again to give them a nod. He starts to walk towards them, then all of a sudden, he turns away and walks straight towards me.

I put my gaze down to my drink and play with my spoon until the last possible second. I can feel him standing there looking at me. I make him wait a millisecond and then I look up at him with wide eyes of anticipation. He is standing before me in a relaxed stance. His leather jacket is open up enough to see the perfectly pressed tee underneath. He is crisp but casual. Yet in his eyes there is a little vulnerability, like he's not entirely sure how this interaction will go.

"Hi," he says, "I feel like I see you are here all the time and thought I should introduce myself. I'm Colton." When I see him out and about he always looks serious and a little broody, as if he is harboring depths that I couldn't imagine. Looking at him now, his face remains serious but there is a sparkle in his eyes. I think he is holding a smile in there and is waiting for encouragement from me to let it out.

At this point when a guy is trying to talk to me, I will usually put my head down and look at my phone. It doesn't even normally get this far. A cute fireman once complimented me on my jacket as I was stirring my coffee at the counter at this very same Starbucks. I looked at the trash jacket I was wearing, mumbled a "thanks," tossed my stir stick in the garbage, and walked briskly to a table. I didn't look up again in case I accidentally met his eye. I didn't want him to think his jacket compliment had gone to my head. There was a game to be played here but I had never learned the rules.

Dream Zoe doesn't know the game either. The playbook has never been downloaded to my hard drive. But I can at least maintain eye contact with someone and smile appropriately.

"Hi," I say, "It's nice to meet you. My name is Zoe."

Colton gives a relieved smile, like he had actually been nervous to talk to me. It has never occurred to me that someone like Colton Chase could be nervous to talk to someone like me. Despite it being a dream, I am nervous too.

I reach out my hand to pick up my coffee cup but instead of touching the cup, my fingertips are touching the door handle of a car. The dream has morphed, as dreams do, and I feel like we are on our first date. Colton's hand brushes past mine and firmly grips the door handle before I can get to it.

"Let me get this for you," he says. His voice is deep and full, like a purr in his chest. He pulls open the door of a silver Ferrari. I am still wearing my same dress but Colton has changed into a beautifully tailored dark suit. His tousled ebony hair blends with the black of the night.

I seat myself in the low-slung seat. The seats are so far back to accommodate Colton's tall size that my legs are stretched out almost completely straight. I feel long and lanky and super-model lithe. He turns to me and says, "Would you like the top down?" I nod yes, and the roof of the car automatically folds back. I am hit with the cool night air. My hair is blown back by the wind in flattering disarray as we speed away.

We are driving down a winding mountain road. On the passenger side I can see the ocean below. The road has been carved into a tower of granite rock.

I look at Colton's strong profile as he commands the road. There are little lines of concentration on his brow as he shifts gears. I relax back into the butter-soft leather of the seats. Colton glances my way and gives me a little smile. "Are you comfortable?" he says.

"Yes," I say. I take my hair in one hand and twist it around to prevent it from blowing in the wind. "I have to do this to prevent me from having crazy-woman hair," I say.

Colton rewards me with another smile. The handsomeness of his face hits me right in the chest. At first, I feel a flutter of energy in my heart and then the feeling spreads throughout my limbs and lights up my face. He has electrified me. "I wish you were really here," I say quietly, "I wish this were real."

"I'm here," Colton says softly. "This is real." He reaches out, picks up an errant strand of my hair and gently brushes it from my face.

I try to think of the rules of lucid dreaming. I could take charge now and make the dream go the way I would like it to go. But I think it may be an opportunity to learn something about Colton.

Somewhere stored in my mind are observations and things I've learned about him, things I've read or heard from other people. If I allow the dream to proceed on its own, my subconscious may arrange it in a way that is useful to me.

Colton is more than just a good-looking guy who frequents my neighborhood. He's a semi-famous entrepreneur. It's very possible that I came across stories about him before he even set foot in my coffee shop. I know he is famous for starting a company called IntelSoul. I ask him to tell me about how he became a successful entrepreneur.

"I started IntelSoul while I was running another company," he says, as he navigates a turn in the road. "I was working really long hours and realized I was probably talking to Suri more than any living, breathing person. I thought, wouldn't be nice if this thing I'm spending so much time with had more of a soul? Like she could think for herself and have some personality? That's when I started playing around with Artificial Intelligence and came up with the technology for IntelSoul. We market it with the tagline 'Technology with soul.' It gives the technology personality. I think it makes people feel a little less lonely."

I am staring at Colton in wonder. I only look at Suri as my next level of laziness as I ask her for information when I can't be bothered to use Google. I also probably talked more to Suri than actual people during the past year. I ended up working in a grocery store while Colton is running companies.

"Colton," I say, "I can't believe you have done so much and you are so young!"

Colton turns his head to me for a moment and smiles. "Youngest brother syndrome," he says. "My two older brothers are very successful. I always have to run to play catch-up."

As I look at Colton's gorgeous face lit by the moon as we drive, it's hard to think of anyone outshining him. He doesn't look upset at the observation, though; it's like he is only stating a fact.

"I'm an only child," I say, "Maybe the lack of competition is why I've always been a person of no particular accomplishments. Mom told me I was special without any evidence. I think that may be snowflake syndrome."

"A snowflake is beautiful, perfect, and unique," Colton says, "so I agree, you have snowflake syndrome. You have it bad." Colton is grinning from ear to ear.

"I needed some competition in the womb," I say, trying to make a joke, "then maybe I would also be able to harness souls for technology." *Even in dreams do I have to say stupid things? Don't talk to him about wombs, Zoe!*

"I just give them a little personality," Colton says, as he takes one hand off the wheel and reaches for my hand. "Nothing replaces a living, breathing, beautiful person." He takes my hand, raises it to his mouth, and gives it a kiss. He brings my hand down, slowly turns his fingers around until our fingers are interlaced, and our hands come to rest on the console between us. We sit happily holding hands and looking out at the moonlit night as the car speeds along.

The stars over head twinkle and shine. I wonder if I could fly up into those stars with Colton beside me. I suddenly have an idea.

"Colton," I say, "Do you ever dream about me?"

Colton takes his eyes off the road for a moment to give me a grave look. Then he turns his head to look intently at the road again. I see the muscles along his smooth jawline tense and release.

He takes a deep breath and says, "I dream of you, Zoe. But not like this. This is the first time I've been able to hold your hand." He gently squeezes my hand then takes his thumb and lightly strokes the inside of my wrist.

I know this is only a dream and I'm not talking to the real Colton, but maybe there is a chance that he did dream about me. Maybe he and I can connect by dreams like Brandon and I connected by dream. If we were connected by dreams and he really wanted to be with me, I could help him transport up to the ship and save him.

This is how I could save him and who knows how many others. They just have to be connected to me and want to be with me. I wish I had been more popular. Why did I spend so much time being a recluse? I should have been out socializing and saving the world. I should have taken Instagram more seriously!

"Colton," I say, "this is really important. If I should ever visit you in a dream and want to fly away with you, please go with me."

I know this is not even the real Colton but I have to at least try to get this message out. Maybe this gorgeous man is dreaming of me right now and we can connect.

It doesn't matter if I am essentially furniture in his dream and the main player is the supermodel he deserves, I just have to be there. I need to somehow make that connection. I hope the real Colton can hear me.

"The world is not going to last," I say. I take his hand and hold it to my heart as I say this so that he knows this is important. "All the storms, and the fires, and the earthquakes are telling us something. It's falling apart. If I come for you, it's because I am trying to save you."

Colton takes my hand and brings it closer to him in the space between us. He does not treat me like I'm a crazy person. Instead, he nods his head and says, "I know the world is not going to last. I'm trying to do something about it. That's what my new company is about."

"Really?" I say, "What is your company going to do?"

"Do you want to see it?" Colton says.

"Yes!" I say in astonishment.

Colton takes his hand away from mine and puts both hands on the wheel as he accelerates. We go a few miles and then he takes a turn away from the ocean to another road that hugs the mountain.

We drive along the isolated mountain road. Colton slows the car as a driveway comes into view at the side of the road. He turns down the driveway, leading us to an expansive property with a house.

"This is my home where I work," Colton says. It's a large house made of stone set among soaring fir trees. I can see the house goes far back and is built into the wall of the mountain itself.

"I thought you lived near me," I say. "I always see you in the neighborhood."

"I have a penthouse there too. It's a good place to meet investors and developers. This is where I do most of my development work. Do you want to come in and see my office?"

Colton takes his phone and swipes at it. Suddenly, a part of the mountain-side opens up like a door. He puts the car in first and drives towards the opening.

"Colton," I say, "are you a billionaire?"

Colton gives me a sidelong look. "Why do you ask?" he says.

"I just want to know if you're Batman," I say.

Colton laughs and drives the car into the stone opening. We enter a garage with space for at least ten other cars. I see he has electric cars, like a good environmentalist. He parks the car in one of the spaces and we step out.

We disappear into an elevator off the garage. The elevator silently begins its descent and it seems like we are going down into the mountain. This is all feeling very James Bond to me. It appears Colton can read my mind because he explains, "I have an office down here because it inspires me. It's what's down here in the earth that is going to save the planet."

The elevator opens and we are in a well-lit room. The floors and walls are of polished granite. One wall has been painted with a mural of a spring-time meadow that brings sunshine to the room. He brings me over to a table with a computer on it and several bowls of colorful, polished rocks. One of the bowls is filled with glittering gems and what appears to be diamonds. Colton reaches for one of the diamonds and places it into my hand.

"I mine these. I bet they would make gorgeous jewelry," he says with a wink.

The diamond glitters in the palm of my hand. I don't know much about diamonds, but I have seen enough engagement rings on the hands of movie stars to know I am holding a fortune in my hand that could pay my way through university right into grad school.

"Everything we need to sustain us is in the earth," he says. "I was looking at the power of geothermal energy that we use now to heat and cool houses and buildings and wondering how that energy could be transferred to vehicles. Do you know how geothermal energy works?"

I have a vague recall that it is energy stored in the earth. "It's geysers and hot springs, and volcanoes, right?" I say.

"Right," says Colton, "and it's cost-effective, reliable, sustainable, and environmentally friendly. It's most accessible in areas close to tectonic plate boundaries. We are sitting on one of those right here," he says. Colton has opened his computer laptop and is typing something.

"You mean this house?" I say. "But that means we are sitting right on top of an earthquake zone."

"If an earthquake happens, yeah, sure," Colton says as he continues to stay focused on his computer screen. "We'd be at the epicenter. It also means I am close enough to study what kind of energy we have down there and how we can access it. Take a look at this." He turns his computer around and shows me the screen. It is full of incomprehensible mathematical calculations.

"I'm sorry, Colton, I never got past pre-calc in high school."

Colton takes his computer back and closes the screen. "That's okay. I've been working on a program to make the geothermal energy more accessible to areas away from the plate boundaries. It's expensive to drill for these resources. My new company will use the technology to extract energy from the earth's core. I really wanted to be able to get down to the earth's inner layer. If we do that, there is more than enough energy there to power the planet."

"Isn't it impossible to go that deep into the earth?" I say, "Wouldn't we be destroyed by the pressure?"

"Yes," Colton says, "but I have a way to do it. It requires an ore that is not currently in existence on Earth but I have a friend at NASA that let me have a look at a metal that they took back from the Mars space probe. This metal has properties I think could be used to access the energy we have beneath us. It will take a ticket to Mars, which no one is giving out yet, but a person can dream, can't they?"

I remember an inspirational quote I had seen on the wall of my high school guidance counselor's office: "The best way to make your dreams come true is to wake up."

When I wake up I will remember what Colton has told me. I feel that what he is telling me is what I already knew from hearing snippets of his conversations countless times while watching him pitch his company to investors at Starbucks. I hope he can find a way to make his dream come true, and soon. It could be the saving of everyone.

I want to try something with him in case all of this is more real than I know. I want to go outside with him and see if we can fly together. Maybe we can fly all the way to Zeus's ship and one more person will be safe.

My dream has changed again and we are outside Colton's stone house. Colton takes me by the hand and leads me through overhanging trees to a garden that surrounds his home. He has a stone patio with insets of something sparkly that I suspect are more diamonds. There is an outdoor fireplace set up with a burning fire. The embers pop and crackle, sending red lights into the sky. He leads me over to a double hammock that has been lined with pillows and blankets.

"Do you want to look at the stars?" he says.

Wordlessly, I join him in the hammock and he wraps his arms around me. The sky above us is full of twinkling stars. I rest my cheek against his chest and contemplate the moment when I will take his hand and try to lead him to those stars. He gently strokes my hair and says, "You inspire me, you know. You make me want to do great things. You are my muse."

"You will do great things," I say.

"You will too," he says.

I don't know how I could do great things when there is a wave of sadness in my mind always threatening to crash through. I sigh heavily, causing his hand to jump.

"I know you get sad sometimes," Colton says. "I've seen it when I've seen you around."

"I don't know if I only feel sad now," I say. "I think I feel…angry."

"That's okay," Colton says. "Don't be afraid of the dark. It can fuel you. Make you do great things." He is speaking in a low, steady voice that is soothing. He speaks with such confidence in what he is saying. It makes me think that maybe I can turn this all around.

"Colton, will you fly with me?" I say. Colton takes my hand like he knows exactly what to do. We sit up together in the hammock and look up at the sky. Colton places his arm around me and I rest my head on his shoulder.

"I'll fly with you to the stars if you like," Colton whispers into my ear. "Or maybe we can just stay here and I'll show you my world."

"Your world seems nice," I say with a sigh.

"You've hardly seen my world," Colton says, "this is just the surface. There's so much more."

He pulls me close and softly kisses me. Our lips part and I look into his fathomless dark eyes. I want to stay here with him and look into those eyes forever. I close my eyes and we kiss again, his deep, even breathing matching mine. His arm tightens on my waist and we slowly lie back down again. I reach up to stroke his hair and think *flying can wait, we'll fly another day.*

Colton begins to kiss my neck. "Zoe," I hear him whisper into my ear. But then I realize it's not a whisper at all but more of a shout from someone else far away. I hear the voice again and this time I can make out who it is. It's Brandon and he sounds frantic. All of a sudden, I remember why I can't stay here.

I place my hand on Colton's chest, "We need to leave here now," I say, "we need to fly."

"Not yet," Colton says as he kisses me, "let's enjoy the night." I will go in a minute, I think. I'll take his hand and we'll fly away but just another moment here. I look at the black sky with the sea of stars and then at the black hair of Colton. I lean in to kiss him again. I reach for his hand, and then out of the night sky comes an enormous flash of light.

The sky splits in two and the light comes at us, wrapping tightly around the hammock. The light is blinding me. I cannot see Colton anymore and I can't feel his hand. I reach out to grab his hand again but all I feel is air.

"Zoe!" I hear my name shouted. It's Brandon calling again. I reach out once more for Colton's hand. I know now we have to fly, we have to get out of here.

"Grab onto my hand," I say, as I reach up my arms to jump into the sky. But instead of jumping I am falling. The blinding light turns into an explosion of luminescent particles. I close my eyes because I fear the force of the explosion. The particles travel through me and in me, pulling me off balance. Before I can hit the ground, I see a pair of strong arms reach out to cradle me.

"I've got you," I hear a voice say. The particles have stopped moving in my body. I must be back but I don't feel like I am back. I open my eyes and see my own face looking back at me. I am looking at myself lying on the ground. I can see Brandon's arm reaching around, cradling my shoulders to stop me from hitting the hard, concrete floor of the spaceship. His other hand is wrapped tightly around my fingers.

Chapter Seven

I wonder if I am having one of those near-death experiences that you hear about where you are floating above your own body as you straddle the line between living and dying. But then I realize I am that I am not floating above the scene; I am viewing it down on the ground. I came back but I didn't come all the way back into my own mind. I am in Brandon's mind.

Does that mean I've become Brandon and can control his body? I test this by trying to lift one of Brandon's hands and make it pat Brandon's head. Nothing happens. Brandon is still using that hand to tightly hold onto my hand. I try to speak but the only thing I can hear is Brandon's urgent cry of my own name. I have no control over Brandon. I can see that all I am is a visitor to Brandon's mind.

That makes me wonder what is actually in his mind. Can I read his thoughts? How would I do that? I don't know how to reach them.

I look at Brandon's hand as he holds my hand. I see his firm yet gentle grip, the way the tendons of his hand flex. I see his other hand cradling my shoulders. My hair spills over his hand and he lifts my head a little so that my hair doesn't touch the floor. I look at this picture of concern and sweetness and stop thinking entirely. I just let myself feel his care.

Then like a key that has fit a lock, his mind's thoughts are open. I can hear what he is thinking. It's a bit of a mess in there. The thoughts go around and round in his head very fast. I can feel his anxiety. I jump in and try to make sense of his thoughts.

Zoe, please wake up. It's going to be okay. I want to laugh out loud thinking this because here's the truth: We're on a spaceship with a couple of nymphs, a psychotically jealous cupbearer, and a Greek god. We're fleeing the destruction of the earth and the vengeance of your mother's supreme god-boyfriend's ex-wife. Apparently Greek gods are a thing and I know basically nothing about them because I spent seventh grade goofing off in class with my friends instead of paying attention that semester.

Zoe, you've fainted into my arms and I can't say I blame you. You are pretty upset to find out your mom has taken off in a space craft without even saying good-bye. But I don't know, maybe she has a good reason. Marcella is much weirder than I remember her. She was just a mom when I knew her when we were kids and now she walks around like she is some kind of queen of the universe and judging me. It's true that she could be the actual queen of the universe since she's with Zeus so maybe she's earned that.

I look at you, the girl with the golden curls lying in my arms, and know I have to continue to keep it together. For you. You are literally the girl of my dreams. I dream about you all the time since we started working together at the grocery store. We're together all day so it's normal that I would end up dreaming about you. What's not normal is that I have not always been sure they were even dreams. I think some of them have actually happened.

One time I was sleeping and having a dream about you. I woke up and I swear I thought you were actually in the room, sleeping beside me. I waved my hand over you and said, "Zoe, are you there?"

You sort of faded away while I was looking at you. Another time I woke up for a moment and I thought I was in your room. I closed my eyes and immediately went back to sleep. When I woke up later and I was back in my own room alone, I thought I must have been dreaming before. Now that I've somehow ended up on a spaceship after dreaming about you, I think I may really have been in your room while you were sleeping. If Marcella knew this, she would have a legit reason to be mad at me.

I'm not sure what to make of Marcella. Everyone thought Marcella was dead. It's hard to believe she would fake her own death and traumatize her daughter in the process. I heard about the cruise ship accident when I was away last summer. We hadn't been friends for a long time but I was sorry to hear it had happened.

I sent you a DM. I'm not proud to say that I didn't really think much about it after that until I came to work at the grocery store and saw you again. You were beyond sad, you were a shade of your former self.

You were like one of those dryer sheets when you take them out of the machine after they have been through a dry cycle. All the vibrancy had evaporated from you and you were listless and frail.

I lost my older brother when I was younger and I knew the place you were at. The sadness was the only layer of you anyone could see now.

When I lost my brother, I did things to build on top of the sad layer. I worked really hard in school and got good grades so that I could have a student layer. I worked out and played basketball and soccer so that I could have an athlete layer. I spent time with my little sister and my parents and built up my brother and son layers. I went out with my friends and went to parties to feed my friend layer. Little by little I built up my person again and the pain took up a small part of my stomach instead of my whole body. I held onto the layers tightly so that they wouldn't blow away and I wouldn't turn into a shade too.

Your mom was your whole world. It was tougher for you to build enough layers so that you didn't blow away. You wore a lot of clothes that had such a nineties look to them that I'm pretty sure they were real nineties clothes that belonged to your mom. I understood that. I travelled to school with a leather jacket of my brother's. When I wore it and someone said "nice jacket," I heard it as "your brother was cool, you must miss him."

I wanted to help you to access at least your friend layer. I started by complimenting you on your clothing sense. You stared at me and then looked away. I didn't take this personally. When you are building a friendship layer, it's usually best if you look at it like it's paper-mache. Little strips gently applied and smoothed down. I kept trying different things to get your attention and a positive response. You were so immersed in sadness, like a goddess of rain.

The thing that really broke your reserve was the fruit and vegetables. It was my main job to keep on top of the produce. I juggled oranges in front of you as I passed your cash register to restock. I picked up two zucchini and mimed that I was playing the drums on a watermelon.

I put an orange slice in my mouth at lunch break and acted out the Marlon Brando heart attack scene from The Godfather. *I texted eggplant emojis in conversation and I was really talking about eggplants. I was not smooth at all. This is the kind of behavior that will get you firmly in the friend zone. But I was okay with that because that was what you needed.*

After a while of this you laughed one day. It came out of in a short, loud burst like a donkey braying. It sounded like it had been bottled up inside of you for a long time. I smiled back at you and our eyes met. You shook your head and said, "You've fratted out quite nicely, Brandon." Zoe was back. You had some nice friendship layer to build upon. You even gave me an opening with some gentle snark about me being a frat boy. Because of course you assumed I was in a frat.

You were wrong about that. I had been in a frat when I started school but it didn't last long. I didn't drink because of what had happened to my brother and it's almost impossible to be in a fraternity if you don't drink.

Drinking was a competitive sport at my frat house. When I declined to join in their drinking games, there would be awkward pauses and a period of bros hunched over sheepishly sipping their beers. No one wants a sober person around when they are intent on getting wasted.

People who drink are weirded out by people who don't drink and that's a fact. They don't know what to do with them.

I had a girlfriend once who took me to a dinner party with some of her couple friends Braydon and Kelsey. Braydon asked me what I would like to drink and then recited a long list of alcoholic beverages he had on hand. I said thanks but I'll just have water. Kelsey looked mortified and screamed at Braydon, "I told you he doesn't drink! You should have got spritzer! Now he'll have to drink the jam! Get the blender out and we'll puree it!"

"The blender is full of Margarita mix, Kelsey!" They went off to the kitchen and had a full-blown fight. I think Kelsey eventually came back and offered me some balsamic vinegar mixed with spritzer.

To avoid this kind of thing, I usually take whatever I am offered when I am in an alcohol situation and hold it in my hand without drinking. I couldn't get away with this at the frat, however, because hoses directly inserted into the throat were often involved. Young and sober is one of the last frontiers of life-style choices that no one knows how to deal with.

With that in mind, I didn't tell you that I wasn't in a frat. I just wanted to see you laugh again. I became your clownish co-worker and I looked forward to opportunities to joke with you when I was at work.

I had a girlfriend earlier in the summer named Adriana — friend of Kelsey! — and I almost felt like I was cheating on her because when we were out I was often thinking about my day with you and the fun we had. Adriana could read my mind, as girls often do, and accused me of liking you. She asked if we made-out in the stockroom. This was ridiculous. I didn't like the fighting and we broke up. The irony is that Adriana kept coming by the store while I was at work after the break-up and a couple of times she and I made out in the stockroom.

We didn't get back together. It was the summer and I just wanted to have fun so I dated different girls. I didn't want you to be one of those girls. I don't want to do anything to hurt you. Over the summer we've really become friends and I don't want to do anything to ruin that. What happens when you have a girlfriend is you eventually break up and sometimes you don't see each other again. You had become part of a new layer I had built into myself. It's one that makes me happy and offers some buffer against the pit of pain I still have about my brother. You are a protective layer. I looked forward every day to seeing you. I want to always be able to have that happy anticipation.

It would be vain to think that my romantic interest matters one way or another to you because it doesn't. You like someone else. Our neighborhood has become popular with a certain kind of hipster and that of course has led to its gentrification by the douchey rich. The douchiest rich dude of them all moved in so that he could soak up the creative vibes falling off the more gifted and turn them into highly profitable, industry-destabilizing apps. I am speaking of oligarch-in-training Colton Chase.

Guys like Colton run the world. I'm an engineering student so it's guys like me who actually make everything run. I see how you look at him when he stops by the store to get some almond milk for his crushed avocado cereal. Which is cool, I want you to be happy.

Girlfriends and boyfriends come and go at our age. What lasts is friendship. What you and I have is special and it goes beyond anything we have with anyone else. We have some kind of connection that makes it possible for us to dream about each other and travel in dreams together. You and I held hands and made it through the earth's atmosphere into a space-station. We have a connection that traverses space and physics.

The color has drained from your face and I fear your sad shade is beginning to take over again. I need to paper some more layers on you again. The paper-mache needs water.

"Astrape," Brandon says, "Zoe has fainted. Could you please get her some water?" Brandon's voice takes my attention out of his thoughts and to the view from his eyes. I look at what is happening around us. Hermes drops the bag he has been packing and comes over to have a look at me on the ground. I feel like I've been away dreaming and in Brandon's thoughts for a long time, but it must have only been a few seconds.

"She's not feeling well?" Hermes says.

"I think she's upset about her mother leaving without saying good-bye," Brandon says. Hermes nods his head and walks quickly over to one of his bags. I mean *really* quickly. It's as if the wings on his shoes give him extra speed. He goes into his bag and pulls out the winged staff he had earlier. He comes back over to us and starts to point it at my body.

"No!!!" I scream inside. Brandon's hand goes to his forehead. I think he has heard me. I don't want to hurt Brandon's head but I have to stop that winged staff from coming anywhere near me. I scream again and with a jolt I am out of Brandon's head and inside my own head.

I have control of myself again. My eyes open and I see Hermes levelling the staff at me. I put my hand out and say forcefully, "No, Hermes, get that thing away from me. I don't want you to use your magic mood wand on me. I do not consent to you doing that."

Hermes puts the staff down and comes over to talk to me. He takes my hand and helps me to stand. I let him do that, then I remember who I am dealing with and snatch my hand away and take a step back from him.

"It's okay, Zoe," Hermes says, "I was only trying to put you in a better mood. I won't do anything if you don't want me to." Hermes looks about twenty-two and has an innocent air about him. I remember him referring to himself as the Prince of Thieves and realize he is tailor-made to be a con artist.

"Let me feel what I feel," I say. "I want to have a clear head and I don't want to have any kind of alteration to my thinking." Hermes puts his hands up in the surrender pose then goes back to gathering his bags for loading onto the transport ship.

Astrape has come back with the water. I take a big sip then look around me. I look up into Brandon's concerned face and immediately feel pangs of guilt. I knew about his brother dying but I didn't know how much it haunted him and I should have.

I also feel guilty about reading his mind. He certainly didn't consent to me sorting through his thoughts. I don't know how I even landed there. It must have something to do with the connection we have that allows us to dream together.

I hope he can't do the same thing and reach into my mind and read my thoughts. There's lots I wouldn't want him to see. Although he seems to have figured out about my enormous crush on Colton Chase all on his own. I have a sudden thought.

"Brandon," I say, "did I come back alone?"

"You didn't go anywhere," he assures me. "You fainted. You've been here the whole time."

I take the rest of the water and swallow it down with a big gulp. "Are you sure?" I say, "Did it go dark at all? Could there be someone hiding in the other ships?" I put the cup down and walk towards the back of the space station where the transport ships are docked.

"Be careful back there," Hermes calls to me, "Listen, if you are going to be crawling around in the ships, could you take some of these bags with you? We're loading up number seven."

I ignore him and start looking around the ships. I walk around a ship, try opening the doors, and find the ship is locked. I then drop down to the ground and crawl underneath it. The ground is caked with dirt and some of the sparkles on my shoes rub off as I push myself along.

"Zoe, let me help you with that," Brandon says, "What are you looking for?"

I pull myself out from under the ship, brush myself off, then immediately go to the next ship and try to open it.

"It's locked," I say, "Why would they lock all these ships?" I bend down to look under the next ship but I do not climb under it this time. The ship sits quite high off the ground and I can see what is underneath. There is no need to get dirty. I can't see anything under this ship either. I can see beyond to the neighboring ships and see that they all have nothing hiding beneath them. I stand up and feel disappointed.

"Zoe," Brandon says, "if you tell me what you are looking for, I can help you."

I look up at Brandon and shake my head. "I'm being silly," I say, "it was just a dream. Let's go see if we can help Hermes with his packing."

I brush back my hair with my fingers and straighten my dress because it has gotten moved around while I was climbing under the ship. I turn my back to Brandon so I can reach into my dress and discreetly pull up my bra strap.

I'm wearing one of those crazy push-up bras and it's riding up and twisted. Of course, my mom told me to wear this. At the thought of her I feel the sting of tears in my eyes. Then as my hand pulls at the strap, I feel something else. I reach under the fabric and feel something hard and sharp. I carefully pull it out with my fingers.

"What have you got there?" Brandon says. I walk up to him and hold out my hand in shock. In my palm is a large, shining diamond.

"Was that under the ship?" Brandon says.

I shake my head. "It was caught inside my dress," I say. "I brought it back with me from my dream. Brandon, I dreamt about holding diamonds and now I am holding one in my hand."

I clasp my hand tightly around the diamond and begin jumping around with excitement.

"I can bring things back!" I say. "I was on Earth in my dream and I picked up this diamond and now it's back here with me. Do you know what that means? I can bring people back with me. I can connect with them in my dreams just like I did with you and I can bring them back! You probably can too. We can dream about those we care about and bring them back here. We can save them."

I thought about all the people on Earth I would like to save. Brandon's parents, his sister, staff at the grocery store, my classmates, everyone I have ever known.

"Do you know how this dream travel works?" Brandon says, "Did your mother tell you anything about it?"

"She said we would have to be in the vicinity of the Earth and it would only work with people we are connected to. They would also have to want to go with us. Being in love helps too."

When I say this, I feel awkward. We both look at each other. I think I'm blushing. I shake myself because my embarrassment doesn't matter. I want to figure this all out and see how we can apply this to helping save more people.

Brandon is looking at me. He takes the diamond from my hand and looks closely at it. He silently hands it back to me and I tuck it back into my dress again.

"He must not have wanted to come with me," I say. "I don't know how much of that was real but he's not here. Maybe he didn't understand. Maybe consciously he thinks I'm that dumb girl who gives him his almond milk and crushed avocado hemp seed muffins at the grocery store."

"Almond milk?" Brandon says. "Who were you looking for, Zoe? Who did you think came back with you?"

I know that to tell him is going to be embarrassing for me. But I know his mind. He should know mine too.

"Colton Chase," I say with a soft exhale of breath. "In my dream he seemed…" I pause and take a gulp of air, "he seemed like he loved me. I thought he would want to go with me."

Brandon looks at me for a moment then blinks and looks away. "I'm going to see if Hermes needs any help," he says.

Brandon walks off in search of Hermes. He seems like he is almost jealous but I don't know why that would be. I saw his thoughts about me. He only wants me as a friend. I feel like the protective shield that is my Brandon layer has shrunk just a little bit.

Chapter Eight

"Take your seats and do up your seatbelts, everyone," Hermes says from his captain's seat at the front of the ship.

"The take-off might be a little rough," he continues, "It's just a little turbulence, though, nothing to be worried about. Emergency exits are to your back, over the wings." Hermes says this last part into his phone like he is talking into a microphone. "Just kidding. There are no wings and there are no emergency exits. I'm your emergency exit. If something happens, look to me. You can count on me. I'm in charge of delivering passengers to Hades, and I haven't lost a person yet. They are all dead but they were like that when I got there."

"Hermes was the guide to the dead who led souls down to the underworld in Greek mythology," I explain to Brandon. "One of his many jobs."

Brandon looks thoughtful. He motions to me to join him at the back of the ship where there's a kind of storage closet. He opens the closet door as if he's checking it out. The door acts as a wall between us and the rest of the ship.

"I don't want Hermes to hear me," he says quietly to me. "I don't believe he's a god. I think what we are dealing with is some kind of alien species and a mythology has grown up around them. The 'gods' likely appeared before the Greeks with all their advanced technology and could easily get themselves declared deities. Hermes probably pronounced himself deliverer of the dead as some kind of joke. I'm sure he thought it was funny to tell the Greek priests that their final journey was going to be with him."

I nod my head but I remain silent. He could be right. But if they are another species that acts like gods, isn't that the same thing as being gods?

Brandon takes his seat beside Hermes in the co-pilot seat while I take a seat behind them. We had called shotgun and I had won, but I gave the seat to Brandon because he's interested in flying. He studies aviation in his engineering course at school. I think he's looking forward to this up-close experience of watching a space transporter fly.

It's a pretty spacious cabin with sleeping quarters and a small kitchen. There's a living area beside the kitchen that includes a small couch and a table and chairs.

On the table there are old board games piled high along with a few paperbacks. It could be the inside of someone's camper, if someone had a camper decorated in industrial-grade steel and alien upholstery.

Hermes has switched gears now and is pretending to be a dad taking his kids on a trip instead of a flight attendant.

"Has everyone used the washroom? Have you got your snacks? Okay, get ready for take-off."

The ship begins to shake as the engines come on. The deep rumble shakes the cabin as the engines come up to full thrust. A massive set of doors in front of us open up and suddenly we are looking into deep space. The shaking of the ship continues as Hermes steers the ship forward through the open doors. His normally jovial expression has hardened and he looks like he is concentrating. I lean back in my seat and clench my knuckles tightly around the back rim of Brandon's chair. He reaches backwards and holds my hand.

It feels like some extra power is being ignited, giving me a massive kick in the back. Brandon releases my hand and my arms fling backwards. We blast through the doors and we are ejected into outer space.

The engines continue to accelerate and I hear their immense power being released with barely controlled fury. The pressure on my chest is enormous and I wonder if the ship will hold together.

After a minute of this, the acceleration drops and the pressure on my body vanishes. We are flying through space.

Hermes relaxes and turns back into his old self. "Everything okay back there?" he says.

"Is it always like that?" I say. "That was more than turbulence. It would have helped to warn me about what was actually going to happen. I felt like there was a hundred-pound weight on my chest."

Hermes turns around and gives me a smile. "Take-off does have a kick to it," he says. "Now we can sit back and enjoy it. There won't be any cars along the way so we can't play the license plate game to pass the time. How about we play name the rock? There are a lot of meteorites out there now. Do you all know your minerals?"

"I think Brandon does. He's a geologist," I say. I lean forward and whisper to Brandon, "I know you aren't a geologist, but you probably know more than he does. Did he ever talk about minerals on his YouTube Channel?"

Apparently, Hermes has supersonic hearing because he answers like he is part of the conversation.

"I didn't talk about minerals because nobody cares about that. The kids liked watching me build my Minecraft structures. I can see why you watched those, being an engineer. I'm an engineer too."

"Really?" I say with surprise.

"I'm the god of invention and magic," Hermes says. "What else would you call engineering?"

Hermes brings up a screen on the dashboard. He taps it and a map appears. "We have to chart our course," he says. "Marcella and Zeus were going to Olympus. There's enough time between us that if Hera goes there to look for them she won't connect you with them when you arrive. We'll hide for a while and then meet up with them once they have dealt with her."

"Can we go somewhere else?" I say.

Hermes and Brandon both look back at me with surprised expressions. "You don't want to see your mom?" Hermes says. "I thought you would jump at the chance to see her. Are you mad at her?"

"I don't want to talk about her if you don't mind. But that's not it. I don't want to leave Earth without trying to help all those people. Brandon and I have been talking. We think we can figure out a way to get at least some of the people out of there. We want to fly them up like Brandon and I flew up."

Hermes taps the screen in front of him and brings up a video of Earth. It looks like he has caught the middle of a hurricane. Trees are blowing violently and things are flying through the air. As he moves the screen around I can see flattened houses and over-turned cars.

"That's a great idea," he says, "but the logistics of that are not safe right now. You two are special in your receptivity to that kind of travel. We don't have the time to put it into effect for other people. You would have to go back there for a while to live. I can't bring you down to stay when there is this kind of weather going on. It's dangerous."

"Where is that?" Brandon says, pointing to the screen. "It looks like the South Pacific. Is it hurricane season?"

"That's San Francisco," Hermes says.

"The extreme weather that we've been seeing for years is gaining momentum. As the storms increase it gets into a pattern that can't be stopped. It gets to a tipping point and nothing can be done to stop it. The tipping point will probably have come and gone before anyone with the power to do anything decides to act. That is why Marcella was in such a hurry to get you out of there."

Brandon's shoulders slump at this news. I imagine he's thinking of his parents trying to fight a losing battle against the elements. I reach out and give his shoulder a squeeze. He gets up and comes around to sit in the seat beside me.

"It's okay, Brandon," I say, "there may be something else that we can do. When I had that dream about Colton he told me about his new company. I think I may have subconsciously been picking up the things he said about his company in the coffee shop. He has an idea to save the environment by converting energy stored in the earth to fuel. It would take a special metal to be able to withstand the pressures of the earth but he knows where to get it."

"Damn, Colton Chase has a good idea," Brandon says. "I probably would have wanted to get a job with him when I graduated. But I've never heard of a metal that could do that. Where do you get it from?"

"Mars," I answer. I call over the seat to Hermes. "Hermes, can you take us to Mars?"

Hermes ponders this for a moment then says, "Yeah, we could do that. A trip to Mars could work. It's doubtful Hera would end up there. I think we have some lead space suits and breathing apparatus in the back. You have to wear them because your delicate human skin could never withstand the radiation in the atmosphere. If you think take-off was rough, you should try landing in the thin Martian atmosphere. But don't worry. There are landing craters on Mars that have been equipped to approximate Earth's atmosphere. And we have shock absorbers and heat shields."

"What about water?" Brandon says. "There's nothing there. How are we going to survive?"

"There's lots of water there, under the volcanoes," Hermes says. "There's a very famous resort under one of them, Olympus Mons. I went there for a vacation with my ex-girlfriend, Katie. She loved the moonlight. Mars has two moons, you know. We had a place for a while on the shores of Lake Boebeis." Hermes drifts off and appears lost in his thoughts. Brandon and I look at each other, then look at Hermes. I take out my phone, write something, then show him the screen:

I think Katie is the one who got away.

He takes my phone and writes back: **What do you think he did to screw it up?**

I write back: **Cheating.**

He replies: **Definitely. With her sister.**

Me: **With HIS sister.**

We stifle our laughter so Hermes doesn't hear. Hermes brings his attention back to us and says, "Have you ever dated anyone with piercings, Brandon?"

Brandon ignores his question. "So, there's water under the volcanoes," Brandon says, "Elon Musk is going to be happy to find that when he finally gets there."

"Oh, he already knows," Hermes says with a wink. "He's one of us."

"Wait, what?" Brandon says. "What do you mean by one of us? Like he's an engineer or he's a god? What is he?" Hermes winks at us again and smiles.

"What does he mean?" Brandon says to me. "Is Elon Musk a god? How many of his kind are on Earth?"

"Don't worry about it," I say, "he likes to mess with us. The important thing is we get to Mars and get the metal we need. Then we can get the metal and take it back to Earth and give it to Colton." Brandon nods along at the plan even though it looks like he cringes a little when he hears me say Colton's name.

"A quick drop-off of the metal to Earth should be okay if we time it right. The metal you're talking about must be fleuranium." Hermes says, "Vulcan mines it on Mars. He spends most of his time there enjoying the volcanoes, extracting the metal, and shipping it off to other markets. We can get some from him."

"Do you know who Vulcan is?" I say to Brandon.

"Um, is he Spock?" he says.

"No, he's not Leonard Nimoy," I say with a laugh. "He's the god of fire, metal, and volcanoes. He did all the forge work. Vulcan is his Roman name. Hey, Hermes," I say, "why don't you call him his Greek name, Hephaestus?"

"He still goes by Hephaestus, but I like Vulcan better. Hephaestus sounds like Festus. That was the name of a character on an old TV show called *Gunsmoke*. The guy was kind of an idiot. I don't like the association. Branding is really important, but not all the gods get that."

Brandon and I get out of our seats and go sit in the living area. We rummage through the games and decide to set up a game of Monopoly. I was hoping they would have some interesting god-developed games, but this looks like something they would have picked up from Walmart. Brandon takes the airplane play piece and I take the milk bottle. Brandon wins the roll of the dice and gets first turn. It only takes him a few turns and ten minutes to buy up all the best properties. On my next turn I roll the dice and end up in jail. Brandon offers me his get out of jail free card, which I gladly use.

On his next turn he's landed on Boardwalk. If he buys it and starts building homes on that, it is game over. He looks at it and says, "Do you want to play something else? This game always gets mean once it reaches the property baron stage."

"Yes, please," I say, relieved that he doesn't want to bankrupt me.

Hermes joins us and sits down in a chair. "Forget the game," he says, "we need to come up with a plan to get the fleuranium."

"Shouldn't you be driving?" I say.

"Auto-pilot," Hermes says. "Most of the driving in space is auto-piloted. When a crash can cause total devastation, you don't leave much to chance. Although you wouldn't know that by the way you humans let your highways get run. Semi-trailers are basically loaded weapons that should never be in the hands of unassisted people. That's humans for you. You guys should never have kicked us out. We could have helped you with that. We even had a road goddess. That's what Katie did. She would have helped you." Hermes is looking wistful again.

Hermes keeps coming back to Katie. I wonder if he wants to talk about her. I make a note to ask him about it later. But right now, I'm wondering about this plan.

"Can't we just ask Hephaestus for the fleuranium to save the earth?" I say.

Hermes shakes his head and begins spinning the milk bottle game piece. "Vulcan doesn't want to save the earth. There's a story that he's the one who caused the carbon dioxide problem to begin with. We call it Vulcan's Curse."

"I remember my mom calling it that but she called it Hephaestus's Curse." I say.

"He put a curse on Earth after all that went down with Gaia the earth goddess. They had a thing, you know."

I shake my head. "Our Earth is falling apart because of some romance gone wrong between a couple of your gods?" I ask. "How can you be critical of humans when the gods act like that?"

"Don't underestimate the importance of love, Zoe," Hermes says. "It has power beyond your comprehension and it can make people do things, good or bad. You've got to respect that or you'll turn into a bitter harpy. And believe me, I've seen them and you don't want that. They have a woman's face with a bird's wings and claws. Just nasty."

I'm not sure that the earth's problems have anything to do with Hephaestus's love life. Still, I wish the guy had better luck with women. He's probably pretty bitter himself and that may make him harder to deal with. Whatever the stories, Hephaestus isn't motivated to help the earth and that is a problem for us.

"If Hephaestus doesn't want to save Earth, then how can we get him to help us with the fleuranium?" I say.

"We steal it," Hermes says. He looks expectantly at the two of us and we stare back silently.

"Zoe, can I talk to you for a moment in private?" Brandon says.

Hermes gets up and heads to the back of the ship. "You two talk about it. I think I will take a shower and get myself cleaned up," he says. "Elysium Mons has a casino that's pretty high end. We're not talking slot machines. You'll have to check your lead space suits at the door."

Brandon waits until Hermes has closed the door to the washroom and we hear the shower go on, ever mindful of his supersonic hearing.

"Zoe, Hermes is a great guy. I know he is trying his best to help us out," Brandon says.

"He's super-sketchy," I say flatly.

"Yes!" Brandon says. "I'm relieved to hear you say that. We can't be stealing from Hephaestus. You don't want to do that, do you?"

I go over to the Monopoly game and start packing up the game. I put the pretend money back in the cardboard slots and gather up all the player pieces. I fold the board up and put it in the box. Before putting the lid on, I have one last look around for all the chance cards. Those always get left out because people stash them. As I'm taking care to be orderly and responsible with cleaning up, I feel suddenly angry.

"Brandon, do you ever get tired of life picking you up and putting you down like a suitcase?" I say.

"Um, I'm not sure what you mean, Zoe," Brandon says hesitantly.

I can feel the emotion rolling in my chest and for once I don't want to push it back down. "Here we were, living our life on Earth, and all of a sudden we are flying through the air and landing on the floor of a spaceship. We had no choice in what was happening to us. And we had to go on the spaceship because of what was happening on Earth. We had no choice about what's going on there either. The pieces of our lives are moving around and we just go along with it. I'm sick of it. Whether these things have been done by gods or the people who have come before us, does it matter? We don't have any control over our own existence. I want to do this because it will be us doing *something*. It may not work out, but at least we tried."

"Zoe," Brandon says, "I know you are upset about your mother…"

"Please don't talk to me about her," I say. "She clearly has been making decisions about her own life for a long time without regard to me. Or she hasn't and her actions have been dictated by some god who wants to date her. I can't let my existence be so out of my control."

"So what if we have to steal from a god? They have not been looking out for us. Climate change is even called Hephaestus's curse. No one has been looking out for us. No one has been looking after anybody but themselves, and now every human is on a course for some kind of apocalypse. We can get the fleuranium and deliver it to Colton and he can fix things. Then maybe all this will have been worthwhile."

Brandon looks at me with soft eyes while saying nothing. I remember what I saw in his mind, his thoughts of trying to help me out of my sad mood. He's only been nice to me. I hope I haven't come on too strong.

Finally, he says in quiet voice, "Remember when it was you and me against all the boys at the playground?"

When he says this, I am hit with sudden emotion. I have to pause before answering because I can feel my throat constrict and I am afraid the words will come out raspy. It would be humiliating if he saw me choke up because he has reminded me of the water gun fight. The truth is, this is one of the best memories of my life. It was the moment I made my first friend. I was the moment I saw another person make the choice to turn away from the crowd in order to stand by me. It was the moment I knew Brandon.

I don't expect him to feel all the things I felt at that time so I simply answer, "Yes, I remember. You helped me fight off the boys I had stupidly riled up and thought I could take on all by myself."

Brandon smiles. "It was you and me against the world."

I smile back at him and his dark eyes light up. "It's funny that you remember that," I say.

Brandon picks up a chance card that has fallen to the floor. One of us must have dropped it when we were playing. He turns the chance card over in his hand.

"It stuck with me," Brandon says. "That's the Zoe I knew. Fighter of boys, winner of spelling bees. You were always so smart."

I am stunned that he remembers me this way. He must be the only one. It's true that I was the kid in primary school who always had her hand up and could answer the teacher's questions. But things changed when my dad left and my mom had to work all the time to support us. We were now a family of two instead of a family of three and that seemed just too small to be a family. For a while, when the teacher asked us questions, I didn't hear what she said because my mind was elsewhere.

Because I wasn't paying attention, I stopped answering questions. I stopped trying and no one said anything about it. I looked around at the other kids in the class and saw them staring out the window or playing with a toy under their desk and that seemed to be okay with everyone. I saw that you could get by with just doing a little and you could save up your energy and your thoughts for something else but I didn't know what that something else might be. I just knew that I wanted to keep something to myself and not give to the world anymore. It was easy to make this change. No one seemed to care.

Brandon takes the chance card and places it inside the Monopoly box. "I sometimes wondered about you when I moved away for Junior High. I wondered if you were still getting in water fights with boys."

I feel like my brain has short-circuited. "Wait, what do you mean when you moved away?" I say. "We graduated from high school together."

"Yeah," Brandon says. "But my family moved to the interior of British Columbia for junior high because my dad got a job there. We moved back for high school. Didn't you notice I was gone?"

I think back to those years. Brandon and I stopped hanging out in elementary school. His life was on an upward trajectory while my life was on a downward one. I assumed he had been out there somewhere in my school being popular while I became less noticeable. I felt like I had disappeared when in fact he was the one who was gone.

"I'm sorry, Brandon, I honestly thought you were in school with us all that time. I definitely remember you being there in high school. I used to watch you play in all the football games."

"It's ridiculous that you weren't on the cheer squad for the games. Our school policy of allowing the popular girls to pick all their friends for the cheer team left the best cheer athlete off the team."

"You knew I was a cheerleader?" I say in surprise.

Brandon takes the Monopoly game and places it on the shelf. He comes over and sits beside me on the couch. "Zoe," he says. "I know you. Just because we stopped being friends for a while, it doesn't mean I lost interest in you. I knew we would be friends again one day. Nothing bad happened between us, we just were doing different things for a while. I always remembered when it was you and me against the world."

Brandon reaches over and takes my hand. He pauses for a second and looks into my eyes.

"I always knew you, Zoe," he says. "Let's do this. Let's do what we need to do. It's you and me for the world."

I squeeze his hand and the happiness bursts out of me with a smile. Brandon and Zoe for the world.

Chapter Nine

The red, sandy soil of Mars is swirling around my feet. A light dusting of air is always moving, depositing grainy sand over every part of me. I reach up to my face mask and wipe the sand off of my eye shield for the thousandth time. Hermes has left us standing outside at the foot of a volcano, waiting for him to come back.

Brandon and I look around at the acrid spot where Hermes has left us. It is desolate and utterly devoid of life. Hermes had warned us that even though it looks like we are in a desert, it is glacier-cold here. Our lead-lined suits are both protection against the radiation in the environment and insulation against the cold temperature.

It's daytime, but the ever-moving dust cloud that skirts the surface of Mars partially obscures the light of the sun. A burnt orange haze settles over everything. We hiked here from the ship, which we left hidden in a volcanic crater.

My legs ached under the heavy weight of our suits as we trudged along. Brandon and I thought Hermes was taking us to an opening at the bottom of the volcano that would lead us to the resort. But it seems like Hermes was unsure of how to get inside.

At one point he stopped and turned to us and signaled, "Wait here." Then he sprinted off at lightning speed without telling us where he was going. I assumed he was using his extra-fast running abilities to circle the volcano and find the right spot to get inside so that we wouldn't be spending any more time out here. I have the idea that this resort, if it exists, likes to be hard to find.

The wind is picking up. Brandon and I are being pushed backward by the velocity of the air and the ferocity of the flying sand. I reach for Brandon's hand and he tightly grasps it, just in time to prevent me from toppling over. The wind is now coming so fast that the flying sand has become an impenetrable mass. We can no longer see each other. We are in the middle of a full-blown sandstorm.

I hold tighter onto Brandon's hand and with my other hand I reach into my pocket to check for the amulet Hermes gave to each of us before we exited the ship. He told us it is some kind of tracking device and that he can use it to lead him back to us. The amulet is still in place.

Brandon wraps his arms around me and pulls me into a tight hug. I think he's trying to create enough mass between the two of us that we won't be obliterated by the storm. We drop to our knees and huddle together on the ground. The wind howls over our ears and it would be of no use speaking, even if we could talk through our breathing masks.

I try to shut the sound of the wind out of my ears and concentrate on my breathing to remain calm. It's difficult to breathe with the suffocating feeling of the sand. I hold tight onto Brandon and hope he is all right. He is taking the bulk of the storm with his body as he shields me. I want to curse Hermes for leaving us this way.

Through the high pitch of the wind I hear something else. It sounds like it could be barking. The noise gets louder and now it sounds like it's definitely barking. The barking is getting closer and closer. It's at my ear now, and then I am alarmed to feel the paws of a dog press against my leg. More paws against my leg and then the quick thump of a tail hits my shoulder.

There seem to be several dogs. I am fearful that we are being attacked and I hope that our suits can withstand sharp teeth. Panicked bile rises in my throat and I close my eyes tightly, wishing myself far away.

Then I feel reassured because against my ear I hear the sound of a panting dog, the way they sound when they are excited and happy. I reach my hand up to pat a dog and it burrows its head into my glove.

The darkness of the sandstorm is pierced by a light. The sand clears a little in the vicinity of the light and I can see the outline of what appears to be a lantern. The swirling sand slowly begins to clear around the lantern, and I can see that it is being held by a young woman wearing a cloak. A saffron veil surrounds her face and she looks to be able to breathe without the help of a breathing apparatus. Her rather beautiful face is untouched by the raging sand, as if she carries an invisible force field with her. She moves closer to us and the sand clears in her wake.

As she gets nearer, the force field that she seems to carry with her extends to Brandon and me, and the sand churning around us disappears. Our limbs are no longer being battered and we can see again. She beckons to us to come closer. Brandon and I get up and stumble towards her. There are three black dogs trotting along beside us. They leap around us and try to lick at the sand stuck to our lead suits.

We get within an arm's length of the mysterious woman and feel the wind die down. The woman places her hand on Brandon's shoulder and gestures to us to follow her. We plod behind her and watch the sand funnel away at her approach. The dogs continue to leap along beside us and behind us like they are herding us.

The windstorm has subsided, and the sand has returned to its former knee-high swirls. We've reached a place at the bottom of the volcano wall. The woman swings her lantern out and focuses its light on a part of the wall. She points at the wall with her long, outstretched fingers. Under her breath, I can hear her saying a string of words in a language I don't recognize. After she finishes, she blows out a puff of smoke from her mouth. The smoke floats over to the wall and there is a trembling of the wall face. As the smoke spreads over the wall, a section dissolves and an opening to the volcano appears.

The woman waves at us to follow her inside. My legs feel heavy from the lead coverings and from fatigue. I prepare to let myself finally rest as I cross the threshold of the volcano opening, when I hear the dogs start barking excitedly.

I turn around and see a sand-covered specter looming behind us. It's human shaped, but it is so covered in packed sand that no human attributes like clothing or skin are visible. My eyes travel down to its feet and I can see a feather peeking out at its heels. It's Hermes. He pats one of the dogs like it is an old friend and gives it a scratch behind his ears. The woman turns around and looks at Hermes in surprise. As she holds her lantern, I can see her fingers tremble slightly.

"Hi, Katie," Hermes says with a sheepish grin.

We are in the mouth of a cave lit by lanterns attached to the walls. We can hear the sandstorm outside welling up again and the wind howls through the opening created by Katie. She signals for us to get behind her, then she turns to face the roaring gales. She raises one arm towards the opening and fans out her hand. Her fingers move like she is playing scales on a piano, and the hole in the wall begins to repair itself. Rocks and dust come together and soon the wall is closed.

Katie turns back to us and crooks her finger at us. I think she is trying to tell us to take our masks off. As she moves her finger, I feel a tug at my helmet. I lift my mask off and take off my gloves. Red dust from my helmet falls off and sprinkles my hands. I take a deep breath and inhale a combination of Mars dust and volcanic ash, sending me into a coughing fit.

Katie has a concerned look on her face. "We have to walk a bit further to my house and then we can get you some water," she says to Brandon and me. "I will make you a tea as well. It's good for the cough. It was very dangerous for you to be outside like that. If you didn't have those amulets you would have died in the storm."

Katie takes down three lanterns from the wall and hands one to each of us. "Follow me," she says and takes a lantern in each hand to lead us through the tunnel.

Hermes picks up the bags he carried with him and hooks his lantern onto one of the bag handles. He gets directly behind Katie and says, "Thank you for coming and rescuing us."

Katie halts her step and turns to face him. She gives him a hard stare then says, "Of course I came. What choice did I have? I am Hecate." She then turns and strides quickly away down into the tunnel. Hermes could well catch up with her, but wisely decides to hang back.

Hermes' old girlfriend Katie, it turns out, is Hecate, an ancient Titan goddess who rules over storms, magic, and crossroads. She protects travelers on their journeys at night and can create and stop storms. By saving us from the storm she was just doing her job as a goddess.

She has been around longer than Hermes, longer than Zeus, longer than most of the gods and goddesses that we hear about. At the same time, she is one of the few gods who is still actively worshipped on Earth today. As the goddess of magic, she is considered the goddess of witchcraft by modern-day witches. There was even a group of girls I went to high school with who were into witchcraft and called themselves the Sisters of Hecate.

We follow behind Katie with the dogs coming up beside and behind us. There are several channels leading off our path to other parts of the cave, but the dogs prevent us from veering off course by nipping at our heels.

We are walking on a downward slope and seem to be going further underground. It must be a well-used path because there are torches all along the way. Finally, we come to an opening at the end of the cave. We step out into a meadow with a hazy, mauve sky above. It takes my eyes a second to adjust to the muted light after the darkness of the cave. I can see we are in a field of lavender grass with clusters of low, brown trees. Green malachite stones have been set into a red clay pathway bisecting the meadow.

"My house is right here," Katie says, pointing to a smoky-stoned house with generous archways and a large fountain out front. Black onyx benches line the path leading up to the house. The door to the house looks to be plated in gold and it has scrolling carvings, some of which look to be ancient Greek letters, while some of the letters look closer to Egyptian hieroglyphs. With a flick of Katie's hand, the door slowly opens and we walk inside a two-story entrance way tiled in black marble. We are greeted by what looks like a white ferret with red eyes. It walks across my legs and then leaps onto Brandon's shoulder, its long whiskers skirting his cheek. Katie quickly takes it off his shoulder, gives it a pat, and pushes it outside.

"I'm sorry about the polecat," she says. "You can step out of your suits here and then you can clean up. My home is built alongside an underground heated spring. You can bathe in it and then we'll get you something to eat. You are of course welcome to stay here. I have other guests too. Are you here for the gala?"

Hermes answers for us, "Yes, we're here for the gala. But there's more to it than that. I can talk to you about it while they are cleaning up." Hermes pauses and looks down at his feet as he waits for an answer. He has brushed the sand off himself but his clothes look disheveled. The feathers on his winged shoes seem untouched by our ordeal in the sandstorm.

"Does that invitation to stay include me?" he says gingerly. Katie looks at him with cold, dark eyes.

"Of course," she says, "You are in my home. Now we have to obey the rules of Xenia. Under the rules I cannot turn away a guest who shows up on my doorstep. As you well know."

Katie leads us down a hallway to an arched door that opens into what looks like a grotto at a spa. The walls are carved out of stone with ledges holding towels, candles, soaps, and oddly, a few nests of owls. There are several pools and the sound of trickling water. Occasionally, a geyser erupts in one of the pools and steamy water shoots up. Hermes disappears for a second into one of the geysers, then emerges completely cleaned of the sand. He looks at Katie with a smile and says, "Don't I clean up well?" She ignores him and shows us to the pools. She gives us some towels and then leaves us alone to clean up. Hermes follows her out the door, looking pensive.

The spring heats a series of interconnected pools, each semi-private because they are bordered by rock walls made up of amethyst and rose quartz. Brandon and I go into separate pools with sheltering walls so we can each have a private bath. I grab a loofah that Katie has helpfully put beside my pool and start to scrub. The dark water bubbles quietly. I look over the border wall of my pool and can see Brandon resting his back against the wall of his pool with his eyes closed. He's only a few feet away so we can talk.

"I wonder why he couldn't just call her," Brandon says after a while.

"They probably had a bad break-up," I say. "He probably was afraid that she wouldn't let us in if she saw us with him. He knew that if we had the amulet and he was nowhere in sight, she would be compelled to come save us. Hecate was always one of the kindest gods. Do you know the story of Persephone and Demeter?"

"No," Brandon says. "I am regretting not paying more attention to Greek mythology when I was in school."

"Demeter is goddess of agriculture and Persephone is her daughter, goddess of spring. Persephone was out gathering flowers one day with her maidens when she got separated from them. The earth opened up and Hades sprung up on his horse-drawn chariot from the Underworld. He snatched Persephone and took her down to the Underworld to be his wife. When Demeter couldn't find Persephone, she was grief-stricken. She wandered around crying, but two gods helped her. Helios, the god of the sun, who saw the whole thing and told her what had happened, and Hecate, who saw it too. She stayed with Demeter and they travelled the world together looking for Persephone."

"Did they find Persephone?" Brandon asks.

"They found out she was in the Underworld," I say. "Demeter was so upset over the loss of her daughter that she stopped doing her job and the crops died. Zeus had to step in. He asked — guess who — HERMES to go to the Underworld and fetch Persephone. Persephone came back but she couldn't stay up top full-time because she had eaten a pomegranate seed in the Underworld. If you eat food in the Underworld you have to stay. They struck a compromise and Persephone spent two-thirds of her time with her mother and one third of her time with Hades. When Persephone is not with her mother, Demeter mourns again and that's how we get winter."

Someone has helpfully left fruit smoothies for us to sip on at the other side of my pool. I paddle over there to get myself a drink. As I am sipping from my glass I see a woman enter from the doorway to the room. She has a towel wrapped around her. I think she must be looking for a pool to enter. She drops the towel and she is standing there naked. I mean, sure, she's having a bath. We're all naked underneath the water. I grab my glass and wade back over to where I was talking beside Brandon, so she doesn't think I am staring at her.

I don't want to shout over the wall to talk to Brandon while there is another person in the spring. I take a sip of my smoothie. It is so good; it tastes like strawberry and banana.

I wonder how Hermes and Katie got together originally. Hermes must have met her when he was bringing Persephone back to her mother. Or they could have met down below. I know that Katie became a friend of the family and spent time with Persephone in the Underworld. Hermes was always going back and forth with the dead. I am sure that Hades, Persephone, and Katie are all friends.

I wonder how Brandon is. I look over the rock wall to see what he's doing. There beside him in the pool is the naked woman. In his pool — like there are no other choices for her bath. They are chatting and sharing a bowl of grapes in the water. She is very pretty. Her long hair is piled on top of her head, loose tendrils framing her face in a becoming fashion. She pops a final grape into her mouth, and then casually gets out of the pool, still naked. Brandon politely averts his eyes but I don't think he missed it. She wraps her towel around herself and then strolls away, but not before giving him a wave good-bye. He waves back and smiles.

I want to stick my head over the wall and ask him all about her, but I am afraid I will sound jealous and stupid. Instead, I duck down in the water to do a final rinse. As I slowly bring my head up, I catch sight of a pair of winged sandals padding by. Hermes has invaded our hot tub area. He sits down on the side of my pool and puts his feet in.

"This is so nice," he says. "Are you kids enjoying the water?"

I swim over and begin splashing Hermes. "You nearly killed us!" I say.

"I didn't do anything," Hermes says, "I don't make storms."

"Mars always has storms," I say. "You set us up so that we would be caught in the storm, and Katie would sense our amulets and come and rescue us. I am so sick of having my life messed up because of the romantic lives of you gods. Why couldn't you just call her and ask her to let us in? Oh, I know, probably because you did something that made you think she would never talk to you again. What did you do? Cheat on her? Ghost her? Cheat on her and then ghost her?"

Wordlessly, Hermes lifts his feet out of the water, and stands up. His usual quick movements are completely in check, and his step is heavy as he walks over to the side of the pool and finds the towels.

Hermes takes a few of the towels and brings them back to the pool. He takes one to dry his feet, and he dumps the others on the side of the pool beside me.

"You two should get dressed," he says in a quietly tense voice. "Katie would like to talk to you. And no wandering around the house. I'll come back to take you to the dining room."

On the way to the dining room, we are intercepted by Katie. In her arms she is holding a black lamb. I pet its woolly head, and it bleats a soft cry that sounds remarkably like a baby's cry.

"Zoe, can you come with me?" Katie says as she puts the lamb on the ground. The polecat comes dashing in and takes a playful swipe at the lamb. The lamb runs down the hallway with the polecat coming up right behind.

Katie smiles at them indulgently.

"Don't worry, Baba and Honey are friends. I would like to help you get ready. I have a beautiful gown that I think would look wonderful on you. Hermes, there are some clothes that you and Brandon can change into downstairs. After everyone has changed, we can meet back in the dining room. You must all be famished! We have some roasted Martian pheasant and Venusian eggs that I'm sure you'll enjoy. The raisin and currant cakes are good. We have blackthorn berry tea as well."

Unencumbered by storm gear, I get my first good look at Katie. She's dramatically beautiful, with long, wild curls and the dark eyes of a sorceress. She has rimmed her eyes with smoky layers of shadow, and stained her lips a deep red. She is like the sexy witch in a Halloween movie.

Katie takes me into what I assume is her dressing room. It looks like a big closet with rows upon rows of gowns, shoes, scarves, and hats. The walls are draped with silky pink and orange fabric overlaid with large gemstones, including sapphires and moonstones. The room is furnished with a pillow-strewn, red-orange velvet circular couch that surrounds a sheepskin rug.

Katie runs her hands across the lines of dresses and the gowns flutter awake at her touch. She seems to have magic pouring from her fingers at all times. She selects a black, low-cut dress that is run through with silver threads. It is very va-va voom.

"That's beautiful. It will look great on you, Katie," I say.

"It's not for me, it's for you. Do you want to try it on?"

I hold the dress in front of me and run my hand over the silky fabric. Just thinking of wearing such a dress gives me a secret thrill. But I don't think I could ever pull it off.

"It's gorgeous," I say, "but that dress is way above my pay grade. I spend most of my time in hoodies and pajamas. This is a big leap for me."

"Then leap," Katie says. "Isn't that how you learned how to fly? Try it," she says with gentle insistence.

I don't want to be rude, so I put the dress on. It hugs my figure, but not too tightly. It's very low cut. "This is going to need some double-sided tape." I say, as I pull at the fabric around my chest.

"No problem," Katie says. She waves her hand over the dress front and back.

I feel the dress make slight movements, as if an invisible tailor is taking nips and tucks here and there. The right undergarments for me to wear magically appear under the dress. I think I'm even wearing Spanx.

Katie sits me down at her makeup table and picks up a brush for my hair. The perfect curls that Bronte had worked so hard to create are now a tangled mess after time spent crushed under my helmet and wet in the pool. Katie picks up a bottle of something and sprays my hair. I brace myself to feel hard tugging as she tries to work through the matting. Katie takes the brush and runs it smoothly through my hair. One brush stroke and the matts are completely gone. She brushes my hair a few more times and in the make-up mirror in front of me, I see my curls are now a straight sheet of silken tresses. She didn't even use a blow-dryer. Katie must have a magic hairbrush.

Then Katie goes to work on my make-up. I think she's going to use the same kind of smoky hues she uses on herself, but instead I see her reaching for pearlized whites and pale shades. She is sitting in front of the make-up mirror so I can't see what this looks like as she applies powders to my face. After a few moments, Katie says, "Now the reveal. Come with me to my tall mirror. Close your eyes."

I close my eyes and Katie leads me to a mirror on the far wall of her changing room. She places something weighty on my head. "Open," Katie commands.

Katie has given me some kind of witch goddess make-over. My blond curls have been brushed out straight and pour down my back. It even looks like she somehow added highlights. I am wearing the black dress shot through with silver threads and it looks like it was made for me. Around my head, I am wearing a baroque silver headpiece with a shining jewel in the center. My make-up is as dramatic as Katie's but my features have been lightened instead of darkened. It has the effect of being ethereal and mysterious at the same time.

"Thank you, Katie," I say. "I love it!"

Katie has a small smile, pleased at her handiwork. "The head-piece is from my collection of Hephaestus's work. He will feel flattered when he sees you wearing it."

"Have we got a meeting with Hephaestus?" I say. This is great. Maybe we can avoid the whole heist.

"Let's go to the dining room and talk to Hermes and Brandon. We can tell you the plan."

I go into the dining room intent on showing off my new look to Brandon. What they call the dining room is more like a luxurious cafeteria. The walls are adorned with jewels and silks like I saw in Katie's changing room. Chandeliers are over-head and fairy lights are strung across the ceiling. Three long buffet tables are organized in a U-shape, and they are over-loaded with food. The buffet tables are decorated with orange and yellow gourds holding willow branches and sprigs of tuberose. About twenty circular tables are set up with place settings and there are people eating at about half of them.

It appears Katie has a lot of people living here. Most of them look to be women, and they are glamorously dressed in long gowns and jewelry. There are a few men as well, and they are wearing modern looking clothes that have the distinction of looking well-made and expensive.

I see Brandon's back to me as he's loading up his plate at the buffet table. Feeling dramatic, I stand posing with one leg coming out of the slit of my dress movie-star-at-the- Oscars style. I will Brandon to turn around and look at me so that we can laugh at this together.

It almost works because he starts to turn around, but he's stopped by a woman in a long blue dress slinking up beside him. She whispers something in his ear and he turns away from my direction to talk to her. It's that naked woman from the baths.

At least she has clothes on this time. I feel deflated nonetheless. I walk over to the buffet to get some food for myself and stand in line behind Brandon and the woman. They have their heads together and they are discussing the food.

"Try this one," the woman says, "the Mayan turtles are to die for. The recipe is ten thousand years old. I have a dessert recipe I like to make. It's traditionally eaten at midnight. Maybe I'll sneak into the kitchens tonight and make it for you," the woman says with a sly smile. She tosses her head and walks right by me without even acknowledging my existence. It's the supermarket all over again.

Brandon turns around to follow her with his gaze as she walks away and almost knocks me over.

"Zoe!" Brandon says, "I'm sorry, I didn't see you there. I was talking to a friend of Katie's that is staying with her."

He stops talking for a moment and notices what I am wearing. He takes a step back to look at me. "Whoa, Zoe," he says, "what's that you are wearing?"

"Katie dressed me and did my hair and make-up. It's what you wear to meet Hephaestus, I guess. Is it too much?" I ask.

"You're beautiful," Brandon says. I am momentarily rendered speechless. I notice that he has changed, too, into something decidedly more rugged. He's wearing a short leather tunic like a Grecian warrior, exposing his well-toned legs and arms. He has on leather cuffs that go to his elbows and a leather headband around his forehead. I am just about to say "nice dress," then think better of it. "You look good too," I simply say.

"Did you see the shoes?" Brandon says, gesturing to his thigh-high lace-up sandals.

We go to sit down with our plates. Katie gracefully seats herself in a chair beside me and we start eating. Hermes is suddenly in the room helping himself to food. He can move so quickly that sometimes it appears as if he has apparated.

Hermes loads up his plate and joins us at our table. "Here's the plan for getting the fleuranium from Vulcan," Hermes says.

Katie gives him a look. "Fine, I'll call him Hephaestus. Anyway, *Hephaestus* is sponsoring the annual Martian Gala this year and Katie is helping him with the details. Katie is very good with figuring out the details of things."

Hermes is looking at Katie when he says this and she is looking right back at him. Something is going on here, but I have no idea what. I'm never very good at figuring out couple subtext. Do they hate each other, or did they just make-out in the stock room? I don't usually know what is going on between two people, and that includes when I am one of the two people.

"That makes sense, that you would help Hephaestus with the gala," I say. "Figuring out details are one of the things associated with your divinity."

Katie raises her teacup to her lips and takes a sip of tea. "I'm associated with ghosts too, and you don't see me doing any ghosting."

Ooooh, that is definitely a burn. Hermes is shifting back and forth in his seat, the shifty bastard.

I whisper in Katie's ear, "Is everything okay with Hermes? Do you want to go to the ladies' room with me and talk about it?"

"Thanks, Zoe, but everything is okay. We have bigger things to worry about. We have the earth to save. The gala is in only a few days, so we have to put things in place quickly to pull off stealing the metal from Hephaestus. The Martians do not like people from Earth visiting, and all official visitors have to be documented and under the auspices of a god or a Martian. We have to create a reason for the two of you being here. Zoe, you are going to go see Hephaestus with me and pose as my assistant."

"And Brandon," Katie says, "we are going to say you are part of the entertainment for the gala. I've called Athena in for back-up. She is goddess of the arts, so we'll say you are with her. I hope there's no god emergencies back on Earth because with Athena on her way here, there will be no one to help coordinate their ships travelling through the atmosphere."

Athena is coming here? It seems like every god is Katie's friend.

Brandon gets up to go to a food table to help himself to some more bacon. One of Katie's dogs is following him around, and he gives him a piece. I jump up to get a second helping, but mainly so that I can whisper to Brandon. "See, didn't I tell you she was great? She's got ex-boyfriend drama over for breakfast, but she doesn't let that ruin everyone's life."

Katie finishes her tea and glides over to where we are standing. She smiles warmly at me and says, "That headpiece looks really nice on you, Zoe. I have some cuffs that would go well with that. I'll go find them and bring them to you. You and Brandon can enjoy your food. We have a while before we go to see Hephaestus." Katie leaves in search of the cuffs.

Brandon takes some more bacon back to the table, with the dog following him again. The dog has rolled onto his back and is wanting a tummy rub. Brandon reaches down to scratch him, and then I hear a whistle and the dog leaps up. Hermes is beside him and he is getting the dog to do tricks.

"Here, Drake, up, up," Hermes says, as the dog dances around on its hind legs. The dog then does a roll over for Hermes and shake-a-paw. Hermes rewards the dog with a piece of bacon from Brandon's plate.

"Hermes, I was going to eat that," Brandon says.

"You've got to stay lean for your performance. Are you ready to go outside, Brandon?" Hermes says. "It's time for you to start your training."

"Sure," Brandon says, with some hesitation. "Let me go find my facemask."

"Not outside, outside," Hermes says. "The outside on Mars is under a biodome. Mars is uninhabitable. But many millennia ago, Martians built a network of biodomes through the canyons and craters that cover Mars. Up until now, these have been undetectable to Earth probes and the Martians built up their society in peace. There's also inhabitable space that's been developed underground on Mars. We are living right now underground on the perimeter beside Katie's own volcano, Hecates Tholus in the Elysium volcani province. It was named for her because Katie is awesome everywhere she goes."

“Her volcano is pretty far away from anything else. The people staying here are Katie’s followers so we can trust them. She flies them up from her Earth covens for the gala. We can get you trained up in secret before we have you perform at the Martian Gala at Olympus Mons.”

“What kind of entertainment are you going to train me to do?” Brandon says apprehensively.

“Everyone enjoys a good fight,” Hermes says. “We’re going to watch you in a match. Let’s see how good those big muscles of yours are at fighting, Brandon. We’re going to teach you how to be a warrior. Prepare for battle.”

Hermes says this with a hard clap to Brandon’s back that causes the last piece of bacon to fly off his plate and into the mouth of a waiting dog.

Chapter Ten

Is Brandon going to have to compete in some kind of death battle? If Brandon is going to learn how to fight like a Grecian warrior, I think I have to see this.

"Can I come?" I say.

"Sure," Hermes says, "you have time before you meet Hephaestus."

"What do you mean by you are training me to be a warrior?" Brandon says. "Am I going to be fighting someone? Like in a tournament?"

Hermes cryptically smiles but says nothing. He takes us through the big gold front door and out onto the clay and malachite pathway leading back to the cave. Before we go back in the cave, Hermes turns and asks us, "Do you both have your amulets on you?" We answer yes. He reaches down to his shoes and extracts two small feathers. He hands each of us a feather. "Take these too. Keep them safe with your amulets. You may need them."

"What do we need them for?" Brandon asks. Hermes ignores him and keeps walking. "How do we even use these?" Brandon calls after Hermes.

We are back in the dark cave. This time we don't have our own individual lanterns, and we have to stay close to Hermes so we don't get lost. We come to one of the channels we passed on our way in, and Hermes turns to take this path. We walk in silence in the warm tunnel for ten minutes until we see a light-filled opening up ahead.

Hermes leads us to the underground outside. We step out of the tunnel, and for the first time I can relax and have a good look at this world we are visiting because I'm not escaping a deadly sandstorm.

The temperature is mildly warm and comfortable for walking. We are walking on a purple gravel pathway bordered by lavender fields of grass. Amber and blue colored wildflowers are scattered amongst the lavender like marbles. Throughout the gently blooming meadow, there are small, brown clusters of trees. Boulders of different, bright colors are haphazardly strewn throughout the fields, their jewel tones glowing. The light is muted but the boulders still sparkle, which makes me think they may be actual jewels.

We walk for about half an hour through the flat terrain. We reach a wide-open field with a silver-white shed. Hermes runs off to the shed, then reappears with two large staffs in his hands. I think I know what he is going to do with them and Brandon does too.

"Don't try hitting me with those," Brandon says.

Hermes throws Brandon a staff, and he catches it. "Just one time," he says, "so I can see where you are at."

Hermes takes his staff in his hand and plays with it.

"I can tell you where I'm at," Brandon says, "I've never hit anyone with a giant stick. Don't do it!" he warns Hermes. Brandon holds his staff defensively in front of him. He stares at Hermes with a determined eye, and I don't think he will let Hermes hit him easily.

Hermes drops his staff and smiles. "I'm a lover, not a fighter. I'm not going to teach you. We have got someone better for that. You are going to be part of the entertainment at the gala and you are going to be performing the warrior art of Omedis, which is a mix of dance, gymnastics, and fighting. It takes strength, speed, talent, and courage. You're going to be great." Hermes flashes us a brilliant smile and his eyes twinkle as he nods his head encouragingly at us.

"And you expect me to learn this in how many days?" Brandon says.

"Do you know parkour?" Hermes says.

"I've tried it," Brandon answers.

"Have you ever done any dance?"

"We had to take it in Phys. Ed in high school."

"Then all you are missing is the fighting. I've seen your moves, I know you can do it. And you will have the best teacher for it. Athena will be your coach. She knows fighting and she knows the arts. She trained some of the greatest warriors in the world in battle. She will turn you into an Omedis master. Now, excuse me while I text her to let her know she's doing this."

"You can text her this far away?" I say.

"It's intergalactic coverage," Hermes says. "You pay extra for it and there's a lag." Hermes is scrolling through his phone. He stops at a message and stares at it for a moment with a perturbed look on his face. He looks up at us with knitted brows. "Change of plans. Athena hacked into the surveillance system on Zeus's ship. She sent me a video. We need to show this to Katie."

Hermes gestures to both of us to hop on his back.

"We're in a hurry," Hermes says. "You're too slow. Get on my back and I'll carry you."

"I don't want to piggy-back on you, Hermes. I'm fast, I can run," Brandon says and takes off running in the direction of the cave.

Instantly, Hermes scoops me up and throws me over one shoulder. Within another second, Hermes has thrown Brandon over his other shoulder like he is a ragdoll instead of a tall, unwilling man. Hermes seems to have suddenly grown big enough to comfortably carry us both.

"Hold on," Hermes yells, and I reach for the back of his shirt. He runs so quickly that all the fields and flowers we passed on the way out go by in a blur. When we reach the cave, Hermes goes low so that we slither through it like a snake. Once outside the cave, Hermes resumes his sprint and within seconds we are at Katie's door.

Hermes drops us to the ground in an unexpectedly gentle way. I straighten my dress, then look at Hermes and he has shrunk back to his usual size. He takes a moment to straighten the feathers on his shoes and smooth back his hair, before opening the door to Katie's house and going inside.

"Stay here," he warns us, as we stand in the front doorway.

Hermes disappears as he moves at high speed throughout the house looking for Katie. He returns shortly, and says, "She's in the library." Hermes gestures for us to hop on his back.

"We can walk," Brandon says, "it's not that far."

"Fine," Hermes says, "I'm just trying to help. I don't want you getting lost in Katie's house."

Hermes does not want to let us out of his sight. I wonder if that sneaky thief has hidden something here that he doesn't want us to find.

The library is a large, circular room with shelved walls of books that look to be twenty feet high. The shelves are made out of some kind of dark, shiny metal and are inlaid with large, colorful jewels. Couches upholstered in orange fabric and circular, stone coffee tables fill the center of the room. Katie is seated on a couch looking over papers as we walk in. She looks up at us and smiles. "I found the cuffs for you, Zoe. Try them on."

I take the cuffs from her and slip them over my wrists. They are heavy and ornately carved. I feel like I could use them to fend off bullets.

"Look at these cuffs, Brandon," I say, as I hold my wrists up for him to see. "I feel like Wonder Woman." I cross my wrists back and forth in front of me like a shield.

Brandon traces his hand over the carvings. "I wonder if you could deflect bullets with these," he says.

I suddenly have an idea. "Katie, did you know Wonder Woman? Wasn't she an Amazon warrior?" I ask.

"I knew a *version* of Wonder Woman," Katie says, "but every self-respecting Amazonian would love to have those cuffs you are wearing. They are made of fleuranium. It's a metal with properties that resist gravitational pressure. That makes them good in a fight as well. I have put a spell on them so you can wear them, otherwise your arms would break."

Brandon and I stare at the fleuranium cuffs, then look up and our eyes meet. I feel a sudden stab of fear, and I wonder if he can see it in my eyes. We are in a strange place, surrounded by people and things with powers we don't understand. I want to ask more about the powers of fleuranium, this metal we are supposed to steal, when Hermes starts to speak.

"We can talk about Diana and her bracelets later," Hermes says. "We need to show you a video Athena sent me. It shows Hera made it to Zeus's spaceship."

At the mention of Hera, I feel my throat tighten and a knot forms in my stomach. Nervously, I cross my arms in front of me and hold onto each of the cuffs, as if they could be my shields right now. Katie glances towards me solemnly, and then looks at Hermes.

"Is the video on your phone?" Katie says. Hermes nods yes. Katie waves her hand towards the phone in a lifting motion and lifts the video right out of the phone into her hand. She then flicks her hand back and a ten-foot screen appears with the video on it. Katie throws her arms out, and with a scooping motion she seems to pick us up and actually put us into the video. I see the landing bay and the line of transport ships. It's as if we are back on the spaceship again.

"What's happening?" Brandon says, "Are we back on the ship?"

"No," Katie says. "It's a simple immersive spell. We're watching the video from inside the video."

The video changes and we are in a room of the ship that I haven't seen before. Astrape is in the room. She has her back to us, and she is testing the door on what appears to be a cage. She swings the door back and forth with a satisfying clang. She pulls a key from her pocket and proceeds to test the lock. After giving the door a few more shakes, she unlocks it and throws the door to the cage open again.

"It's ready!" she yells, while putting the key back into her pocket.

She turns around to face our direction, and Brandon and I jump back. Flames are shooting out of Astrape's eyes. Brandon puts his arm protectively around me before we remember that this is a video and we aren't really here.

"What happened to Astrape?" Brandon says.

"She's the goddess of lightning," Hermes says.

"I thought she was Zeus's assistant," Brandon says.

"Well, she is," Hermes says, "but she's also a goddess. She and Bronte are thunder and lightning goddesses. They're the keepers of Zeus's thunderbolts. I knew they'd be angry that Ganymede took one. He would have been safer going back to Earth."

A clap of thunder and lightning fills the room, shaking the cage. Astrape takes one of her perfectly manicured hands and runs her nails across the bars, sending sparks flying. Her eyes narrow and burn red, while she breathes out a dark puff of smoke from her dilated nostrils.

With a flash of light, a door opens and Bronte bursts into the room dragging Ganymede behind her. He has his hands over his ears and he falls to the ground.

"Please, no more thunder," he begs. "It's too loud! I'm sorry I touched the thunderbolt!"

Bronte shimmers like an electric specter. Her white hair crackles and small bolts of lightning shoot through the strands.

"*You* don't tell *me* to be quiet!" Bronte roars, as she pushes Ganymede into the cage. Astrape leaps forward and slams the door shut. She clasps the lock in her hand, and her hot touch causes the metal to become molten and the edges melt away.

Ganymede curls into a ball in the corner of the cage and sobs. I think Astrape and Bronte might take mercy on his pitiable form, but I'm wrong. The two of them circle the cage and shoot slivers of lightning through the bars. Ganymede leaps out of the path of the fire and narrowly avoids being burned.

"Please," Ganymede says, "I thought we were friends!"

Astrape's eyes shoot two flames on the floor before the cage door. The flames quickly burn out, leaving two simmering holes in their wake. "Only at our pleasure did you get to serve alongside of us!" she screams. "We're goddesses! You don't touch what is ours. This is a high crime and you will be tried for it!"

Astrape flicks her fingernails like she is warming them up for another round of fire, sending sparks flying. She lifts her hands up and points her fingers at the cage like claws. Before she can let loose another flame, Bronte stops her.

"Wait, Astrape, we have to go. I just got a message that a transport ship is docking down below. It must be Hera. We better clean up so we can greet her."

The two goddesses turn to each other and hold hands. They close their eyes and take deep breaths together, then begin to chant. I watch as the electricity that seems to reside in them begins to retreat. Their hair stops sparking and their skin stops shimmering. Before long, they look like normal women again.

Astrape opens her eyes and the fire in them is gone. Bronte turns to address Ganymede, and her voice has lost its thunderous edge.

"You'll stay here until we get to Olympus," Bronte says in a calm, steely tone, "and then you'll stand trial. Now, let's go greet Hera."

The video changes and we are in the docking area we were in earlier. A sleek, silver and white ship is taxiing down the landing area to where the transport ships are parked. Once it is parked, the ship's door opens and out pops a languid leg. A slender hand grasps the edge of the door, and then a glossy head follows.

The head turns and we can see the beautiful, haughty face of Hera. She seems to pause in this awkward posture as if she if posing for a photo shoot. Her feline gaze shoots left and right and then all at once, she is out of the ship and onto the ground without a hair out of place.

There is something familiar about her. If gods are real, or at least they have had a real part of our history, maybe we have a collective memory about them. Maybe when the actual purported queen of the gods shows up, we know who she is because there is some scrap of memory of her in our DNA.

While I am pondering this, I see Brandon shake his head in confusion. "Isn't that the lady whose cookbooks we were selling at the front of the supermarket last week? We had her video playing too. Isn't her name Tamsin Kelsey?" Brandon says with surprise.

I look closer and Brandon is right. Hera looks familiar because we saw her on TV last week under another name. Tamsin Kelsey is a lifestyle guru who has made a fortune acting superior and telling the masses what to do with their skincare and their accessories and how to eat.

I bought my mom one of her cookbooks for Christmas once because it was a bestseller, and I didn't pay enough attention at the time to realize she was a total fraud. One of her "clean" recipes for broccoli was actually this:

Boil water to a bubbly masterpiece, drop in Earth-nurtured broccoli, cook to al dente perfection, enjoy!

"Do every single one of you have high-profile jobs on Earth?" I ask Hermes.

"Do you really think a goddess like that is going to be able to retire to a quiet life?" Hermes replies.

"Her company and website are called Juno, the Roman name for Hera," I say while shaking my head in wonder. "All this time Juno has been hiding the actual Juno in plain sight."

Tamsin, aka Hera, sashays her way about the docking area with the quiet confidence of a born mean-girl. I reach out to Brandon and hold my hand to his ear so I can whisper to him quietly.

"She would eat me for lunch," I say, "Tamsin Kelsey makes girls cry with her passive-aggressiveness. And then they buy the stuff she sells. I hope I never meet her. At the same time, I wonder what she uses to get her hair to shine like that."

Astrape and Bronte enter the room looking like their old selves. They smile broadly when they see Hera. Bronte lets out a delighted squeal.

"Hera, how wonderful to see you!" Bronte says. Hera strides forward and holds out her hands to both goddesses. She smiles at them beatifically and they bask in her glory. She pulls both of them into an embrace.

"You are both looking so beautiful, as always," she says. "Just perfection! I would love to get you to model for my company. Why haven't we done a photo shoot with you yet?"

Bronte looks confused. "We did," Bronte says, "we did a shoot where we modelled for your new fall skincare products, remember?"

"Oh, that's right," Hera says, "we didn't end up using them. I think the light wasn't right. Not your fault at all, of course. When you are made of light like you two are, you have to be careful about how the photo is lit. No ring lights for you two! You are naturally radiant."

Astrape looks at her hand and studies it. Bronte puts one of her perfect nails in her mouth and begins to chew on it.

"I want to catch up with you lovelies," Hera says. "Let's go sit down and chat before I go up to see Zeus."

Bronte and Astrape look awkwardly at each other. Hera instantly picks up on their tension.

"Darlings, it's fine. All the strife between Zeus and me is ancient history. It's been millenniums! We are blissfully de-coupled. I was on my way to Mars for the Martian Gala. I thought I'd make a trip there this year to catch the gala and stock up on Martian sand. It has the most amazing exfoliation and regenerative properties. I plan to package it and sell it to my Junoites. Anyway, I was getting my ship ready to launch when I saw Zeus's ship in the radius of the earth. I decided to surprise him and stop by to say hello."

"Oh," Astrape says, "it's too bad he didn't know you were coming. You've just missed him. He took one of the transporter ships and left. He didn't say where he was going."

The smile that Hera has been wearing disappears. She fixes a cool stare at Astrape and then at Bronte. The thunder and lightning goddesses take a step back under Hera's scrutiny. I reach for Brandon's hand with shaking fingers. He holds my hand and whispers, "Remember, we're not really here. She can't do anything to us."

Hera's chin juts out and she tilts her head back, accentuating the sculptured line of her high cheekbones. She paces across the floor and turns her back to us. After a moment, her head drops and one of her hands goes to her forehead. Her shiny hair has been braided into a single plait down her back. A multitude of different jewelled pins have been scattered through her hair, but the end is tied with a simple leather string. Suddenly, she turns around, lifts her head, and she looks composed again. Her smile has returned to her face.

"That's too bad," Hera says. "I should have let him know. But we ladies can still have a visit. My nails are just a mess. Maybe one of you can do a manicure?" Astrape and Bronte look delighted to be able to serve Hera instead of face her wrath. They both run off in search of their sparkly suitcases while Hera settles herself into one of the couches we sat in earlier. Her smile disappears while they are gone and instantly reappears when they return.

Bronte and Astrape set up their manicure station while Hera lounges on the couch. Hera places her hand on a portable manicure table they have wheeled out, and Astrape reaches for it.

"You have such beautiful hands, Hera," Astrape says as she reaches for her nail file.

"That's what Zeus always said. He said that about everything, actually," Hera says with a laugh. "He always knew what to say."

Astrape nods but doesn't say anything. I don't think she wants to pick up on this thread of conversation. She bends her head further over Hera's hand and files her nails.

"Did you know we had a three hundred-year honeymoon?" Hera says, as she sorts through nail polish samples. She settles on a royal purple and hands it over to Astrape.

"Would you like us to do your feet too?" Bronte says in an effort to change the conversation.

Hera slips off her shoe and rests her foot in Bronte's lap by way of answer. Bronte takes out a foot bath from beneath the manicure table and begins to soak Hera's feet.

"This is nice," Hera sighs. "I could use a glass of wine. Where's Ganymede, did Zeus bring him with him?"

Bronte jumps up and says, "I'll get you a glass of wine, Hera. You just sit here and relax." Bronte disappears into one the doors and comes back a few minutes later with a bottle of wine and some wine glasses.

She sets them on the coffee table and begins to open the bottle of wine. Hera, who had been leaning her head back and closing her eyes relaxing, sits up and opens her eyes at the sound of the clanking wine glasses.

"What's this?" Hera says, "Wine glasses? Isn't this ship equipped with Grecian Goblets? We got a huge set as a wedding present. They are supposed to be distributed to all the royal Olympic residences so that Zeus and I can always enjoy our drink from them. Where is Ganymede? He needs to see to this." Hera takes her feet out of the foot bath and leans towards the coffee table in search of her shoes. Her hand blindly reaches out to find the shoes when she swats at something else, and there is a clang under the table. Out from under the table rolls a golden, bejeweled Grecian Goblet.

Hera reaches for it and picks it up. "A Grecian Goblet? On the ground? How could Ganymede allow this? Is he here or did he leave with Zeus? Either way, he must be punished for allowing this to happen."

"He is being punished," Astrape says, "He went crazy and stole one of Zeus's thunderbolts and tried to shoot up the ship. We have him caged below until we can take him back to Olympus for trial."

Hera narrows her eyes and stares intently at Astrape. "Why didn't you let me know this earlier?" she says quietly.

"It just happened," Astrape says. "We have it under control and we're shipping him back. We didn't want to bother you with unimportant details. He's only a Ganymede. He thought he was going to lose his job and he lost his mind. You know how those weak Earthlings can be."

“Why would he think he would lose his job?” Hera says with a furrowed brow, while looking back and forth at both Bronte and Astrape. The two goddesses are silent and frozen in place. Hera gets up and walks over to a window to look out at the stars. The jewels in hair tremble ever so slightly.

“He wasn’t a very good Ganymede,” Bronte says. “He was going to have to be replaced eventually. He figured it out.”

“We’re sorry we didn’t tell you, Hera,” Astrape says, “it was just a personnel issue. We didn’t think it mattered to you.”

Hera comes back from her post at the window looking at the stars, and stands in front of the goddesses. The goddesses are still seated on the ground from where they had been doing Hera’s nails. Their former fire and fury have been entirely extinguished. Hera towers over them and her gaze hardens.

“Everything that happens here is my concern. Everything that happens with Zeus is my concern. He can have other women, but there will never be another first wife. I am queen of heaven. Even the stars are under my command. Do you like the stars?”

“Poor Astrape and Bronte,” Hermes says, “I think she’s going to turn them into constellations. I guess I’ll never have that drink with them.”

“They’re goddesses too,” Katie says. “That’s not something she can do easily.”

Hera appears to have thought this through too, and she abruptly changes tactics. She smiles at Astrape and Bronte and asks if they are finished with her mani-pedi. The goddesses answer yes.

“Thank you,” Hera says, “I wonder if the nail polish will survive the transformation.” As she says this, the air around Hera begins to shake and shift. Her form becomes unfocused, like we are looking at a hastily shot picture taken from far away. The blurring becomes swirling until nothing of substance can be seen. She spins around in front of us like a mini-tornado.

The swirling gradually slows down and lengthens and flattens. Hera’s shape has entirely changed. Standing in front of us is a fully-grown female lion. She looks like she could be straight out of the Serengeti. Brandon and I involuntarily leap backwards away from her. Even Hermes and Katie look nervous. The lion lifts one of her front paws, as if to check on her claws, and it is indeed painted purple. With a swing of her tail, Hera the lion trots off and out the door. From down the hall we can hear her roar.

Chapter Eleven

The video is now being shot from inside Ganymede's prison room. Ganymede is sitting on the floor of his cage with his head in his hands, looking like he is regretting his life choices. Yeah, dude, maybe you shouldn't have pointed an atomic level weapon at our heads. You might like to rethink your attraction to shiny objects too. Being a Chippendale dancer on that cruise-ship must be looking pretty good about now.

Ganymede stretches out his legs and gingerly rests his head back against the bars of the cage. He's careful to avoid touching any of the fresh burn tracks within the cage, some of which are still smoking. He closes his eyes, as if he's trying to sleep. There is a low rumbling sound, like the sound of a big cat purring, and Ganymede's eyes bolt open.

"She's back," he whispers to himself, "she's back with the thunder." Ganymede beings to shake and whimper.

Hera the lion slinks into the room on silent pads. Ganymede sees her and leaps to his feet. He looks terrified. He runs to the far side of the cage and clutches at the bars.

"Oh, my God, she's going to eat me," Ganymede gasps. The lion walks over to the cage and rubs her body against the bars. She crosses back and forth several times, taking her hide across the bars like a housecat trying to satisfy an itch. She emits a low purr as she moves around that reverberates throughout the room.

The steady purr and the soft movements of the lion have a soothing quality. Ganymede looks entranced by the slow pace of the regal feline. He lets go of the bars and his arms come to rest at his sides. He has stopped shaking and his eyes look sleepy. After a while, Ganymede sinks to the ground and simply watches Hera.

The lion makes a few more passes of rubbing her sides across the bars and then sits down and lifts a front paw to her mouth. She slowly and meticulously grooms her paw while she quietly purrs. Watching the big cat at her gentle work is like watching an ASMR video. I find myself feeling more relaxed. I look over at Brandon and he seems calm too. Ganymede is quietly seated watching Hera. His head tilts left as he watches Hera grooming her right paw. She goes to work on her left paw and Ganymede tilts his head the other way to follow her work.

"Purple claws," Ganymede says, "nice."

The lion stops grooming and sits staring into the cage. She is making direct eye contact with Ganymede. The cat has large light brown eyes that stare impassively at the prisoner. Ganymede leans forward so he can get a better look at the lion's face. He crawls towards the front of the cage and he is within a foot of the lion. All the lion would have to do now to injure Ganymede is swipe a paw through the cage bars. Ganymede seems oblivious to the danger and only continues looking deeply into the lion's eyes.

"Zeus left quickly because he knew you were coming and he was afraid to be here," Ganymede says, as if he is answering a question. The lion continues to purr and stare at Ganymede.

"He was afraid you would hurt Marcella, his girlfriend. They left so quickly they forgot to take me. I don't know where they went."

The lion comes closer to the cage and presses her snout against the bars. She opens her mouth to lick her nose and there is a glimpse of her large, sharp canines. She settles down into a prone position in front of the cage and slips her two front paws through the bars. Ganymede comes forward and gingerly pets the paws. The lion squints her eyes and her purring becomes louder.

"He came back here to pick up Marcella's daughter from Earth. Apparently, it's about to blow. Oh, you don't think so? Yeah, there's no real consensus about this on Earth either. Marcella picked up her daughter and some guy. I think he may have been her boyfriend. He was trying to get my job. He was a real weasel of a guy. As if he knew anything about cup keeping. Hermes was with them too. They all took off in another transport ship after Zeus and Marcella left. I don't know where they went. Do you think Marcella and Zeus had a daughter?"

The cat momentarily releases her claws from her paws and they scratch the floor of the cage. She throws her head back and opens her mouth to let out a loud roar. Ganymede drops back in alarm. Some kind of spell has been broken and he realizes he is inches away from a fully-grown lioness. The lion withdraws her paws from the cage and leaps to her feet. She paces around in a tight circle until she is moving so quickly she is a blur of fur and claws. Then all at once, she comes into focus again, and the goddess Hera is standing in front of us. Ganymede's mouth drops open and he begins shaking again.

"Ganymede," Hera says soothingly, "what a terrible experience for you. You thought you had lost the favor of Zeus and couldn't sit at his side any longer. We all know that is the worst thing that could happen to a person. The court is going to see that and will rule firmly on your side. There's no hurry to get you back to Olympus for trial. I'm heading to Mars for the Mars Gala. Would you like to accompany me?"

Ganymede looks shocked. "You want me to come with you?" he says. "I feel so honored. Yes, I would love to come, thank you!"

Hera smiles. With her high cheekbones and large eyes, I can see a hint of the feline that she was moments ago. "It will be fun," Hera says. "The gala is always a great party. A handsome man like you is wasted on a spaceship. You need to be where you can be seen. Let's get Astrape and Bronte in here to clean you up. We'll have to pack some clothes too."

At the mention of Astrape and Bronte, the color drains from Ganymede's face. Hera doesn't seem to notice, and pulls out her phone and texts them. The two goddesses come into the room. At the sight of Ganymede, Astrape's eyes begin to turn red, and the ends of Bronte's hair are sparking.

"Ganymede is coming with me," Hera says. "Please get him ready so he can go to the gala with me."

Astrape breathes out a puff of black smoke and her red eyes blaze. Hera looks at her steadily, and Astrape blinks back the red in her eyes until they turn brown again. "We will see to his trial later," Hera says quietly to the two goddesses. "I have need of him where I'm going. He could be useful. Remember, any servant of Zeus's is a servant of mine." She's talking about Ganymede, but the way she says it makes me thinks Hera considers herself the boss of Astrape and Bronte as well. Astrape and Bronte exchange looks and I wonder if they can communicate with each other telepathically. After a moment, Astrape reaches into her pocket for the key to the cage.

The video of the spaceship ends and the scene evaporates around us. We are back in Katie's library.

"I am surprised she's coming here," Katie says, "she never goes to Mars. She avoids my house here as much as you do, Hermes."

Hermes ignores the jab. "Not to mention, her son is on Mars right now," he says. "She should know that Hephaestus is sponsoring the gala. That should be enough reason for her to avoid coming to Mars at all costs."

"Hephaestus is her son?" Brandon asks. "Why wouldn't she want to see her son?" Hermes and Katie ignore his question and go off to the end of the room behind a stack of books to talk privately.

"Let me tell you a story about Hera's motherly love," I say. I sit down on a love seat and pat the space beside me as a signal for him to join me. His leather tunic squeaks against the seat as he sits down.

"Hera had Hephaestus out of spite," I say. Brandon lifts one eyebrow in confusion. "She was mad at Zeus and wanted to have a child without him so she had Hephaestus. But when Hephaestus was born, he wasn't good-looking enough for Hera and she rejected him. She tossed him down the side of Olympus and according to the myths, he permanently injured his foot." Brandon shakes his head and his eyes grow large.

"What's this lady the goddess of again?" Brandon says.

"Birth and marriage," I say. "I know. She's terrible at it. Maybe the gods should have had job interviews instead of relying completely on nepotism."

"Poor Hephaestus was abandoned by his own mother," Brandon says. I feel a catch in my throat and I cough to make it go away.

"His story gets sadder," I say. "Zeus didn't think he could get his own wife, so when Aphrodite came along, Zeus arranged a marriage between them. Aphrodite is the goddess of love and beauty. She's drop-dead gorgeous. Zeus thought it best to have her married so that the gods wouldn't fight over her. But, of course, he didn't ask her what she wanted, and she did not want Hephaestus. He tried to be a good husband. Hephaestus doted on her and made her beautiful jewelry. She didn't care. She cheated on him constantly. The poor guy was rejected by his mother and then his wife."

"Now I feel bad again that we are planning to steal from him," Brandon says.

"Yeah, but keep in mind what we're doing it for," I say. "We'll have to make sure he doesn't catch us because he did have a vengeful streak. When he had to grow up without his mother's love, he created a beautiful golden throne for Hera as a gift and had it sent to Olympus. He couldn't take it there himself because, of course, he was banned."

"Hephaestus was the blacksmith and jeweler. He could make anything. Hera loved the gift, but when she sat her mean ass down on the seat, invisible, unbreakable chains appeared and Hera was trapped in the throne. She was trapped there for days and Hephaestus wasn't going to let her go. None of the gods could persuade him to release her. Eventually, Dionysus, the wine god, got Hephaestus drunk on sweet wine. Lucky for Hera, Hephaestus is a nice drunk, not a mean drunk. He finally let her go."

"Did Hephaestus get punished?" Brandon asks. "The consequences of tying up the queen and Zeus's wife must be pretty bad."

"Not at all!" I say. "That's when Zeus decided he should marry Aphrodite. They gave him a gorgeous palace on Mount Olympus too."

"Hera must have been angry about that," Brandon says.

"I don't think it helped their relationship at all. Hephaestus also got back at his cheating wife," I say.

"When Aphrodite was having an affair with Ares, the god of war, Hephaestus crafted a golden net to catch them. The net dropped on them when they were naked in Hephaestus's bed and kept them trapped. They couldn't get out! Then Hephaestus invited a bunch of the gods over to look at them and laugh. Slut-shaming has a very ancient history."

Hermes seems to have heard that last part. “Ares was trapped in the net too,” Hermes says, joining our conversation. He walks over to where we are sitting and continues. “He was actually banished from Olympus for a while for his affair with Aphrodite and what he did to Hephaestus. Ares is my brother and Zeus’s son. Hephaestus isn’t even related to Zeus. But Zeus backed him over his own son. Dad liked Hephaestus.”

Katie joins Hermes and comes over to talk to us.

“There’s been a change of plans,” Katie says. “We think Hera definitely is coming here looking for Zeus, and what she said about the gala and Martian sand is just an excuse. Ganymede has also let her know about you, Zoe. She was always going to have it in for your mother, but now she may have it in for you too. Ganymede has planted the idea in her head that you may be Zeus’s daughter.”

I burst out laughing. “No one’s going to believe that! It’s ridiculous,” I say. “Besides being impossible. My mom only met Zeus a little over a year ago.”

“Hera doesn’t know that,” Katie says, “and technically, it’s not impossible. Time works differently for gods and goddesses.” I am momentarily speechless. I look over at Brandon for reassurance. He looks stunned. His mouth has dropped open and the color has drained from his face.

Hermes sits down on the arm of the loveseat beside me. “No one is saying Zeus is your father,” he says.

“Good,” I say, “because that would be gross.”

Hermes leaps up from the loveseat and is quickly met by Katie. He has a look of fury on his face. He looks ready to explode on me, but Katie is at his side whispering things in his ear. She pats at his arm and then his hand until Hermes appears soothed. She leads him to a couch and he lies down. She sits beside him, patting at his brow and making soft sounds. Within seconds, he has fallen asleep.

Katie turns to me with a serious expression. “I’ve cast a Zen spell on him,” Katie says as she continues to pat Hermes, “he will have a short nap while I pat him and will wake up calm.”

“I should have been more careful,” I say sheepishly. “Zeus is his dad. That wasn’t very nice of me.”

“That was plain dangerous of you,” Katie says. Her dark eyes look gravely into mine. I am reminded that she was once one of the most revered goddesses, a Titan who ruled over heaven, earth, and sea.

"Zeus is king of the gods," Katie says. "That may not mean anything anymore on Earth, but here it means something. To his gods it means something. To gods, the sin of hubris is the greatest sin of all." I bite my lip and stare down at the ground. I did not mean to offend Katie. I will have to be more careful about what I say around her and all the gods. Like it or not, we are living by their rules now. Katie gives me a silent look, then bends down and strokes Hermes' brow again.

"Hubris?" says Brandon to me quietly.

"For ancient gods, it's when you think you are better or as good as the gods," I whisper back. "Anyone who thinks they are better than the gods got severely punished. There was once a really talented weaver named Arachne, who thought she was even better than Athena, the goddess of weaving. Arachne bragged about it and challenged Athena to a weaving contest."

"The whole town came out to watch. The two weaved intricate tapestries at high speed. Athena was good, but Arachne was a little better. When it looked like Arachne was going to win the contest, Athena changed her into a spider and that is where spiders come from."

"Athena?" Brandon says with alarm under his breath. "You mean the one I'm supposed to train with?"

"You'll be fine," I say, "just don't be too prideful about your Omedis abilities."

"That will be easy," he says "I have no Omedis ability." Brandon taps his fingers distractedly against his thigh. I can feel his nervous energy as he sits beside me.

"What's wrong, Brandon?" I say. Brandon looks like he wants to say something, then bites his lip. I think I know what is bothering him.

"Zeus isn't my father," I say wearily.

"I know," Brandon says quickly. "But…is it possible? I never met your dad."

"He left when I was really young," I say. "But he was definitely my dad. If my father was an actual Greek god, don't you think I'd know it? That would make me a demi-god. I would have some special abilities. I have none. I can't even win at Monopoly!"

Brandon laughs when I say this, then looks serious. "I don't know how it would work, Zoe, but I think you need to consider it as a possibility. You're young and haven't had a chance to do many things yet. All your abilities haven't come out yet. And you are really pretty. Like a goddess."

I almost burst out laughing again, but then look at Brandon and see he is serious. I look down at my fleuranium cuffs as I say, "Thank you, you are really sweet. But I'm not a demi-goddess. However, please feel free to treat me like one," I add with a smile. Brandon smiles back and seems to relax. "But not in front of Athena," I say. "Seriously, she would hate that."

Katie has stopped patting Hermes and left the couch. The god of thieves begins to stir. He swings his feet onto the ground and sits up.

"I must have fallen asleep there," he says pleasantly with a yawn, "it's been a busy few days. Anyway, we wanted to let you know there's been a change of plans. In light of the fact that Hera is going to be looking for you, we think it's best that Zoe stay at Hephaestus's house and that Brandon stays here."

"Hera thinks you are a couple so it will be easier to hide you if we keep you apart. She will never go to her son's house, and she doesn't like going to Katie's house either. That will minimize the chance of her running into either of you."

"I'm surprised she doesn't like going to Katie's house," I say. "It seems like all the gods like Katie."

A warm expression comes over Hermes' face as he looks at Katie. "Yep, they do," Hermes says, "even my difficult step-mother. But Hera stays away from here because of some of the house-guests Katie likes to have. Katie entertains people who don't necessarily get along with Hera."

"Wouldn't that be everybody?" Brandon whispers to me and I try not to laugh.

"You have an open-door policy," Hermes says with a fond look at Katie, "because you have a good heart." Katie receives this compliment with a quiet smile. Her dark eyes have softened again.

"My friend Lamia is staying with me now," Katie says. "She's had a rough time of it, but she is doing a lot better now. She's staying in my east wing."

Hermes absentmindedly untwists the man-bun he has been wearing in his hair. He shakes his hair out and runs his fingers through it. He looks more god-like with his long, flowing locks. They would have been a beautiful couple when they were together.

"What kind of rough time did Lamia have?" Brandon asks.

Katie hesitates. She walks over to a mirror that is on the wall near the entranceway to the library. When she stands in front of it, the mirror suddenly lights up and she is bathed in a beautiful golden glow. She artfully arranges her long, dark curls in cascades down the front of her shoulders. It has the effect of framing her exceptionally lovely face. I can see it has an effect on Hermes too, and he appears to be staring intently at her.

At last Katie stops trying to divert attention with her hair-arranging and decides to answer the question.

"Brandon, Zoe," she says, "you know enough about our history to know some very bad things went on. When the gods interacted with humans, humans inevitably got hurt." She looks at us and pauses. She is waiting for some kind of reaction. Brandon and I both look at each other and I want to say "duh." Instead, we both look back at Katie and nod our heads in agreement.

"Hera, in particular, caused some bad things to happen to women because of all the jealousy she had over Zeus's affairs. Lamia was a woman who had an affair with Zeus and had children by him. When Hera found out, she killed all of Lamia's children."

I see Brandon beside me clutch his hands into fists at this news. He looks over at me uneasily. He is obviously horrified at this particularly terrible act of Hera's. This is not one of the stories I remember from school, but I had heard plenty of others about Hera's persecution of Zeus's children conceived with other women. If Hera thinks I am Zeus's child, I am in as much danger as my mother.

"Lamia went mad at the loss of her children," Katie continues. "In her madness, she turned into a monster. She had the body of a snake, but the head and upper torso of a beautiful woman. She could still attract men by wearing long dresses that covered her monstrous lower half. She would go after young men, and make them think she wanted to seduce them. She would spend a lot of time with them so that she could fatten them up. Then when they were nice and fat and they were ready to sleep with her, she would pounce on them and eat them."

Brandon has been leaning forward to listen to Katie's tale. He almost falls off the couch when Katie gets to the part about Lamia eating young men.

"Has anyone in a long dress offered you food around here, Brandon?" Hermes says slyly.

I remember the woman from the pool and from breakfast. I remember she was wearing a long dress and she was trying to make him eat.

"Does she wear a long blue dress and like to make midnight snacks?" I say.

"That's her!" Hermes says, "you met Lamia." So, her naked flirting was just a ploy. She's probably dreaming about wrapping Brandon in a crepe.

"Remember I told you about not wandering around in this house?" Hermes says.

"I wasn't wandering around," Brandon says, "this was at breakfast before you all came in."

"She's fattening him up like the witch in 'Hansel and Gretel'!" I say with indignation. "She was just going to knock on his door late at night and make a meal of him."

"But she has legs," Brandon says, "I saw her in the pool."

"She's recovered," Katie says, "She doesn't do that stuff anymore. She had a madness for a long time because of what happened to her, but she has gotten better. Her snake form is gone and she is no longer a monster. She just needs a quiet place to rest and be cared for. I provide that for her here. You are safe to eat with her."

Katie moves next to Hermes. She brings her face close to him and speaks softly.

"I believed in her and she has changed. It is safe to be with her now."

Hermes holds her gaze and answers back, "Your belief in people is a wonderful thing. Does everyone deserve a second chance?"

Katie looks at Hermes for a long time before answering. "Yes. Everyone," she says finally, "If they want to change for the better. If they can see beyond themselves and look at the whole. If they try." Katie's dark eyes become shiny and bright. The moon goddess is channeling ethereal energy as she locks eyes with her former lover. Hermes moves slightly closer to her until their chests almost touch. Katie's fingers twitch and Hermes brings his hand closer to hers.

"This is why I came here," Hermes says, "to help save the earth, so they can have another chance. I knew you would help because that's what you do. You see the whole story. You have compassion, and out of that things are reborn. If Earth has that second chance, it would be the luckiest planet in the whole universe. It would change for the better. It wouldn't take its gifts for granted. It wouldn't be selfish. It would do things right this time."

Katie's beautiful face is soft and warm. Her full lips curl into a smile as she tilts her head up at Hermes.

"*Atlantiades*," she says in a voice like a sigh and holds out her hand to the god.

The two of them hold hands and smile while staring into each other's eyes. They are in a world of their own. Brandon whispers to me, "I think we should give them some privacy."

Chapter Twelve

Brandon and I decide to head back to the lavender-grassed meadow Hermes had taken us to for Omedis practice. We retrace our steps through the tunnel until we find the passageway that leads to the training field.

As we head out along the purple gravel path that should lead us back there, I am struck by the eerie silence of this place. On our two trips outside Katie's house we have not run into any other living soul, and we have not seen any evidence that outside of her house anyone else is alive. The stillness makes it feel like a lonely place and I am so glad to have Brandon by my side.

As we walk along, the silence is broken by a buzzing in my ear. I swat at it, thinking it must be a fly, although I haven't seen any insects here yet. It buzzes by my face again and it seems awfully large. I wonder what kind of insect it is. I remember getting bit once by a horsefly and I don't want to repeat that.

I duck my head and start to run ahead on the path to avoid it. I turn around to look for Brandon, and see that he is staying back and trying to catch the thing. With a quick snatch of his hand, Brandon captures it. His two hands encase it, the buzzing angrily increasing in volume at being trapped.

"Zoe, come back and look at this," Brandon calls to me. I walk back to him and he opens his hands slightly so I can see what he has caught. It is a tiny flying vessel, about the size of a matchbox car. It looks to be a miniature drone. He opens his hand and the little aeronautic vehicle shoots out of his palm and flies away, like it was waiting for its chance for freedom. We watch the drone take a final circle of us, and then it speeds off out of sight.

"I think someone is spying on us," Brandon says.

We look around and we don't see anyone else. All we can see are miles and miles of lavender-grassed fields. The grass is very tall in places and it is possible that someone could be hiding in it. As I stare out into the landscape, I think I may see a sliver of movement rippling through a field.

"Do you see that, Brandon?" I say, pointing to the far-off field.

Brandon cranes his head to look to where I am pointing. The field is still now. Brandon shakes his head no. We continue walking when out of the corner of my eye I see the field ripple again.

"Did you see that?" I say to Brandon.

Brandon crosses his arms and trains his focus on the field. "Yeah, I did," he says. He bites his lip and seems to be considering what to do. "Come, on, let's keep walking," he says.

It could have been an animal in the field and not a person. An animal could be worse. I have no idea what kind of animals could be living on Mars. I hope they are vegetarians. I feel Hermes really dropped the ball in not giving us lessons on the life and history of Mars while we were flying here. All he wanted to do was cheat his way through the board games that were stashed on the ship.

I wonder what kind of people live on Mars or if they are even people at all. It's obvious that there is some kind of civilization here, but it chooses to remain hidden. It's been built in craters and valleys and subterranean habitats. I wonder if they are some kind of mole people who crave dark corners.

We have arrived at the meadow where Hermes and Brandon left their weapons. I pick up one of the staffs they hurriedly discarded and twirl it around.

Brandon picks up the other staff and throws it across the field like a spear. I throw mine in the same direction and it lands somewhat short of Brandon's staff. We begin a staff-throwing contest to see who can throw it the farthest. Brandon can throw much farther than me.

"How are you so good at that?" I ask Brandon.

"I think you are good too," Brandon says, "you are just constrained by that dress. I'm the one wearing javelin- throwing clothes."

We lose interest in throwing the staffs and decide to look at what other additional weapons Hermes has stored out here. They have been laid out in a shed that he erected. There are swords, knives, shields, spears, and several varieties of clubs. They all look decidedly dangerous. As I reach out to touch the handle of a spiky club, I hear a sound coming from outside.

Brandon hears it too. We go to the door of the shed and peek around the doorway while still trying to remain hidden in the shed. We see a tall, beautiful woman in full Grecian armor throwing spears across the field. She throws with the grace and power of an Olympic athlete. This must be Athena.

She turns and looks towards the shed. We try to quickly pull our heads back so she doesn't see us hiding and staring at her, but it is too late. Without hesitation, she takes one of her spears and hurls it at the door. It lands precisely one inch before the doorway where we are standing, causing us to jump back. She then picks up her shield and strides towards us with a stern face.

When I have seen depictions of Athena, she is almost always wearing a gold helmet, armor, and carries a shield with Medusa's head. The Athena heading towards us is carrying an ordinary shield and has foregone a helmet. Her long hair is in a practical braid down her back. The short metal and leather-armored dress she is wearing allows her to take long, powerful strides as she comes towards us.

When she reaches us, she stands in the doorway and the shed goes dark because she is so large she blocks the whole entryway. She bends her head to look us up and down with her intelligent gray eyes. I already feel small in her presence but I feel even smaller under her scrutiny. Then she closes her eyes and it seems like she begins to shrink. Her form gets smaller and smaller until she fits in the doorway and the light is able to come through. Her graceful figure is scaled down until she is just a little smaller than Brandon.

"You should not look at gods unawares," she says calmly in a low, melodious voice. "It could blind you."

If Hera scares me, Athena straight-out intimidates me. She is intelligent, strong, and majestic. She is the goddess of wisdom and war, an unmarried deity whom the ancient Greek heroes sought out for help and advice. When it came to battle, Ares, the god of war, was the brute force but Athena was the tactician. She was one of the most powerful gods of the ancient world, and it was mostly due to her brain power.

She was even cerebral when it came to her birth. Her mother, Metis, was Zeus's first wife. When Metis was pregnant with Athena, Zeus heard a prophecy that their next child would overthrow him. Zeus's solution was to swallow Metis whole. Strangely, this story did not stop Hera from marrying Zeus or from telling everyone that she was his first wife when, clearly, she wasn't. She's the one everyone remembers but she wasn't the first.

One day Zeus complained of an unbearable headache. It became so bad that Hephaestus took an axe and split Zeus's head open. Athena sprung from his head fully formed, armed, and ready for battle.

Zeus was very proud of her and seemed to forget the whole "your child is going to overthrow you" prophecy. I think he was actually a good father to her.

Zeus, however, continued to be guided by prophecies about being overthrown by his offspring. He gave up on marrying the sea goddess Thetis because it was prophesied that she was destined to bear a son who was mightier than his father. Zeus made her marry a mortal man, the king of the Myrmidons of Thessaly. Thetis gave birth to Achilles who played a big part in the Trojan war. Athena acted as a mentor to Achilles during the battle. She also came up with the idea for the Trojan horse. Brandon is being trained by one of the history of war's great strategists.

As Athena enters the shed, I feel like I should bow or curtsey or something in the face of the overwhelming power and authority that emanates from her. I awkwardly do a sort of combined curtsey-bow and say, "You must be Athena. I am Zoe and this is Brandon. It's an honor to meet you. Is it okay to call you Athena?"

"Athena is fine," Athena says as her eyes quickly skim me and then scan the room, "although three thousand years ago I would have expected you to kiss the floor first before speaking to me. But these days I work in technology with people who sometimes steal my chair, so things change. You are the two I'm teaching, I presume?"

"It's nice to meet you, Athena. I think you'll just be teaching me," Brandon says. "Zoe is going to be working with Hephaestus on the gala."

Athena walks over to the wall of weapons and starts surveying them. "And has anyone taught you what the gala is all about?" she asks while examining the point of a sword.

"No," I say, "they haven't said much about it."

"Then I will be teaching both of you," Athena says. "How does anyone think this mission will succeed if you haven't been taught anything?"

Athena tests the weight of different staffs before selecting two of them. She takes one and hands the other to Brandon. She motions for us to follow her outside.

Athena methodically paces back and forth in the field, flattening the long grass where she treads. She is building a training surface. She begins to talk as she works.

"First of all," she says, "have any of the Martians contacted you?"

"We haven't seen anybody," Brandon says, "but we think they may be watching us. On our way here, we saw a small drone following us."

"It was probably the Martian resistance," Athena says.

"What is the Martian resistance?" I say.

Athena rolls her eyes. "Didn't Hermes tell you anything about the planet? The gala is an annual fundraiser benefiting native Martians in their bid to fight takeover of their planet. The Martians are a small population of mainly indigenous people who make their homes underneath the surface of Mars and in its craters, canyons, and lava tunnels. They created a biosphere and make use of the naturally occurring underground springs and streams. It's a very delicate, balanced system. They deeply fear getting taken over so they formed a resistance."

"Who do they think is going to take over?" Brandon asks.

"You," Athena says, "people of the earth. It hasn't escaped their notice that Earth has been sending up probes for years. They also know that there are people on Earth who are planning settlements here."

"They don't like the idea that after messing up Earth, people are looking at Mars as a safety net. They don't want Earthlings coming over and doing the same thing here."

"But what about trying to help people," I say. "Do they have any interest in taking refugees?"

"First of all," Athena says, "they don't feel like they are being given a choice to accept people. They haven't been consulted at all. And second of all, they feel like they did their part for refugees when they took in the monsters of Tartarus after one of the wars of the gods."

"What's Tartarus?" Brandon says. "And did you say monsters?"

"Tartarus was a dungeon of torment and suffering in the deepest part of the Underworld," says Athena. "The gods imprisoned the Titans there after they had a war. But there were also other beings who chose to live outside the bronze walls of Tartarus after being released from prison there, such as Cyclopes. These are creatures you would call monsters. They were not part of the prison system of Tartarus and were intelligentsia and artists. They provided us with some of our greatest weapons. They did not like being caught in the middle of godly wars and having their home constantly disrupted."

"They sought a new home on the surface of Earth and sent emissaries to check it out. It should have been easy for them to live peacefully on the surface because there are few of them and they are solitary. They could live scattered throughout the earth and not be impactful on the general population. They like to keep to themselves in caves. But they didn't have the ability to blend in as the gods and they were tormented by the Earthlings. Earthlings have no acceptance of the other."

Athena stops talking and puts her hands on her hips as she looks at the field she has built. She looks dissatisfied. She goes back to the shed and returns with a scythe. With long strokes of the blade, Athena cuts down more grass and expands the size of the practice area. She takes the edge of the scythe and whittles away at the stray grasses on the sides of the square she has built. As she does this finer work, she starts up talking again.

"The Cyclopes were driven off the face of the Earth and they fled to Mars. The volcanoes and caverns and underground streams of Mars reminded them of home. The Martians were welcoming to them because they were so much more advanced and brought their technology with them. The Cyclopes built the biospheres. Before that, the native Martians were eking out an existence in the habitable corridors underneath the volcanoes."

"There also weren't that many of the Cyclopes so they didn't pose a threat to the Martian civilization. They became citizens of Mars. The Cyclopes of Mars called themselves Tatarussians in honor of the Cyclopes who chose to remain in the Underworld."

Athena takes a pair of gloves from a pouch on her dress and places them on her hands. She pulls out a second pair and hands them to Brandon.

Athena continues with her story. "The gods like to vacation on Mars and mine its resources. We have worked out a peace with all the Martians, including the displaced of Tartarus. The Earthlings have done nothing to extend peace and show respect. The Martians believe Earthlings are only interested in conquest. These are sensitivities we have to be very aware of when we're mingling with the Martians at the gala."

"Do they hate us?" I ask.

"Pretty much," Athena says, "but they are okay with documented Earthlings helping out with the gala. That's something that has happened before. You have to have the proper documentation, and Hermes is taking care of that. You also have to have an approved reason for being here. In years past Katie has brought up people from Earth-bound witches' covens to help with the gala."

"They come help and then Katie puts a memory charm on them so they forget the experience when they go back to Earth. Zoe, you should be telling everyone who asks that you are from one of Katie's covens."

"Do I have to pretend to be a witch?" I ask. "Won't they expect me to know magic?"

Athena puts down her scythe and comes over to look at me. She cocks her head at me as she studies me with her deep gray eyes. Finally, she says, "You are very pretty. Almost like a goddess. Do you have some nymph in you?"

Brandon shoots me a look. I don't want Athena to think that I in any way compare myself to a goddess. I quickly shake my head and say, "No, I had ordinary parents."

"Your mother is the consort of Zeus," Athena says. "This is not ordinary." I feel embarrassed by the word "consort" and look away from her penetrating gaze. Athena turns her attention to Brandon.

"You look like a straight-up Earthling. Now we will have to train you to look like an extraordinary one — a hero. You have to perform the warrior art of Omedis. It's tradition at the gala to have a demonstration exercise."

"I wish Hermes had come up with a better idea for you. He has no appreciation of the years of training and discipline it takes to master Omedis. It is the artistic representation of the warrior. When Omedis is performed well, you feel the strength, the bravery, the talent of the true warrior. Well, we'll see what we can do. Take this," Athena says handing Brandon a staff.

The two of them walk into the center of the field Athena has turned into a training ring. Athena holds her staff in front of her horizontally between her two hands. "Pick up your staff and hold it like this," Athena says. "The components of Omedis are simple. You are going to use your staff to fight, dance, and perform gymnastics. You will do this in a mock battle with an opponent."

"Okay," Brandon says. "I'm glad it's a mock battle. Up until now, I wasn't really sure what the plan was. I'm glad I don't have to fight someone for real."

Athena takes her staff high into the air and brings it down hard onto Brandon's staff, knocking it out of his hands.

"When you are dealing with weapons it is always real," Athena says angrily. "Do not take this lightly and do not ever let your guard down. It is always possible to get hurt or worse. I lost my best friend Pallas in a mock battle like this. I accidently killed her because we weren't paying enough attention."

Athena had been speaking very loudly and fiercely but now she suddenly becomes quiet. She puts her staff upright into the ground like it is a pole and lets herself slide down it into a crouch position. She leans her head against the staff and grips it tightly in one hand.

"We would have been together forever had I not been so careless," Athena says quietly. "I have taken her name in her honor and my full name is Pallas Athena. When I was worshipped in the temples of Athens the priests said her name with reverence, which is what she deserved."

Athena grows silent. She takes several deep breaths and closes her eyes. I imagine she is far away, a young goddess roaming the hills of Greece with the person she loves best in the world. Athena opens her eyes and seems to remember we are here. Then she bounces up, holding the staff in the ready position in both hands.

"I never wanted to hurt Pallas," Athena says in her usual pragmatic tone. "You will not be fighting anyone who will be so motivated to keep you alive. Now pick up your staff and don't let me knock it out of your hands again."

Brandon picks up his staff and holds it defensively in front of him.

"In combat you use your staff to block, thrust, and strike," Athena says.

She takes a step forward with her staff and tries to strike at Brandon's leg. Brandon is able to block it by bringing his staff down in front of him before she can hit him. Athena then takes her staff and brings it up and tries to strike Brandon's head. Brandon blocks her strike and knocks her staff down. He then lifts his staff over his head and thrusts it at Athena's torso.

Athena looks surprised and avoids the strike by cartwheeling away with her own staff. She throws the staff in the air then does a back-tuck and catches the staff in her hand. She aims to strike at Brandon's torso, then fakes and brings the staff back down beside Brandon's ankles. Brandon neatly jumps over her staff, quickly recovering to bring his staff up again to strike at Athena. She blocks it and then holds up her hand to halt the fight.

"That was a very good start," Athena says with surprise. "You seem to have a natural ability to block my strikes. Later, I will show you the aerial moves I have been using to add to your defense and offense. To be Omedis, you will need to eventually add dance and gymnastics moves."

Brandon crouches down in a defensive position with his staff. "How about we add them now?" he says. "I would like to try them." He is smiling and clearly enjoying himself.

Athena looks shocked at his confidence. She ignores his request and continues to practice fighting moves with him for the next two hours. Brandon is really good at this. He's able to block most of her blows and almost gets in a few of his own.

"Let's take a break and get some water," Athena says. "I, of course, don't need, it but humans have to be fed and watered at regular intervals. It's one of your weaknesses. It's why I always have pistachios on my desk at work. I offer them to the engineers during a mid-morning meeting and it always goes smoother. They don't fuss as much."

"Brandon is studying to be an engineer," I say, as we trudge back to the shed in search of water bottles. Athena looks over at Brandon but does not comment. Athena locates a stash of water bottles in the shed beside some spare spear heads. She tosses one to each of us.

"There is a stream near-by that we can hike to," Athena says. She looks at my long gown. "I cannot tell if you are athletic under that very impractical dress. Can you walk?"

"This is not a normal look for me," I say, "I can definitely walk."

After about ten minutes of walking we arrive at a trickling stream of fresh, pale-pink water. Athena assures us that the water is okay, pink is just the color of water on Mars. We fill up our water bottles and sit by the side of the stream. Athena reaches into her pouch and pulls out a bag of almonds.

"I packed these for you," she says as she passes us the bag.

"Thank you," I say. I take a few almonds out of politeness as I am not very hungry. Brandon has worked up an appetite and takes a handful of nuts. I am nervous sitting in close proximity to the goddess.

. As I keep my eyes focused on the babbling stream in front of us, I can feel her looking at me. I decide to break the tension by getting up and moving around. I take off my shoes and dip my feet in the stream. Holding up the hem of my dress, I splash around in the cool, shallow water.

"Are you a Naiad then, a water nymph?" Athena asks.

"What? No," I say reflexively, then immediately regret my rudeness. "I am not a Naiad, your, um, Majesty. I am an ordinary person. There is absolutely nothing special about me." I keep my head down and try to look submissive.

Athena looks at me with her scrutinizing stare. Her gray eyes narrow and seem to darken in intensity. "You don't like these comparisons to the gods?" Athena says, "A nymph is not on par with a god, you know. But it is superior to a human." As Athena says this, she strokes the handle of the dagger she holds in a casing at her waist. I fear I have angered her and the dagger will soon be soaring my way.

Athena gets up and takes her sandals off to join me in the water. She walks over to where I am standing and openly looks me up and down. She pulls out her knife and points it towards my chest.

"May I?" she asks. Is she asking for consent to stab me? Brandon drops his almonds and runs into the stream without having time to remove his shoes.

"Athena, what are you doing?" he says with alarm.

Athena looks unperturbed. "I am asking to cut a lock of her hair," she says to Brandon. She turns to me again and says, "May I cut off a small piece?"

I remember that Athena has a thing about hair. The Gorgon Medusa was once a beautiful woman with thick, luscious hair that she took great pride in. She made the mistake of having sex with Poseidon in Athena's temple. Athena punished Medusa for this transgression by turning her beautiful hair into writhing snakes. I wonder if taking a piece of my hair was the first step in affecting some hideous punishment on it. I wished Katie had left it as a matted mess.

I stand frozen and do not know what to do. Athena takes a step forward with her knife. "What is the matter with you?" she says. *Well, Athena, you have a knife in your hand and you seem to want to use it on me.* I open my mouth to speak but nothing comes out.

Athena steps back and puts the knife back at her waist. "Oh, you are afraid," she says, "that makes sense. I could annihilate you, so you are right for being cautious. It's been so long since I've been with humans who know who I am that I forget that I can inspire fear. I just want a lock of your hair so that I can inspect it. May I?"

This is weird but I nod my head yes. Athena takes her knife out again and reaches for one of my cascading locks and cuts off a small piece. She takes the lock and plunges it into the water. She lets the running stream flow over it for a few seconds then takes the lock out of the water and holds it tightly in one hand. After squeezing on the lock in her hand she opens her palm and looks at the hair. She gazes curiously at it and gingerly moves it around with her index finger. Finally, she appears annoyed and throws the lock on the ground.

"This isn't even real!" she exclaims. "This is doll hair!"

"I think that might be a hair extension," I say. "Katie fixed my hair for me. I thought she would have used real hair."

"Witches," Athena scoffs, "so much of what they do is illusion. Well, you are definitely not a Naiad. They would never need help making long hair. Their hair grows naturally long and full. They often don't wear clothes so it's back-up wardrobe to cover themselves in front of unexpected guests. They are modest." Athena steps out of the stream and we follow her.

Once we are on the shore, Athena looks derisively at Brandon's wet shoes. "You must take better care of your equipment," she scolds, "wet shoes can be death for a soldier. Now, I heard your girlfriend say that you are an engineer. Can you fly planes?"

Brandon and I exchange awkward looks at the word *girlfriend* but neither of us correct Athena. It seems pointless to explain contemporary dating dynamics to an ancient deity.

"I am studying to be an engineer," Brandon says. "I have an interest in aerodynamics and know a little about flying. I am really interested to learn how your ships work."

"Good," Athena says, "I will teach you about them, then. We have a few days together, and I will spend some of the time teaching you how to fly my ship. You are a better fighter than I would have imagined. It's probably due to your girlfriend. Heroes fight better when they are in a quest for a woman. I think if she's watching and you can show off for her, you will do all right. You're more likely to survive."

That was a lot of information to process. What did she mean by survive? Wasn't this a demonstration fight? Brandon and I are rendered momentarily silent.

"Why are you two not answering?" Athena says, "Is it because I said she was your girlfriend? You Earthlings are so infantile about love. I hear my co-workers talking about this. You don't like labels. Well, labels allow for expedient conversation and effective strategy."

"I was more concerned about what you said about survival," I say. "Is Brandon going to be fighting someone dangerous?"

"Where do you think you are?" Athena says, "You don't make the rules here. Not even the gods make the rules. We can guide you, but we cannot control everything. We are trying to achieve something by stealth. But it is a noble cause. You are trying to save the earth. I am always on the side of the noble cause and of heroes. You will be joining the pantheon of great heroes. When we say Achilles, Heracles, Diomedes, we will also say Brandon and Zoe."

Athena walks a few feet and then stops and surveys the field up ahead. "My ship is not far from here. Let's make good use of our time. You two may continue resting and I will retrieve the land shuttle from the ship. I will drive Zoe to Hephaestus, and then Brandon and I can resume training.

"I was supposed to meet Hephaestus with Katie," I say. "Shouldn't we go back to her house?"

"I can provide the introduction to Hephaestus," Athena says. "You don't have time to go back there. We must get you safely to his home right away. I have been tracking Hera's ship. She is already on Mars."

Chapter Thirteen

Athena dashes off to get the shuttle, her long braid swaying back and forth with every charged stride. Brandon and I walk beside the stream for a few moments in silence. Brandon has his head down and his brow is furrowed. I don't know how much Brandon knows about the heroes Athena talked about, but they did not have an easy time of it. We are a long way from fighting preschoolers with water-guns.

We come to a grove of small, brown leafed trees and decide to sit down under their shade. As we approach the grove, I look up at the leaves of one of the trees and see movement. I think it might be a breeze blowing the leaves, but then I hear chirping. Looking closer, I can see that concealed within the leaves are a dozen or so pheasant-sized creatures. We get to within a few feet of the tree and up close I can make out the details of the first wild animals we have seen since our arrival on Mars.

"What are those?" I say, pointing at the creatures.

Brandon cranes his neck and stands directly under the tree. "I thought they were birds, but they don't have feathers," he says. "They're like the hairless-cat version of birds. They have wings but they are covered in skin."

There's a flutter of movement from the tree and then two of the creatures fly out of the tree and land on the ground a few feet in front of us. They begin pecking and scratching at the red soil. Now that they are closer I can see that they have long, curved beaks, scaly brown and lavender skin, and hard, beady eyes. Brandon crouches down until he is at their level.

"Zoe," Brandon says with wide eyes, "I think these are dinosaurs." Brandon puts both hands on the ground and he reminds me of a rabbit that is getting ready to leap away from trouble. I join Brandon in his crouch and look closer at the creatures pecking the ground.

"I think you're right," I say with shock. Although small, the leathery animals have a dangerous look to them that birds their size don't generally possess. I remember the theory that birds on Earth are direct descendants of ancient dinosaurs. Maybe Mars once was home to the giant animals and their evolution went a different way.

One of the creatures turns to me, and as if noticing me for the first time, opens its beak and hisses at me with a black serpentine tongue. It unfolds its wings, which are deceptively long, and flies back up into the tree. Its companion cocks its head and stares quizzically at us for a few seconds. Then it too opens its wings and leaps into the sky. It does a circle of the grove before joining its flock back in the tree.

"Maybe we can sit under a different tree," I say nervously and Brandon nods in agreement. I don't want to be dive-bombed by a velociraptor cousin. We walk along until we find a smaller tree that looks to be free of mini-dinosaurs. Brandon sits down under the tree and leans back, with his arms supporting his head. I sit down beside him as he looks up through the leaves on the tree and at the sky above. He hasn't shaved for a while and has the beginnings of a beard. His skin is glowing from the exercise with Athena and his hair is in loose, tousled waves. He seems lost in thought and I wish now I could so easily dip into his mind and see what he is thinking like I did when I fainted.

"Are you okay?" I ask Brandon.

Brandon turns his head to look at me. He has a frown line between his brows and the muscles of his jaw are tensing. He takes a deep breath before answering. "I'm okay," he says. "I think Athena just wants to prepare me for all the possibilities of working with weapons. But I'm sure it will all be fine." The grim line of Brandon's mouth tells me that all is not okay with him. It occurs to me now this may be a good time to let him know I had unwittingly had access to his thoughts.

"Brandon, remember when I fainted and I had my vision of Colton Chase?" Brandon says yes and I see a slight downturn of his mouth at the mention of Colton's name. "Something else happened then," I continue. "I think I may have left my body because when I came back to consciousness I didn't come back to my own mind right away. I was, uh, briefly in your mind, and I could see your thoughts." I can feel myself blushing as I confess this. I didn't mean to do it, but the fact remains I invaded his brain.

Brandon sits up straight and looks at me with open-mouthed shock. "You could read my mind?" Brandon says.

"Not all your thoughts," I say, "only just a few of them as I passed through. Your thoughts were all over the place in there and I couldn't look through them easily. I think the mind is actually a pretty messy place. If yours looks like that, imagine what mine looks like. It's probably an episode of *Hoarders*."

Brandon doesn't smile at my attempt at a joke. "What did you see in there?" he says. He shifts his body to look directly at me.

"I really didn't see much at all," I try to reassure him. "The thoughts were coming at me, and I couldn't control what I saw. You were worrying about me passing out. Then you thought about our friendship and remembered all the nice things you did to try to shake me out of my depression. I don't think I have ever properly thanked you for that."

Brandon is looking deep into my eyes. I reach for his hand and our fingers lock together.

"I should have said this a long time ago," I say quietly. "I want to thank you. You've been a hero to me. I don't know where I would be without you. I was walking around like an unwashed zombie."

"But you invented cabbage toss and bowling for oranges and I wanted to come to work every day just to play with you. And look how things have changed — now I have hair extensions," I say, while holding up what I think is one of the fake locks. Brandon smiles and seems to relax.

"You don't have to thank me," he says, "I'm sorry you were having such a rough time. It must have been really hard when you thought your mom had drowned." At the mention of my mom I feel my stomach clench. I try to ignore it because I don't want to get distracted from what I need to say to Brandon.

"Brandon, I saw something else in there. I saw your thoughts about losing your brother. I have been an idiot. I am so sorry that I have been so wrapped up in myself that I have never talked to you about that. We weren't friends when your brother passed away but I heard that it happened. I am really sorry that I have not been there for you as you deal with your own grief." Brandon puts his head down and covers his mouth with his hand as I say this. After a moment he puts his hand down beside him and looks directly at me. His large brown eyes are shiny and he blinks a few times before answering.

"It was a long time ago," he says. "I was nine when it happened. Liam was eighteen. I can't believe he was the same age as I am now. He seemed so grown up back then."

Brandon pauses and looks down at his hand on the ground. He allows his fingers to fan out in the grass. "When you lose somebody," he says, "the missing and the sadness never goes away. It's weird because in some ways it's like the person never goes away either. When I lived at my parents I used to walk down the hall to my brother's room and I always felt he was about to step out from behind his door and throw a nerf ball at me." Brandon shakes his head at the memory. He picks up a lavender blade of grass and rubs it between his fingers. Suddenly he breaks it in half. He turns to me and asks, "Do you know what happened to him?"

"I heard he had an accident," I say. "I thought he fell off of the fence around the walkway of the stadium."

Brandon nods his head and says, "He had been drinking. Liam was always chasing the party. He used to drive my parents nuts with all his partying and drinking. They never knew what to do about it. They would ground him but he would find a way to sneak out and get drunk again with his friends."

"He was even grounded the night it happened. My parents had just discovered he was not in his room when the police showed up at our door." Brandon turns to gaze out at the field. I look at him, but remain silent to give him a chance to talk and get out everything he needs to say.

While still looking out at the field, Brandon says in a flat voice, "I'm not sure it was completely an accident."

I feel myself go still and hyperaware at these words. I notice faint chirping from the trees behind us. "What do you mean?" I say.

Brandon sighs and looks at me. "I'm not saying he did it on purpose but I don't think Liam was happy. Looking back, I think Liam was depressed and he didn't know what to do about it. I think that's why he always drank and partied. To get away from his own thoughts. He was always such a popular guy who made sure everyone around him was having a good time. He was his school president, he was captain of the football team, he was like his own welcoming committee for everyone he met. But when he was alone in his room he was a different person. I'd hear him crying sometimes late at night. I think he liked to see other people having fun because he couldn't stand to be alone with his own thoughts."

There is nothing to say to this so I put my arms out and I hug Brandon. He puts his arms around me and hugs me back tightly. I rest my cheek against his shoulder and close my eyes. The leather armor he is wearing has a cured scent that I breathe in. I feel his chest rise and fall, his breathing gradually moving from shallow to long, slow breaths. After some moments we naturally come apart and I pull back to look at him. His eyes look sad but I notice the line between his brows has all but disappeared.

Liam sounds like he was a lot like Brandon in his popularity. They both seem like guys who were fun to be around. Brandon turns to look at me with a small smile.

"It's very strange to know you have looked into my mind," he says, "Did you find anything embarrassing? Was I replaying fights with Adriana?"

"You were thinking about a dinner party you went to with her. But her friends were doing the fighting," I say.

Brandon shakes his head and smiles. "I remember that," he says. "And what about my thoughts about you?" he says nonchalantly, while plucking at another blade of grass. "I hope I was a gentleman."

"You are always a gentleman," I say, "don't worry. I saw nothing but pure thoughts about me."

Brandon raises one eyebrow and looks at me quizzically. "I'm not joking," I say. If his brain was divided into zones I would definitely be living in the friend zone.

Brandon is looking out into the fields again. A pair of the mini dinosaurs have left the tree and are flying over the field. They are flying together but apart in interconnected infinity patterns. Where their patterns connect, they briefly touch then fly off again. Together they are methodically covering the field, looking for whatever food it is that sustains them.

Brandon plays with the blade of grass in his hand. He twists it in his hand until it forms a long lavender tube. He takes the ends of the blade and knots them together. Taking my hand, he presses the knotted blade over my fingers and onto my wrist like it's a bracelet. It sits delicately on top of my fleuranium cuff.

"Thank you," I say with a smile. Brandon smiles back. He then looks down at the bracelet he has made and gently strokes it.

"I think you're my family," he says quietly. He turns his face toward me and tilts his head, a soft lock of hair falling across his brow.

"I think you're mine too," I say. His hand slides up from the bracelet until our fingers meet and interlink. Our bodies move imperceptibly closer together so we are touching all the way down, from shoulder to ankle. The loneliness that has gripped my heart for so long falls away. It feels like I have a friend forever to hold my hand.

I look into the sky and can see the infinity-circling dinosaurs are coming back our way. They land together in front of us and twitch their heads back and forth as they stare at us. They are almost cute with their small size and their easy companionship. Then one of them sticks out a long, black tongue and hisses at us. Its mate follows suit, its black tongue stabbing the air like a spear. Then the two of them begin to charge us.

"Oh my God!" I say, jumping up. "Let's get out of here." I grab the hem of my skirt and start to move away. Brandon stands and looks at them for a moment with his arms crossed. "Brandon, come on," I call. "We don't know what these things are. They could spit poison."

Brandon takes heed and decides to join me. We walk-run past the grove of trees out into the open field. The dinosaurs are in hot pursuit. They are surprisingly fast. If they get any closer, we will have to start sprinting to get away from them.

In the distance we can see a rectangular, wide vehicle driving through the fields looking like a super-sized SUV. I know it belongs to Athena because on the front of the vehicle a large insignia of an olive tree has been stamped into the metal. Olive trees are one of the symbols of Athena. The vehicle speeds up and comes roaring towards us. We pick up our pace so we can quickly join her and get inside the vehicle. When she has almost reached us, she suddenly veers away and circles the transporter behind us.

"What the hell, Athena?" I say to Brandon. I would never say this to her. I'm not crazy.

I turn around to see what she is doing. Behind us, I can see that the pair of dinosaurs has grown to a flock of dozens and they are gaining on us. Athena is trying to cut them off with her vehicle. She drives in circles around the dinosaurs and the confused creatures huddle closer together.

They form a compact herd with Athena keeping them in place with her vehicle. After a commotion of hissing tongues and flapping wings, the dinosaurs decide to give up the fight and take to the sky. The mass of them fly into the air and up and away. We watch as they soar away until they are out of sight.

Athena jumps out of the vehicle. "I rounded them up for you," she says jubilantly. "If you had a bow and arrow that would have been a perfect time to shoot them. If we have time with your training, Brandon, I'll show you how to use a bow. It's not a weapon we use in Omedis, but it's good to know. Hop in and we'll go see Hephaestus." Athena seems in good spirits. I think her happy place is any time she can combine strategy with a fight.

"Hephaestus lives under another volcano," Athena say. "It might be quicker to get there by canal up top but you don't have your lead suits and some of the trip would be outside the biosphere. We are going to go via an underground dried lava channel. It will be dark in there because they are usually only used by the Martians. But it's okay because this transporter has Tartarus-grade headlights."

Athena drives us back to the cave entrance. Our vehicle barely fits inside. We putt along in the cave until we come to another channel.

Athena turns the transporter to go into the channel. It's unlike the other channels we have visited because it immediately takes us on a steep drop. Our vehicle is almost vertical as we drive down into the channel. We would be sent crashing out the front window if we weren't strapped in with a harness system like we are on a ride in Disneyland.

We are plunged into darkness because this channel is without lanterns. The high-powered headlights of the transporter come on to light our way in front of us so that we are prevented from crashing into a wall. Still, it's not smooth going and we bounce back and forth against the sides of the channel. After traveling downwards for a while, we hit some kind of bottom and our vehicle is able to travel mainly horizontally again.

We continue along in the black of the tunnel until Athena comes to a sudden stop.

"I see something up ahead," she says. She flicks a switch on the driving panel and the headlights increase in brightness. The intense light fills the cabin and hurts my eyes. I have to squint to see what Athena is looking at. Through the tunnel I can see glowing red in the distance. It seems to be ebbing and flowing, like it's alive. It looks like the campfires I used to see across the lake when I would go to summer camp.

"Is that a fire?" I say.

"Some of it is fire," Athena says. "It's a lava flow. We're going to have to cross a live river of lava up ahead."

"I thought all the volcanoes on Mars were dead," Brandon says. Athena snorts and rolls her eyes. "This just means we are near Hephaestus. He's the god of volcanoes. His presence activates them. Hopefully he and his men have been hard at work on a bridge so we can get over this. He's an excellent craftsman."

Athena starts the transporter up again and we roll slowly forward. We get closer to the lava river and can see its bubbly, orange-red mass. It flows in a slow, steady river of fire and lava. The edges fan out so that small streams of lava shoot off from the sides before trickling out into steaming black rock.

There's a primordial quality to the relentless flow of the lava. It's not hard to imagine that worlds were formed by the hot, insistent push of the molten liquid. Steam rises from the sizzling river and is clouding our window. Athena keeps applying the wipers so that we can see.

As we get close to the lava flow crossing our path, a black iron structure comes into view. Hephaestus has indeed built a bridge across the river of lava.

It's a beautiful structure with ornate filigree metal sides moored by black Ionic pillars. The bridge is guarded by a pair of golden lions at one end and a pair of silver dogs at the other.

“Doesn’t he do beautiful work?” Athena say admiringly. The golden lions guarding the entrance to the bridge are intricate in their detail. With the headlights shining on them I can see that each strand of hair on the lions’ heads has been individually carved out of gold. I marvel at the majestic expression that has somehow been fashioned out of gold on the lions’ faces. As I am looking at one of the lions, my attention is caught by its snout. The nostrils are moving open and closed.

Before I can point out to anyone that the golden statue of the lion appears to be breathing, the lion jumps to its feet and throws its head back in a roar. Athena immediately accelerates to get the transporter quickly across the bridge. Before we can get very far, the lion has leaped onto our windshield, blocking our view. The lion is hanging on with its claws as Athena tries to knock it off by steering the transporter back and forth. The lion lets out a roar of anger and frustration, its long, golden teeth looking like highly polished, sharp daggers. Snarling teeth scrape and scratch across the window.

We hear a loud thump overhead of us. The other lion has jumped on top of the vehicle. The sound of metal scraping metal can be heard from above.

“It’s scratching the roof!” Athena exclaims. “That lion is going to ruin my transporter.”

Athena brakes the vehicle. She gets out of her seat, runs to the back of the transporter, and opens a utility box. She takes a large animal skin and wraps it around herself. This must be the famous aegis that is supposed to be like a shield protecting the gods. She reaches into the box again and pulls out a sword still in its sheath. She straps the sheath to her belt.

Athena runs to the middle of the transporter and climbs on one of the seats. She stands up and presses her hands on the ceiling. I notice for the first time that there is a hatch in the roof of the vehicle. After two, quick, hard pushes, Athena has opened the hatch. She pulls herself up and out of the opening. We hear a roar of the lion before Athena has shut the hatch, locking us inside.

There is a loud, heavy thump on the roof. The lion has fallen under Athena’s sword. The far lighter sound of footsteps on the roof follows. Then a crashing sound from the hood of the vehicle. Athena has jumped onto the other lion’s back.

She pulls at its mane and the lion throws its head back to let out a snarling roar. She grabs the snout of the lion with one hand, forcing its mouth open even further. With the other hand, she takes her sword and thrusts it deep into the lion's mouth. She leaps off the lion and it falls lifelessly onto its side.

She kicks a few times at the golden carcass until it falls off of the hood of the vehicle. With the hood of the transporter now cleared, she widens her stance and turns with her sword at the ready to face the direction of the light. She's prepared to strike because the silver dog statues at the other end of the bridge have come alive and they are running at Athena.

Two silver muscular dogs the size of Rottweilers are racing towards Athena in a paired attack. As they get closer to her they separate, one going to each side of her. Athena pulls out a knife from around her ankle so that she now holds a blade in each hand. The two dogs leap simultaneously, their mouths open and growling. I brace myself for the expected attack on Athena. Then in mid-air, the dogs' legs splay open and they crash to the ground. They lie motionless on either side of the bridge.

Athena brings her arms down and walks over to one of the dogs. She gives it a kick and checks that it is dead. She must think that she needs to be sure that it won't attack again because she brings her sword up above her head so that she can stab the dog.

"No, no, no! Stop!" We hear a voice yelling. "You don't need to do that! I've turned it off." Athena freezes and turns to look at the direction of the yelling. We see the figure of a man at the end of the bridge. He looks like he is trying to move quickly over to us but he is having some difficulty walking. He has an awkward, halting step and I realize he is walking with a cane.

"Steropes, can you meet them and explain," the man yells. A larger figure is running behind him and it quickly catches up to him. Now in full view, I can see the bigger figure is huge. He's about eight feet tall and powerfully built. As he gets closer, I can make out the details of his face. Instead of two eyes he has one giant eye beneath a single thick, bushy brow.

I turn to look at Brandon's shocked face. "That's a Cyclops," I say.

"Are they good guys?" Brandon asks.

"Sometimes," I say feebly.

The Cyclops runs with heavy feet towards Athena and holds up his hand for her to stop. Athena lowers her sword and converses with the Cyclops.

After a few moments, she comes back into the vehicle and speaks to us.

"Steropes apologizes. He was having a little joke. Hephaestus installed the animal statues with animatronics so they can come to life. He says most people when they cross the bridge find it very entertaining when the animals start to move. Steropes may have accidentally hit the kill switch."

"Hephaestus does robotics?" Brandon says.

"He's actually a technology nerd," says Athena. "He made robots to serve the Greek gods. He was revered in the manufacturing and industrial centers of Greece, particularly in Athens. We have worked together many times. Come outside and you can meet him."

We climb out of the vehicle and get on the bridge in time for the arrival of Hephaestus. I look at his face and try to see why his mother would ever have found him to be unlovable. He does not have the finer features of the other gods I have met but he is far from ugly.

He has rugged good looks and the down to earth energy of someone who knows how to work hard. He's gray haired yet vital looking, with a leanly muscled build and sure movements now that he is not trying to move fast. If he was on Earth he would be a silver fox.

Athena walks over to Hephaestus and gives him a kiss on the cheek. Hephaestus kisses her back and holds both of her hands in his. "Athena, my dear, I am sorry about the lions and the dogs. Don't worry about slaying them. It's nothing we can't fix."

Athena introduces Brandon and me. "This is Zoe," she says, "she's from one of Hecate's covens. She's going to be on hand to help you with any last-minute things you need for the gala. Hecate's house is filled up, so would it be alright if she stays here?"

Hephaestus looks at me and smiles. "How nice of you to come all the way here to help me. I'm glad your coven could spare you. It won't be much work. Thalia, the goddess of festivity and rich banquets, does all the heavy lifting. But she's very busy and there's always details that I think of at the last minute that I need help with."

"Hephaestus looks at me and smiles. "How nice of you to come all the way here to help me. I'm glad your coven could spare you. It won't be much work. Thalia, the goddess of festivity and rich banquets, does all the heavy lifting. But she's very busy and there's always details that I think of at the last minute that I need help with. The guys around here aren't very good with that sort of thing. You can stay in my cave. It's better than that sounds. I just love a good volcano, so when we started mining here I decided to build a home in the wall of a volcano instead of living under the biosphere. It's very cozy and I will tell the Cyclopes to turn off the forge at night so you can sleep."

I smile and nod at what Hephaestus is saying. I had been nervous about staying in his house, but he is making me feel very welcome.

Athena next presents him with Brandon. "This is Brandon of Earth. He is an untried hero, but he has taken on the training of Omedis so that we can have the traditional Omedis performance at the gala for entertainment."

"Good, good," Hephaestus says while shaking Brandon's hand. "I believe we have a Cyclops as your opponent in the fight this year. It's a Cyclops, isn't it, Steropes?"

The Cyclops says something in a language that I don't understand. It sounds like he is growling while chewing glass. After he finishes speaking, Steropes turns to Brandon and glowers darkly while saying a few more growly, chewed glass words. I think loosely translated it means 'come at me, dude.'

"Steropes says we have one of the best Cyclopes training for battle. It should be a good fight," Hephaestus says. He turns to Athena and says in a quieter tone, "Is this young man going to be taken back to Earth and have his memory wiped as per usual?"

"Yes," Athena says, "he won't remember a thing,"

"Good," Hephaestus says. "I know the guy Steropes is talking about, and he won't want to remember that. Can you give us a lift to the cave?"

Chapter Fourteen

The black stallions charge at me, snorting fire and straining at their bits. The masked man yanks at their reins as he struggles to control them. They are coming down the hill too fast. I want to run and hide but my feet are frozen in place. I open my mouth to scream and it feels like my voice is trapped in my throat, a hard knot of sound that threatens to choke me. I gag and pull at my neck, trying to open my throat up. With a push from deep inside my belly, my throat opens and I can breathe. I try to yell and it comes out at first as a howl, like I am a ghost in a haunted mansion. I push harder and it gets louder and stronger. I open my mouth as wide as I can and I scream. The eyes behind the metal mask of the man look angry at my resistance but I do not relent and I continue to scream.

The screaming fills my small room and startles me awake. I hear the low hum of a motor as my nightmare evaporates. I'm not sure where I am at first then I remember I am sleeping in the guestroom of Hephaestus in his cavernous home built under a volcano.

The low humming is coming from a Roomba-sized robot that is rolling back and forth over my legs as I lay in bed. This little guy usually wakes me up here by butting the door open and dropping off a breakfast tray, but today has decided to roll all over my bed.

Having been woken up from a deep sleep, my body is fighting getting up and is feeling sluggish. I want to lay back down on the pillow and attempt to catch some more sleep. I lean back on one arm and try to remember why I have to get up. The little robot must have me figured out because it rolls up close to my ear and revs its motor. I am shot back out of my sleepiness and want to bat the robot off the bed. Like a cat that refuses to change its path just because you are in the way, the robot passes over my chest then zips down my covers, onto the floor, and out the door.

I get out of bed and shut the door so that I can eat and get dressed privately. Hephaestus has been nothing but kind to me since I have been staying with him, but he has a lot of males hanging out in his caverns. I wouldn't want to be caught changing by a satyr or a cyclops on their way to the forge to do some welding.

Hephaestus has constructed the original man cave. It's an actual cave that's been outfitted with leather sofas and chairs for when his friends want to lounge and play video games. Robots serve their snacking needs and come by regularly with trays of food and drink. Tables rise up out of the floor anytime someone wants to sit while they eat. A whole section of the cave is what they call the forge. It has tools for welding and smelting and general metal construction. Hephaestus spends most of his time in the forge designing and building metal working projects. It's usually pretty noisy in there from all the work being done, so when I want to talk to him I have to stick my head in and he comes out and we go somewhere a little quieter.

Hephaestus has put me to work helping to greet and organize out-of-planet gala guests who stop by his cave to visit. These are guests who are clients for his mining business, or who could be future clients, and he wants to make sure they are taken care of.

Katie sent a bag of clothes over for me the first day, but most of them are a little fancy for the job. She packed several pairs of beautiful silk pajamas that I have hacked into being day wear by layering them with leather vests and jackets Hephaestus has in his mud room.

I select a pair of beige silk pajamas and top it with a slightly beat-up brown leather jacket. Whatever Katie did to my hair seems to have stuck and I only have to run my fingers through it to be presentable.

I make my way to the front hallway to see who may be coming in today. First on the list are a group of Nereids who are coming with someone from another planet. Hephaestus has asked me to let him know when the Nereids are going to arrive so that he can be on hand to greet them. Nereids are sea nymphs and they hold a special place in Hephaestus's heart. He was raised by two Nereids, Thetis and Eurynome, in a cave on the shores of the River Oceanus when he was so cruelly rejected by Hera. These two ocean nymphs gave Hephaestus the motherly love he lacked from his own mother. With them, far from the glory of Olympus, Hephaestus learned and practised the art of metal working.

As I read through the guest list I hear the clip clop of hooves. Hephaestus is entering the room on the back of his pet donkey. He jumps off the donkey with his walking stick when he sees me. He pulls a carrot from his pocket, gives it to the donkey to eat, and the donkey ambles off towards the door outside.

"Could you get the door for him, please, Zoe?" Hephaestus says. I open the door and the donkey strolls outside.

"Thank you, Zoe," Hephaestus says. "I know it's silly to be riding him indoors but I think he feels a little out of sorts when he doesn't get to do something once in a while. When we lived on Olympus I would ride in on him for parades and big events while the other gods entered by chariot. I think he misses the pomp and circumstance sometimes."

Hephaestus takes a look over my shoulder at the list for today. "The Nereid group should be here soon," he says. "Thetis will be with them so I want everything to be special for them. She is like a mother to me. Do we have the gift bags ready?"

I pick up a box of gift bags I have stashed under a table to show Hephaestus. When various guests arrive, we give them a gift bag full of treats. There are a pair of gold tongs, several pieces of his exquisitely crafted jewelry, a miniature pewter anvil, and a vial of Mars sand which is known for its cosmetic properties. My job is to track their arrival and check that they are staying in accommodations that will suit their needs. Nereids, for example, are water based and need to stay somewhere that has big bathtubs and not just a shower.

Next, I usually call one of the Cyclopes to give them a tour of the forge. Guests often want to order more jewelry once they see all the things being created by Hephaestus in his shop. If they are interested, they can then go down to look at the mines as well. The mines are completely operated by robotics and visitors are often curious about Hephaestus's ingenuity.

"Everything is ready for Thetis and the Nereids," I say. "I even found some dried seaweed and coral to tie around the bag handles for decoration."

"That's very thoughtful of you," Hephaestus says, "you do have a talent for thinking of my guests. You are quite different from the other witches Hecate has sent me. They were always tying the bags with bat whiskers or trying to sneak in magical dolls that weren't really very nice. I think they were made from burlap and straw and they came with pins you could stick in them. Those witches must have been from the sorcery side of witchcraft. You seem to be more of an enchantress."

I don't try to disagree with him. I hate telling a bold-faced lie to Hephaestus, but at the same time I like the idea of being an enchantress. I am so glad he has never asked me to do any spells to prove myself.

"I am enjoying meeting everyone," I say. "I've met so many interesting Olympians. I see the Nereids are bringing people from a planet outside of our galaxy. I'm looking forward to that. On Earth we weren't sure that people on other planets exist. They don't really visit us."

"Oh, they visit you," he says, "but usually only by accident because they were coming here. Our galaxy is a long way away for anyone else to come visit. Visitors are only traveling out this way because of the fleuranium on Mars. I am so glad they are willing to come this far because it keeps me in business. That's why I'm happy to sponsor the gala. It's a way to show my appreciation for my out-of-galaxy customers since I can't come to see them."

"Why can't you visit them?" I ask.

Hephaestus looks at me like I'm a complete idiot. "Gods can't leave our galaxy," he says, "what do they teach you in school? Don't you know about the Law of Milky Way Transfiguration and Deification? That's just appalling." I shake my head and feel both confused and embarrassed.

Hephaestus checks himself and speaks in a gentler tone. "The gods are tied to the Earth and the celestial objects within the galaxy. The Earth is our planet too. We only created Olympus so we could have a break from Earthlings. Your species is incredibly needy when they are in the mood for needing someone. Then when you don't, you just throw them away. It takes an unbelievable amount of effort on Athena's part to keep Olympus undetected from your Earth authorities. Maybe that's why she doesn't apply her goddess of wisdom talents to the education system. She can't do everything."

I am remembering about what my mother said about the gods living on Olympus and coming to Earth for their entertainment. It sounds like my mother got it wrong. Or maybe it was a matter of perspective. From my mother's viewpoint, it would seem that Olympus is the home of the gods since that is where most of them live.

"Did you want to stay on the earth?" I say.

Hephaestus's eyes go wide and he throws his hands up.

"Do you know who the earth is?" he says. "It's Gaia! Gaia, who is Mother Earth, and the mother of everyone. Gaia was the first woman I ever loved. But I wasn't allowed to marry her because she was one of the old gods and part of the old ways. My family wanted me to marry one of the new Olympian gods. So, they arranged for me to marry Aphrodite. She was young and beautiful. She came from the sea, which is so much newer than the old, rocky parts of the earth. I tried to make her happy but she didn't want me. She left me for my brother Ares. And my wonderful Gaia just checked out. She went to sleep. She's been asleep for a long time. No one can wake her. She has no idea what has happened."

"Do you mean what has happened to the earth?" I say.

"It's the same thing!" Hephaestus says, "Gaia is Earth, Earth is Gaia. Listen, I am sorry to get so worked up about this. These are concepts it takes a long time to learn and obviously the education system has failed you. But I know you understand about the dependence on celestial objects and that is something I wanted to talk to you about."

"Witches need to commune with the moon as part of their rituals. You haven't had a chance to see the moon and that must be affecting you. We have two beautiful moons on Mars. I'll arrange for a lead suit and one of the guys can take you to see them." Hephaestus smiles at me expectantly.

I don't want to get in a vehicle with one of Hephaestus's friends. "Thanks for the offer, but I don't need to see the moon or, um, the moons. I'm not very observant of witch customs. I'm more of a free-thinker."

Hephaestus is quite a lot taller than me. He leans against his walking stick so that he can bend down to look me straight in the eye without losing balance. Up close I can see the strong, vertical lines on his cheeks that run from his chin to his cheekbones. He has crinkly lines at the corners of his eyes that map many years of smiling.

"Zoe, you don't have to see the moon if you don't want to, but I'm concerned about you. You've been having nightmares. The robot who brings you your breakfast told me."

"They report on me?" I say.

"They do a complete diagnostic on you when they go in the room, yes, but I don't pay attention to most of that. You could use some iron. But I am most attentive to your happiness.

"It's very hard for Earthlings to go without sunlight. I think you may have a case of SAAD — Sunlight Anti-Absorption Disorder. It's very common for visitors here. I think we need to get you to the planet's surface for some natural light."

I don't want to leave Hephaestus's cave. I am happy helping to organize the gala. It's really not much work, and it's fun to see all the people getting in the mood for the party. Sometimes the party planner, the goddess Thalia, will come by and she gets me excited about what she is doing. She's planning to have fireworks to cap off the event. There's even talk of an ambrosia fountain.

I can't deny that I am having nightmares. I've been having dreams of the helmeted man every night since I've come here. I'm embarrassed that my screaming has woken people up and is being documented by the robots. It's hard for me to know why I am having nightmares.

I wouldn't say that I feel depressed the way I felt when I thought my mother had died. I couldn't say exactly how I feel about my mother now. Whatever I feel is in a tight ball in the pit of my stomach. If it tries to get out I clamp it down. I can't let it get out because if I do, it could explode and I may be rendered incapable of doing anything. I have the earth to save. I have to keep it together.

I try to keep my answer vague. "I think I'm just getting used to sleeping in a different bed. I'm really feeling okay."

Hephaestus stares intently at me. He presses his lips together and squints his eyes in thought. “I don’t mean to pry, but is it boyfriend trouble? With girls your age it’s usually boyfriends. Or you are fighting with your mother. Often it’s both.” He nods his head sympathetically.

I feel the pit in my stomach travel and start to press up against my sternum. Hephaestus is not going to let this go. Maybe I can tell him a little and it will satisfy him while offering me some relief.

“I don’t have a boyfriend, but…” I begin.

“Wait, you don’t have a boyfriend?” Hephaestus says, “How is that possible?”

“I don’t know,” I say, “my mom was asking that too.”

“The boys in your high school must be under a localized indifference spell,” Hephaestus says. “There’s obviously something wrong with them.”

“It’s not just them,” I say, “I’ve had a crush on someone for a long time and I didn’t think he noticed me, but now I think he may like me too. But there’s also a chance I’m completely fooling myself.”

The corners of Hephaestus’s mouth twitch upwards. “Zoe, I don’t think you have to worry. I’m sure Brandon likes you.”

“Brandon?” I say. “No, I’m not talking about him. There’s another guy back on Earth. Brandon is…I mean he’s wonderful. He’s probably the best person I’ve ever met. Because I can’t honestly say for sure I’ve definitely talked to Colton, but I think if I did, he would also be the best person I’ve ever met.”

Hephaestus puts his chin in his hand and nods his head. “So, two guys. That’s okay, that makes sense. And Brandon is the one who came here with you. That’s an important point. And the mother? How is she figuring into this?”

I look into Hephaestus’s warm eyes and I can’t help myself. I start crying. “I don’t know where she is. I missed her for so long and then she came back and left again right away. I don’t know if she left because she had to, or if she was kidnapped or if she just wanted to be with her boyfriend. I don’t know if I should be worried about her or mad at her. I don’t know what to feel so I try not to feel anything.”

Hephaestus gets me a box of tissues from a drawer in the table. "Zoe, let me ask you this. Was there a god involved in all of this?"

"Yes!" I say. I wipe at the tears under my eyes. "How did you know?"

"There always is," he says with a sigh. "Listen, you don't need to figure anything out right now. I've known a lot of people and I talk a lot with the guys in the shop. No one knows anything most of the time. The trick is to accept that the unknown will always be with you. Sit with it, everything will become clear eventually, in its own time. The things that you know for certain though, those you must hold onto and cherish."

"Brandon is one of those certainties. He's here, he cares about you and you care about him. He's something you need to hold onto. I'll tell you what I will do. I'll speak to the Cyclops he will be fighting. I'll tell him to be extra-careful and go easy on Brandon."

I want to jump in the air and give Hephaestus a hug. Instead, I settle on giving him a big smile. "Thank you, that would be amazing," I say. "I have been so worried about Brandon's fight."

"Well, you should be," Hephaestus says, "Cyclopes are tough. If you don't want to go up to the surface, how about I offer you a change of scenery? I want to make sure the Martian Tartians are going to be happy with the gala. It will be hard for you to check in with them because they don't really like Earthlings. They are at a reception tonight near the volcano and I thought maybe you could go to it and circulate about the room. You could see what they are saying. See if anyone is complaining about anything so we can fix it."

"But, how will I do that?" I say. "Would they even let me into the reception?"

"I left out an important part," Hephaestus says, "you can go and be invisible. I made a helmet for Hades that allows him to be invisible when he chooses. He has the helmet but I made a prototype when I was testing it out. It doesn't have all the inscriptions and scrolls and I hadn't worked out the shape yet but it will make you invisible. I have it back in the shop."

I took an online quiz once where they asked what special power would you rather have: the ability to fly or the ability to be invisible. In the last week I've had the chance to do both. I immediately agree to become invisible and gather Martian gala intel.

"Good," Hephaestus says, "I see someone dressed in an arctic char-skin coat coming up the path. That must be the Nereids. I'll go greet them and show them around. Then I'll get the helmet and bring it to your room so you can try it on." Hephaestus takes his walking stick and pauses at the door.

"Zoe, you're going to be told throughout your life to follow your heart and that's a good thing. But your heart doesn't just mean love. It means compassion. Try to always find that compassion in your heart. It will lead to great things." Hephaestus leans onto his walking stick and jauntily walks out the door to meet the guests.

When Hephaestus was rejected by his mother he constructed a throne with magic ropes and kept her bound. He wouldn't release her at first. When he was told he owed it to his mother he responded with his most famous quote:

"I have no mother."

Dionysus convinced Hephaestus to have compassion for Hera. The god of smiths listened to the god of wine. In compassion, Hephaestus released the bounds of his loveless mother. And then Hephaestus finally ascended Olympus, where he had been cast off as an infant. On Olympus he became the beloved maker of the tools of the gods. He finally had a palace to call his own.

Chapter Fifteen

I don't get a chance to go back to my room and try on the helmet until dinner time. Groups of visitors stopped by to see the forge and factory all day. The biggest group to process was Dionysus and his forty followers. They stumbled in calling for wine and cheese like they were on a Napa Valley wine tour. Hephaestus was worried they would fall into a vat of molten metal and told them the forge was closed for maintenance. He took them to his underground springs where they could drink and eat all day. He had several of his robots constantly circling the springs so that they could rescue any revellers who passed out in the pools.

Hephaestus has left the tarnished bronze helmet on my bedside table. It has a rough, unfinished look to it. It's far from Hephaestus's usual standard of design and is unembellished with the flourishes he likes such as intricate scroll work and lettering. I guess when he was making the prototype for the helmet he was concerned with whether its magical properties could work and he would fix the esthetics later.

I take the helmet over to the mirror in my room so that I can watch myself disappear when I place it on my head. The helmet is large and heavy. I think it will probably slip off of my head when I'm walking around in it if I'm not careful. I take a fur scarf that I found in my closet and stuff it into the helmet to help it fit better. For the first time in my life I am not worried about helmet head because of whatever magical thing Katie did to my hair to make it look like I get daily blow-outs.

I pick up the helmet and place it carefully on my head. I look in the mirror and expect myself to disappear into non-existence but nothing happens. Thinking that maybe I don't have the helmet on quite right because of the fur, I jostle it back and forth. Still nothing happens. Maybe this thing doesn't work anymore. I give it a reasonably firm smack on the top of my head to make sure it is all the way down. With a flash of bright light that momentarily blinds me, the mirror is gone.

I am not in my room anymore but instead I am outside in a meadow. It doesn't look like a Martian meadow because the grass is green instead of lavender. Is it possible that the helmet has caused me to travel somewhere as well as make me invisible?

I hold out my hands and wriggle my fingers. Since I can see them I guess I must not be invisible. I look down at my clothes and I am no longer wearing my leather jacket and pajamas. I am dressed in a long, white gown and there are sandals on my feet. I reach up to feel my helmet and it seems to be gone. I pat my head and can feel I'm wearing a flower crown. The flowers trail through my hair and I have flower bracelets around my wrists.

I'm not sure what to do in this new place. Not knowing where I am, I wonder if it is better to stay put and wait for someone to come looking for me. It's a beautiful spring day and the meadow is full of wild flowers. It has a quiet that's unlike Mars because the environment is more active. I can hear the sounds of a light breeze moving through the grass and the chirping of birds is more varied and pronounced. This is a place that is alive and fertile. This feels like Earth. I think I must be having some kind of vision of home. My own planet was so beautiful and I feel a stab of guilt that I didn't appreciate it more.

"Kore!" I hear someone calling. I turn around to look for the voice and not far behind me are a group of four girls in long, filmy dresses.

One of them waves at me and then picks up the hem of her dress so that she can run towards me. The other girls see what she is doing and run after her. The four girls arrive before me with big smiles and flushed cheeks from running.

"We couldn't find you, Kore!" the same girl says. I know this girl. Her hair is long and flowing to the waist, which is different from her usual style, but I know her, as well as the others. I used to cheer with these girls back at my old cheer club. We were on the same stunt team. I haven't seen them since I quit cheer in my senior year because the season was over and I thought I would be leaving town to go away to university after graduation.

They were nice girls who I enjoyed cheering with, even if I didn't become very close to them. We were all-star cheerleaders, not high school varsity cheerleaders. That meant we cheered as a competitive sport and not for our school teams. We didn't even go to the same high school. We cheered for a cheer club and did pretty well in competitions.

Sometimes I would watch nineties teen movies with Brandon and the female villain was always a cheerleader. She was stealing boyfriends and barring girls from the cheer squad because they weren't popular enough.

This was not my life as a cheerleader. In all-star cheerleading there are no pompoms and being popular will get you nowhere. What you need is a good back hand-spring and the ability to form a strong pyramid.

Lauren, Paige, Hailey, Jamie, and I had legendary pyramids. We had perfect form and our flyer Hailey never had to worry about us dropping her from ten feet in the air. Cheerleading is a sport and I will fight anyone who says otherwise. Yes, we wear make-up, teased pony-tails, and sparkly uniforms, but to execute our routines we needed strength, balance, grace, and synchronized gymnastics skills. Movie cheerleaders are socially terrifying. All-star cheerleaders are all about sit-ups and push-ups.

I feel a pang in my stomach when I look at them. I think what I'm feeling is loss. I hadn't even realized that I missed them. We made promises to get together when I left the team but not long after that my mom died — or so I thought. They texted and phoned but I didn't have much to say. I sent short replies and didn't answer their pleas to go out. Lauren showed up unannounced at my house one time, and I turned up the TV and hid under my duvet until she went away. After a while they stopped calling me. Their life went on without me and my life just stopped.

I wonder if they all hang out together all the time without me. They have flowers in their hair like they are going to Coachella. Maybe I'm going to get to see a concert, that would be fun.

"Hi, Hailey," I say.

Hailey furrows her brow. "What's hihailey, Kore?" she says.

"I don't know what you mean," I say. "Why do you say Kore after everything?"

The girls burst out laughing. "Kore, what's wrong with you? Did you drink something?" Paige says.

It dawns of me that they think Kore is my name. "My name is Kore?" I say. The girls look at each other with concern. Paige seizes my arm and says, "Seriously, Kore, what's wrong with you? Did you slip and hit your head? Do you know my name?"

I'm pretty sure I will get this wrong but I go ahead and say it. "You're Lauren, Paige, Hailey, and Jamie," I say. The four of them look at each other like I'm crazy.

"Kore," says Jamie. "I don't think those are even names." She stands closer to me and speaks very slowly to me. "I'm Europa," she says while pointing to herself. She then gestures to the other girls. "This is Asia, this is Ephyra, and this is Rhodos."

I don't know what is happening but I decide to roll with it. I laugh and say, "I know, I was just kidding. It was just a joke." The four of them laugh and look relieved. They have baskets in their hands that are full of flowers. I look around to see if there is a basket on the ground that I should be holding. I see one a few feet away and go over to pick it up.

"Did you find any yellow flowers?" Jamie/Europa says.

I look in my basket and see purple, orange, and red flowers but nothing yellow. "No," I say, "but these are really pretty."

"Yes," Europa says, "but you said you wanted to find yellow flowers for your arrangement. Are you sure you didn't get too much sun?"

"No, I'm fine," I say. I swing my basket over my elbow. Lauren/Asia smiles and links arms with me. We all set off together through the fields in search of, I guess, more flowers.

We walk along picking sprigs of flowers for our baskets. The girls seem to have specific projects in mind and are hunting for particular flowers. I remember I am supposed to be looking for yellow flowers. The area we are in doesn't have anything that is yellow so I walk a little further ahead.

A butterfly with amber and black wings flutters by. It's been a long time since I've seen one of those. It flies ahead of me and I can see it land. I run up there so I can have a closer look.

The butterfly has landed in a patch of flowers, its kaleidoscopic wings slowly opening and closing as it precariously balances in place. I bend down to have a closer look. The black antennae of the butterfly move up and down over top of its bulbous eyes. I reach out my finger, thinking it might hop on like a pet bird. It looks for a minute as if the butterfly is considering it as its legs and antennae twitch concurrently.

The butterfly shoots up into the air and I follow. It flies in a zigzag pattern and I am surprised at how far it can fly without needing to rest. Then I remember that butterflies can migrate and that this one can probably fly much further than I can walk.

I continue to follow it as it flies away. It lands again and I run up to it to try one more time to catch it. When I reach the butterfly, it looks like it has landed in a sea of yellow.

Small, yellow flowers are everywhere. They look pretty and delicate and would probably be perfect for whatever project I was planning to make. I wonder if I can sneakily ask one of the girls what kind of arrangement I was going to make. I look behind me to talk to them. I don't see anybody there. The field is empty.

I must have walked further than I realized when I was chasing the butterfly. I better go back and look for them. Still, I have finally found some yellow flowers. I think I would like to take some of these and maybe even put them in a planter. I take out a small garden spade that is in my basket.

As I dig at the plant I think about the name the girls were calling me. *Kore*. It's an odd name that I am unfamiliar with. I carefully remove the flower by its roots and place it in my basket. I take some extra dirt and pack it around the plant. As I am patting it down, I remember that I have heard the name Kore before. Kore is the original name of Persephone. It's the name she went by before she was kidnapped by Hades and taken to live in the Underworld. The girls think I'm Kore.

As I think this, a cloud appears overhead and moves across the sun. The sky grows dim and the air has the acrid, electric feel that comes before a storm.

I need to get out of here right now. I grab my basket and turn to run in the direction of where I left the girls. Tightly grasping the basket, I only make it a few steps before the ground begins to shake. I try to keep running but I fall as I lose my footing on the rumbling earth. The ground before me ripples upwards in a wave of undulating soil.

I try to get up again so that I can run far away from here. I am knocked back down as the earth shudders and folds. I lay in child's pose on the ground, bringing my hands onto my head to protect myself. The tremulous soil beneath me buckles and quakes, feeling like a pounding beneath my belly. All at once I hear a giant crack and I know that the earth is splitting apart.

I look up to see that a chasm has opened in the earth before me. It splits apart and roars towards me like a flooding river. I roll out of the way before it can reach me and I fall into its cavernous depths. The torn earth falls wide open, and black smoke billows out. I cover my mouth to prevent myself from choking on noxious fumes. Flames shoot from the chasm, followed by a thunderous sound. In an explosion of movement, four black stallions leap into view as they struggle to escape the scorching abyss. They are pulling a chariot driven by an armored man in a bronze, carved helmet.

He's the man from my nightmares. I can see his steely eyes through the slit of his visor. He is urging his horses on as they strain to release the chariot from the hold of the earth. The surging beasts breathe ashes and smoke. They tear the chariot from the earth's fiery red maw. Sparks fly from the wheels of the chariot as it bears down on me. I want to run and hide but there is nowhere to go as the earth disintegrates around me.

The chariot comes alongside me and the masked man reaches down with one arm to scoop me up beside him. I twist to get away from him but there is no escape. I am pressed up against his chest, the hard edge of the armor cutting into my side. We are eye to eye and his eyes are so dark they are fathomless. I lose myself in those eyes and it all goes dark. We are dropping into the chasm and the earth is closing over us. I open my mouth to scream.

"Zoe, are you all right now?" It's Hephaestus and he is looking down at me with a concerned face. The deep lines on the sides of his face add to the grimness of his downturned mouth. I am lying on the floor of my room in his home. He reaches out his hand to help me get up and directs me to sit on my bed. I slump down on the side of the bed feeling exhausted. With some difficulty, he crouches down in front of me and takes out a flashlight and shines it in my eyes.

"I'm just checking to see that your mind is all there," he says. "It looks okay. But you had a strange reaction to that helmet. I came in here to get you for the reception and you were on the ground mumbling to yourself. Then you started to scream. Is there something wrong with this helmet?"

Hephaestus picks up the helmet which he had flung on my bed. He looks inside of it and pulls out the fur scarf I had used to line it so that it would fit better.

"Did you do this?" he says while holding the scarf out to me.

"Yes," I say, "it was too big and I was afraid it would fall off. I put that in there to help it fit better."

"Oh, no, no," Hephaestus says while shaking his head, "these are delicately calibrated instruments. You shouldn't do that. Any change can set everything off course. It's not your fault. You didn't know that. I should have been here to help you put it on, then I could have made any adjustments needed myself. You must have set something off. What was happening to you? You didn't become invisible."

I shake my head and think back to the horses spitting fumes, the choking smoke, and then finally, darkness. I shiver at the memory. "I was in a meadow with other girls but I left them and then I couldn't find them. There was some kind of earthquake. Then a man in a chariot came out of the earth and grabbed me. He was taking me away. He forced me into the chariot and then the earth opened up and swallowed us." I look down and my hands are shaking.

Hephaestus rubs his chin with his hand. He puts the hand down and drums his fingers on top of the handle of his walking stick. "Could you see what the man looked like?" Hephaestus says.

"He was wearing a helmet. I couldn't see his face," I say.

Hephaestus's eyes open wide and he looks like he is having a dawning realization.

"That was Hades," he says, "you were having a vision from Hades' life. I think you were seeing the kidnapping of Persephone. Everything I make is made specifically for the individual. When I made this for Hades, it of course took on some of him. This was a vision left behind. You were seeing basically a movie of what happened."

"But it wasn't like that," I say, "It was more than a vision. I could feel everything. I could feel the heat from the horses as they breathed fire. When I picked flowers, I could smell them." Hephaestus taps his walking stick on the ground and takes a turn around the room. He scratches his chin and looks at me while shaking his head.

"That is unusual," he says, "left-over visions aren't normally multi-sensory like that."

I hesitate before telling him the whole story. I take a deep breath and tightly clasp my hands to prevent them from shaking.

"I've seen the helmeted man before in my dreams. I've been dreaming of him for a long time. Since I got here, it has been every night. It's always the same. He's coming to get me in his chariot and he's about to grab me. It looks exactly like the vision I just had."

Hephaestus drops his walking stick on the ground. He picks it up and holds it with both hands to steady himself.

"You've been dreaming of Hades?" he says with alarm. "And it matches the vision you had in the helmet," he says as he begins to pace the room.

Hephaestus walks back and forth across the room three times as he gathers his thoughts. Suddenly, he stops and looks at me. "I know what it is," he says with a satisfied smile on his face. "You must have called Hades up when you were doing one of your witchcraft spells. I've been telling Hecate for years that she must put some controls on her witches. When you are dealing with magic, you never know what forces you are unleashing. But not to worry. You weren't seeing the real Hades. Only a dream image of him. It's just coincidental that you accessed the vision when you put on the helmet. It's all fine," he says with a smile.

I open my mouth to reply but quickly close it again. I can't tell Hephaestus that I am lying about being a witch. He would question me further and then I wouldn't know what to say and he would find out that we are planning to steal the fleuranium. I am not a master of deception — I'm not Hermes! I swallow hard and try to give Hephaestus a smile signalling that he has made me feel better.

But I don't feel better. Hephaestus has put into words what I have long suspected — the god of the Underworld is coming for me.

Chapter Sixteen

The gala is being held at the casino beneath the great Elysium Mons volcano. Hephaestus has dropped me off here a few hours before the gala is to begin in case anyone shows up early. The casino comprises a large gambling room and a banquet hall. Thalia, the goddess of festivity, and I walk through the venue to ensure everything is ready. Her nymphs, dressed in iridescent, slinky short dresses, are in the gambling room. They are rearranging casino tables and slot machines with the help of a pair of Cyclopes to improve the flow of the space.

Next door to the gambling room, the banquet hall is set with tables on tiered platforms lining the room. The platforms are like high-end bleachers so that guests can watch the entertainment in the middle of the room. I hope it is good luck that the casino is named after the volcano that houses it, Elysium Mons.

The Elysium Fields were the heaven of the Underworld in Greek mythology. Few people made it into the Elysium Fields. Heroes were some of the ones that could expect entrance. I hope this place treats Brandon well as tonight's hero-entertainment.

I hear the sound of fluttering wings and a bird calling. I look up to see a hawk and an owl fly into the ballroom and circle the room together. They swoop over the stage at the far side of the room before flying up to the ceiling and landing on an overhanging chandelier.

The two birds coo at each other as they survey the room below. With a shuffle of its feet, the hawk gets close enough to the owl to groom the owl's wing with its beak. The owl only reacts by slowly swivelling its head to look at the hawk. It's unusual for two predators to co-exist so peacefully. Fluttering its wings, the hawk leaps from the chandelier and flies out the door with the owl closely following.

A few moments later, Katie and Hermes enter the ballroom. They had told Hephaestus they would come early under the guise of wanting to help out. They arrive holding hands and look like they have worked out their problems. Katie is resplendent in a long, royal purple dress embroidered with silver snakes and white owls. A silver cape attaches at her shoulders, elbows, and wrists so that when she raises her arms it resembles wings. Her contribution to the room's décor includes a series of large standing torches blazing on pedestals throughout the space.

Hermes is wearing a black tuxedo with a white shirt and black-tie. His omnipresent feathers can be seen discreetly peeking out from beneath the hem of his pants at the back of his shoes. He has chosen to wear his helmet tonight with wings. His long hair scrapes his shoulders and his beard is closely trimmed.

"I see my pets are behaving well tonight," Katie says, as she points to gold-plated cages on each table containing a live raven that serve as centerpieces. The ravens caw as we pass them. Katie waves her fingers at each bird in turn and their cages briefly light up and shine. She bestows each raven with a shiny coin-sized disc that they instantly leap on and put in their mouths.

"I like your helmet, Hermes," I say. "Is that your god formal wear?"

"It is," Hermes says, "it's also going to help me pull off this heist tonight. Hades made this for me a long time ago to help me fly and go faster. While you are all at the gala watching the Omedis demonstration, I have to sneak out of here with Athena and get to Hephaestus's mine. Athena will temporarily disable the robots and stop production so we can break in. The two of us will load up our ships with fleuranium and then bring them back here and hide them outside the volcano."

"We'll be back here before anyone notices we are gone. Right after Brandon performs, we're all going to get out of here and onto our ships. Katie is coming with us so she can put a force field around you and Brandon so that you can go outside without needing a lead suit. She'll also protect you from any storms on the surface." Hermes looks at Katie and squeezes her hand.

I feel my heart quicken as Hermes describes the plan. I can't believe this is actually happening and we will soon be back on Earth.

"How are we getting back to Earth without being detected by Earth authorities?" I say. "I thought it was Athena's job to hack into their systems to help the gods leave and enter Earth. Can she do that from here?"

"Athena can probably figure out anything but she didn't leave that to chance. She programmed the system before she left to give her a window of opportunity at a scheduled time when all of the Earth's space systems are temporarily deactivated. We have everything perfectly timed so that we will have no trouble getting back on the Earth. The how is not the issue. It's the where. Your hometown was hit with an earthquake and then a typhoon. We can't return there right now."

I clutch my throat upon hearing this news. I'm about to enjoy a feast and everyone I know is fighting for their lives. I immediately think of Colton and hope he found safety in his rock-bound home.

"Are people okay? Did anyone get hurt?" I ask.

Hermes gravely nods his head yes. "People got hurt. We don't know yet how many or who. We will take you to the Greek island of Nisyros. It's where we prefer to go when we are landing on Earth. We have underwater caves there where we can hide our ships. It's an actual active volcano but don't worry, it's not bubbling right now. We can go there and plan how we will find your friend Colton and bring him the fleuranium."

I cringe a little when Hermes refers to Colton as my friend. I still don't know for certain if he is aware of me in any way beyond the girl who elbowed him at the frozen yogurt shop. I sometimes wonder if I entered another dimension when he finally looked me directly in the eyes and said "Hi, Zoe" after all those months of me pining after him. That's when everything got weird, and maybe it was set in motion by the weird act of someone so handsome and rich acknowledging my existence.

The diamond I brought back from our night under the stars I gave to Hephaestus to make into a pendant for me. It's hanging by a gold chain around my neck. If it's still there when we return to Earth, then I will know all of it was real.

The next guest to arrive is Athena. She's wearing an emerald green dress with a large bronze belt that emphasizes her athletic and graceful figure. Her hair is styled in an elaborate twist of braids at the crown of her head. In contrast to her party wear, she has a long, sheathed sword hanging off of her belt. It seems like an odd thing to bring to a party, but I guess for the goddess of battle a discreetly worn sword is part of the formal wear.

Athena is flanked by a Greek soldier in full armor and helmet. He walks in pace beside her as they enter the room, his mouth and chiselled chin the only things visible beneath his full-face mask. I watch the confident stride of the pair of them with admiration. They look totally at ease with themselves and their purpose, two warriors who can take on any challenge. It takes me a second to realize the noble warrior is Brandon. He notices me at the same time and breaks into a big smile. We immediately start to walk swiftly towards each other.

I realize now how much I have missed him since we've been separated. Every night when I went to sleep, I had hoped he would visit me in my dreams. Instead, I had been visited nightly by visions of Hades. Looking at Brandon now as he takes purposeful strides towards me, I feel that he would fight for me if Hades really did come for me. He would keep me safe.

We meet in the middle of the room and I stop and stare up at him with wonder. Is it possible that he grew in the time we've been apart? He looks like a hardened soldier, not someone who was stocking fruit ten days ago. I feel suddenly awkward in his presence and I'm not sure how to greet him. Should I salute him? I start to raise my hand and Brandon reaches out and grabs it.

"Are we reduced to shaking hands, Zoe?" Brandon laughs and then pulls me by the hand close to him. He wraps his other arm around my waist and draws me in for a hug, careful not to crush me against his metal breastplate. He takes off his helmet and shakes out his hair. Here is the handsome Brandon face that I know so well. But there is a slight change in his visage. His cheeks are a little leaner and a fine line is developing between his brows. It's like his sped-up basic training added some maturity to his face.

"I want you to save a dance for me later," Brandon says.

I eye his armour and say, "I guess there will be no slow dancing with what you are wearing."

"There will be slow dancing," Brandon says. "The armour comes off right after the fight. You look really beautiful, Zoe. You are the prettiest girl in the room. A true goddess." Brandon holds out his arm and I take it. I feel like I am being escorted to the ball by a handsome prince.

Brandon looks around us with interest, taking in the full scope of the Olympus Mons ballroom. The casino has been built into the base of the volcano, much like Hephaestus's home. The walls are made of polished granite of different hues. They are a patchwork of grays, taupes, and blacks flecked with silver veins and shiny, hard grains of stone. It is austere and opulent at the same time. The heavy stone finishings of the room are prevented from being too dark by dozens of crystal chandeliers that hang from the ceilings.

"Is there a god of polished crystal?" Brandon says, while looking up at the lights.

"I think the lighting is for our benefit," I say. "Apparently, the Martians prefer the dark. I saw one in the ballroom earlier and he had to wear sunglasses to protect his eyes in here."

"What did he look like?" Brandon asks.

"He was really small, about four feet tall. He had green fur all over his body and he didn't wear much in the way of clothes, just a loin-cloth type thing. He seemed uncomfortable wearing it."

Brandon nods his head. "I saw one going into the cave behind Katie's house," Brandon says, "but I didn't get a good look. Lamia said they were small."

When he says the name Lamia I feel like I've been stung. In between training sessions, he's clearly been hanging out with the goddess of casual nudity. I look up at Brandon and try to ascertain if Lamia has been working her seductive ways upon him, but he is not giving anything away.

Athena walks over to us and to my surprise she gives me a hug. "You look very lovely, Zoe," she says. She tilts her head and surveys me with her deep gray eyes. "You two enjoyed time in the grove of trees, didn't you? I think you may have some tree nymph in you. You are part Alseid."

This is impossible. I have spent the past week meeting real nymphs of every kind as they visited Hephaestus's house ahead of the gala. They were an endless parade of breathtaking beauty. I think Athena has been working among ordinary people on Earth for too long and forgets what nymphs look like.

"Thank you, Athena, but I have absolutely no relation to any type of nymph. I am just an Earthling, just like Brandon," I say, gesturing to Brandon beside me.

"Ahh, but you'll see," says Athena, "he is more than a regular Earthling now. He has learned very well. I think at the great battle of Troy he would have been a commander. But only if you are on his mind. That insipid Lamia kept coming out and trying to distract him. Hecate has asked her to stay home so she won't be triggered by seeing Hera. The sight of Hera could bring back the monster in Lamia. I don't want her around Brandon tonight either. I want him to be able to see you when he is performing so he can access your magic." I have no magic to give him, but it's fine with me if I don't have to have Lamia around.

Athena claps her hand on Brandon's breastplate. "Did you see this?" Athena says. "I gave him my aegis to wear. That will protect him in case his opponent slips and hits him too hard."

"I thought the aegis was the animal skin you put on to fight the lions back at the bridge," I say.

"Do you have more than one dress?" Athena asks. "There is more than one aegis. It is simply the word for a magic-infused protector in battle. Hephaestus made me several types. There is one you may have heard of that is a shield with Medusa's head on the front. It is particularly effective because anyone who looks in Medusa's eyes is immediately killed. But that can be very dangerous for an audience watching the battle."

Two hours later, most of the guests have arrived and the party is underway. Brandon is circulating and I try to stay close to Hephaestus in case he needs anything. Hephaestus is wearing a tuxedo and using an elegant walking stick topped by an onyx handle. We are standing by our table on the highest platform above the ballroom floor. Hephaestus turns to me with a smile, "This is an excellent turnout, Zoe. Thank you for all your help."

I smile back at Hephaestus. I am glad to see him so happy. He's looking ruggedly handsome tonight. The gods must have impossible standards if Hera could reject him on the basis of his looks.

It's a big crowd of mostly deities and some visitors from other planets. I am enjoying looking at the opulent gowns and jewelry worn by the revelers. I am betting that Hephaestus made a small fortune filling last-minute orders for his designs.

"When do the Martians get here?" I ask him.

"Oh, there won't be any indigenous Martians attending," Hephaestus says.

"Why not?" I say with surprise. "I thought the gala is a fundraiser to benefit Mars."

"It is. But the indigenous find the gala to be too loud and bright for their sensibilities. They have very weak eyesight and instead rely on echolocation to get around. Much like your bats, Zoe," says Hephaestus, with a nod to what he believes is my witch status.

"Echolocation uses sound-waves to determine where objects are in a space," Hephaestus explains, "To echolocate, the Martians send out sound-waves and when they hit an object, they produce echoes. The noise of the gala is disruptive to this and the light hurts their eyes. And the noise they make for this is ultrasonic, which you would find uncomfortable. It's just not a good mix."

Hephaestus waves at a Cyclops I recognize from the forge.

"All the guys from the forge are here tonight. Most of the Cyclopes here were originally from Tartarus. The Martian representation at the gala really falls to the displaced Tartians. Even though the indigenous Martians and the Martian Tartians are different species, they have similar temperaments. They both evolved in dim, underground caverns near flames or volcanoes. They like the quiet and the dark."

Hephaestus looks fondly at his friends from the forge. His painful memories of his mother must be a distant memory now that he has found acceptance from his fellow lovers of volcanoes.

"Oh, look there. Here's a treat for you, Zoe. A Hecatonchires has shown up."

I look to where Hephaestus is pointing and my mouth drops open. An eight-foot-tall creature with a hundred hands is chatting with a pair of Cyclopes.

Hephaestus speaks to me in a confidential tone. "They are the best at making weapons. Master craftsmen."

Music plays as people mingle and Hephaestus taps his walking stick to the beat. Hephaestus suddenly stops tapping his walking stick. I look over at him and the smile is gone from his face. He is looking darkly out into the crowd. I follow his gaze and I see a smoothly coiffed head near the entrance to the ballroom. Hera has arrived.

She is dressed in a gold Grecian style gown that flows down her sinewy frame like liquid metal. Her neck is layered with gold necklaces and her face shimmers with gold highlighter. At her side is a blond-haired man who has his head turned towards her and away from me as he listens intently to what she is saying. She finishes speaking and takes a sip of her drink from her bejeweled goblet. The man turns his head away from her and looks my way. With a sharp intake of breath, I realize it's Ganymede. I want to jump off the dais and run away.

Hephaestus hears my gasp. "It's alright, Zoe, don't be concerned about Hera. I won't get upset. I've moved beyond her. She doesn't want to stand next to the son who got old anyway."

I don't answer because I am focusing on using my amulet in my pocket to call on Katie. The plan is when Ganymede shows up, Katie will intercept him and work a memory charm so that he won't be able to identify Brandon and me. I try to focus on calling her to come by my side. Within seconds, Katie arrives in the company of Hermes. I think he helped her get here so quickly.

Hephaestus is staring out at Hera and hasn't noticed the arrival of Hermes and Katie yet. Hephaestus has left his walking stick leaning against the table. Katie flicks her finger and the walking stick falls to the ground. Hephaestus leans down to pick it up and while he is doing that, I point out Hera and Ganymede to Hermes and Katie. They run off and go to meet Hera and Ganymede before Hephaestus has even stood up again.

Hermes pulls his stepmother into a hug. She seems touched by his step-progeny affection and turns to give him her full attention. She stands chatting with Hermes while chugging back her wine. She has her back to her escort Ganymede, and he stands there awaiting the further command of his queen.

Katie moves in on Ganymede. She puts her hand on Ganymede's head like she is admiring his hair. Ganymede smiles preeningly at her, then his face goes blank. Katie must have worked her memory charm on him. She disappears into the crowd, leaving Ganymede staring blankly into space. After a while, Ganymede rouses himself. He shakes his head and flips his long hair back. In the process, he elbows Hera.

Hera turns away from Hermes and casts an annoyed look at Ganymede. The marriage goddess shakes her empty cup and hands it to the cupbearer. Ganymede takes the cup and heads off to the bar for Hera. Hermes stays to talk with Hera. After a brief chat, Hermes moves on, leaving Hera to find her next social conquest. Her eyes scan the room and then she looks upwards at the tiers of tables.

She suddenly stops scanning when she reaches Hephaestus and me. I think she is drawn by the silver white of his hair. I expect she will soon realize who she is looking at and move on. But she stays looking at us and fixes us with a hard stare. In a flash, the hard look is gone and she smiles up at us. Ganymede has returned with her drink. She graciously takes it and sips at her wine while staring at us. She turns to whisper something to Ganymede and then the two of them head our way.

I feel a knot of fear in my throat as I watch that trash mother and her long-haired lackey walk towards the platforms. I want to get Hephaestus and me out of here before he even has a chance to see them.

"Hephaestus, did Athena tell you she was lending Brandon an aegis? I'm sure it would benefit from a fitting from you. Do you want to go and find him with me?"

"She did what?" Hephaestus says, "Now, why didn't they come by the forge first? They're not the same size. I don't know why no one understands you can't just use an instrument that is custom made for someone else and expect the same result. This is disastrous. Luckily, I brought a tool belt with me. I see him. I'll go get the tool belt and meet you over there."

Hephaestus takes his cane and weaves his way through the tables and down the back steps that lead to the kitchen. He can move surprisingly quickly when he wants to. He's gone and out of sight before Hera and Ganymede come up the front steps to our table. I put my head down so I can walk past them without them noticing me. I catch a glimpse of Hera's sloe-eyed beauty as I lift my head slightly. Her eyes are magnetic and I want to look at them again. I lift my head and take a second look. Her rosebud mouth curls slightly upwards as I lock eyes with her.

"Watch it, doll hair!" Ganymede snaps at me. I have accidentally run into him while I was distracted by Hera's gaze. "Take your tacky-ass extensions and get away from here. Can't you see that this is a queen? I almost spilled her drink. The cup is sacred!"

I mumble an apology and try to slip past him but Hera intervenes.

"Ganymede, please, it's alright," she says. Hera puts a manicured hand on my arm. "I apologize for my companion. He doesn't mean anything by it. And you have beautiful hair. There's no shame in not being able to grow long hair." She smiles at me with perfect white teeth. I lift a lock of my hair and examine it. It doesn't look that fake to me.

"Thanks," I say and try to move past them. Hera blocks my way. "Is it Wiccan?" she says.

I don't know what she's talking about. "I'm sorry, I'm not sure what you mean." I say.

Hera comes closer to me and looks me in the eye. Her long-lashed stare is grave and unblinking. "That looks like a Wiccan weave," she says. "You must be a witch. Are you visiting from Earth?"

I don't want to tell her anything about myself, but I am being compelled to answer. It's like she is pulling the answer out of me with her eyes. I feel I could fight it but I decide it may be best to let her have her way. "Yes," I say, "I am visiting from Earth."

With this information, Hera releases me from her stare. "You must be one of Hecate's girls, then. It's such a waste of your beauty to make potions and howl at the moon. I would like to talk to you about working for my company. I'll find you later and we can talk about what you can do for Juno." Hera flashes her eyes at me one final time before waving at some people at another table and sashaying away. Ganymede carefully cradles her cup and trails after her.

The minute Ganymede and Hera are out of sight, I run down the stairs and onto the ballroom floor. I find Hephaestus with Brandon. The god has his tools out and is making adjustments to the aegis. Athena is hovering nearby like a watchful mother hen. She gives Brandon a final pep talk.

"Brandon," Athena says, "you have learned enough to not embarrass yourself out there. I talked to the Cyclops you are fighting and he is interested in giving a good demonstration of Omedis."

"The only thing you need to worry about is that Cyclopes have a temper. If he gets frustrated, he could forget himself and become rough with you. But if that should happen, you have Hermes' feather and that will give you the speed to leap out of the way. The performance is starting soon. I am going to get a drink. I'll see you on the floor."

I catch her eye and we walk to the bar together so we can talk out of earshot of Hephaestus.

"Hera spoke to me upstairs," I say, "she was questioning me and trying to find out about me."

"She's on the look-out for anyone who could be your mother's daughter," says Athena. "She has the power of hypnosis so it is hard to resist her questions. Try your best to defy her. Don't worry, this is almost over. I am going with Hermes now to load up the fleuranium. We will be back in time for Brandon's performance. And then we will all fly out of here."

Hermes suddenly appears at the bar with us. He orders two shots from the bartender. He hands one to Athena and the two of them clink glasses.

"Drink up," Hermes says, "to successful thievery."

"To valor and victory," answers Athena as she downs the drink. The two of them hold hands, and with a blur of movement they are gone.

I join Brandon as he is getting ready for the fight. Brandon is standing with his eyes closed breathing deeply. As his chest rises and falls, he rotates his head slowly from side to side. He opens his eyes and stares steadily at some point in the distance that I can't see. He seems to be accessing something deep inside of himself, a place of calm and strength.

We are in an area at the back of the ballroom that we curtained off for the performers while they wait to go on. The presentation part of the gala has already started. Hephaestus, as the sponsor, went out first and said a few words of welcome. He then introduced the indigenous Martian I saw earlier. The small, green, furry being held out his hands in welcome and received loud applause. This caused him to clutch his ears and he was gently led away by Thalia.

A troupe of Olympian dancers perform next. Brandon and I watch them from a part in the curtain. Brandon must have noticed that I am nervous for him because he says to me reassuringly, "Don't worry about the fight. Athena has given me a lot of training. She put me in visions of classic battles."

"Oh, you mean like you got to watch training videos?" I say.

"No," Brandon says, "more like I was actually in the battle. I got to spar with Hercules, Ajax, and Achilles. Their visions don't play out in real time so I was there for a long time."

"You *fough*t them?" I say with alarm, "Those are great heroes. You are lucky you survived," I say.

"Sometimes I didn't," Brandon says.

I look at my old friend and wonder what he's gone through in the last few days. Whatever has happened has left him sure of himself and his own talents. I have been worried for Brandon but I now I think I can rest easy about what is about to happen. He's been brave since he was a little kid. He stepped up for his family and helped them through their grief over the loss of Liam. Athena found all the strength inside of him and harnessed it. Now he is ready to do his part in our plan to save the world.

The dancers are almost finished their performance when there is a commotion. A group of Dionysus's followers have drunkenly stumbled into the arena. One of them looks particularly wasted and is trying to get one of the dancers to dance with him.

“Oh my God,” I say, “those are the followers of Dionysus. We should put a leash on them. They can’t resist a party. Hephaestus knew this would happen so he put some of his Cyclopes on security. They should take care of this.”

As I say this, a pair of Cyclopes invade the arena. They glare at the confused revelers and herd them off the stage. One of the Cyclopes picks up the dancing drunk and flings him over his shoulder. The Cyclops stomps off with him to the medic tent.

Brandon steps away from the curtain and stumbles over to a bench we have backstage. The color has drained from his face and there is sweat pouring down his forehead. I move quickly to him and kneel down in front of him so I can check him out.

“What’s wrong, Brandon?” I say, “Are you okay?”

“That drunk guy,” Brandon says.

“Are you worried about them coming back?” I say. “I’ll go speak to Hephaestus. We’ll increase the security around the perimeter.”

Brandon shakes his head. He gets up and paces around the small space. He briefly looks at me with frightened eyes then goes back to sit on the bench. He leans forward and puts his face in both hands.

“Are you sick?” I say. “If you’re not feeling well we’ll cancel the performance.”

“No, I need to perform. Hermes and Athena need the time to get the fleuranium,” Brandon says. He looks at me with wide eyes. He takes two deep breaths and finally says in a low voice, “Zoe, I think I saw Liam. The drunk man dancing out there looked like my brother.”

Brandon’s eyes look as haunted as if he saw a ghost. I know exactly how he feels. My mother also came back from the dead. He may indeed have seen Liam, or it may be that the visions and the stress of training have affected his mind and he is seeing things. I know now that he is in no frame of mind to go out there and fight a Cyclops.

“I am going to get you some water,” I say to Brandon. “I will be right back.”

I step around the curtain in search of Hephaestus so I can tell him that we need to call off the performance. I see him and try to hurry over to him because the dancers have finished up and are leaving the arena.

have finished up and are leaving the arena. Hephaestus is picking up his cane and starting to walk over to the stage when suddenly, the ballroom turns dark. The crowd grumbles and shouts in confusion. Images of giant blue peacocks are projected onto all the walls, and the image of a peacock fills the floor of the ballroom. A single spotlight shines on the center of the floor.

Out of the black and blue darkness steps the regal figure of Hera. She steps into the spotlight and beams her eyes at the tiered tables. She turns in a complete circle and the crowd becomes quiet.

Hera's nude tinted lips spread into a large grin. She stands tall and holds her hands in prayer position. With a flash of her eyes, she raises her arms into the air. The crowd breaks into loud applause. Hera brings her hands down and the crowd goes quiet.

"I am delighted to be here on behalf of my son Hephaestus," Hera says. "We thank the Martians for their generous hospitality. I have spent the last week getting to know so many of you. Some of you are old friends from Tartarus. As you know, I am the goddess of monsters and you are beloved to me."

"Our entertainment brings together your old oppressors the Earthlings, with the highly esteemed Martians, in the art of Omedis. I know this is a sensitive time for Martians, as they quite rightly fear the encroachment of Earth on their beautiful society. Please put that aside for now and enjoy this demonstration of Omedis. It will remind you of the proper place for Earthlings. Beneath the heel of Tartarus."

Chapter Seventeen

The crowd breaks into uproarious applause. Hera pauses in her speech as she basks in their appreciation. She is stirring up Martian hostility to Earthlings. Hephaestus needs to stop this fight. I look around for his familiar silhouette but it is too dark for me to see anything.

"Please join me in welcoming our competitors. Representing the Earth, we have the Earthling Brandon," Hera says. With a flourish of her hand, the curtain opens to reveal Brandon. He looks out to the crowd with a stunned expression. The crowd applauds and Brandon hesitantly walks into the spotlight with his staff in hand. He puts one hand to his eyes and looks out at the crowd. I wish I could offer him some encouragement. With the bright light upon him he cannot possibly see anyone. He gives up looking and stands patiently with his staff at the ready.

"And representing Mars we have a very special Martian Tartian. You all know the tragic story of how Tartians came to Mars. They are originally from Earth where they made their home in Tartarus. They were displaced by war and became refugees. They sought asylum on the surface of their home planet of Earth but instead of being treated with compassion, they were mercilessly hounded by above-ground Earthlings."

"The Cyclops Theodosius tried to live peacefully in a cave on the shores of Greece. He was not harming anyone but his cave was invaded again and again by soldiers. Theodosius fought back. As a result, he was blinded in a vicious attack by Earth militia. He had to flee to Mars where he was welcomed with open arms by the Indigenous Martians. They helped him heal and they gave him a home. Now he has a thriving life on Mars, far from the Earthlings who harmed him. Please welcome the Tatarussian Hero Theodosius."

A spotlight shines on the back of the room. An enormous Cyclops stomps into the light, his heavy step causing the crystal chandelier lights to shake and jingle. Half as wide as he is tall, he looks like a mountain come to life.

He says something to the crowd, and he sounds like a combination of a grizzly bear growling and knives being sharpened. The knife sharpening sound hurts my ears. Hera glides over to him and judiciously offers him her hand as she walks him to the battleground. She looks like a proud mother presenting her beloved son for a playdate.

I hear Hephaestus's walking stick as he hurriedly makes his way to the arena. He reaches Hera and Theodosius as they meet Brandon.

"Stop! This is not right! Clymon was going to fight Brandon," Hephaestus says. He looks up to the Cyclops and says, "Theodosius, I'm so glad you are here, but this is a demonstration battle and the details have been worked out with Clymon. We can't accept substitutes at this late date."

Theodosius snarls and spits some kind of answer to Hephaestus. The Cyclops stands awkwardly under the spotlight. His heavily muscled shoulders and neck meet a head that resembles a cinder block. He has let his hair grow long over his mutilated one eye so that it grazes his nose in matted strands. He takes his staff and twirls it around in a distracted way, causing Hera, Hephaestus, and Brandon to duck.

"Clymon sends his regrets," Hera says. "Theodosius did not want to disappoint the crowd. If you are worried that he can't see — don't. Indigenous Martians have taught him to navigate by echo-location. He is more than capable of fighting an Earthling." Hera turns to the crowd and says, "Please give us your applause and the fight will begin."

The crowd whoops and hollers and claps. Some of them give a standing ovation. With all this noise it will be impossible for Theodosius to find Brandon through echo-location. The Cyclops is fighting blind. Hera has been unclear on how the fight will actually start, so the Cyclops takes it upon himself to start swinging his staff in the general direction of Brandon. Hephaestus is powerless to stop the fight. He and Hera make a quick exit from the arena. My heart breaks for Hephaestus because his mother has betrayed him yet again and is using him to get what she wants.

Brandon stands with his staff at the ready, prepared to cartwheel his way into a performance of Omedis, but it is useless. It's clear that all the Cyclops intends to do is club Brandon with his staff as best he can. Theodosius charges at Brandon and tries to bring the staff down on his head. Brandon is able to duck away using a back-tuck. If Theodosius had succeeded, the staff would have gone straight through Brandon's skull.

It's a timed match and it appears Brandon's best option is to wait out the clock while nimbly avoiding the raging Cyclops with the big stick. As Brandon somersaults and cartwheels his way out of the path of Theodosius, the crowd starts to boo. They came to see a fight. They want Brandon to fight back. He would be crazy to get close enough to Theodosius to try to hit him. Brandon seems to not care what the crowd thinks and continues to duck and roll to avoid the attacking Cyclops.

I look at the clock and there is only three minutes left. Brandon should be able escape this unscathed. It is still dark in here and I can't see if Hermes and Athena have returned yet. Katie emerges from the crowd and helps with the light situation. She visits all the standing torches in turn and magically illuminates them. She then walks by the ravens on the tables and opens their cage doors with a flick of her fingers. The ravens take flight with the silver discs she had given them earlier. They fly up to the rafters and the silver discs turn into lights that light up the ceiling. It's now possible to view what is going on in the ballroom.

I can see Athena and Hermes have hurriedly returned and are watching the fight from the sidelines. I run over to join them. I look for Hephaestus too, but I can't see him.

Brandon is still doing a good job of evading the Cyclops' attacks. He jumps and dances out of the way at every deathly blow aimed at his head.

"That is the training of Omedis," Athena says with pride and a satisfied smile. Her hair is in disarray and her sword is askew. "A good warrior knows when to attack and when to retreat. In Omedis, you retreat while dancing."

Athena seems confident that her prodigy will make it through this travesty of an Omedis demonstration. She adjusts her sword belt and smooths back her hair. "This is almost over. I'm going to go get my ship ready so we can leave right away. I'll meet you outside."

Athena charges out the door. There are only two minutes to go. I am holding my breath until the clock finally ends the match.

I notice there is a commotion on the side of the arena. It's Dionysus's followers drunkenly stumbling again onto the floor. Those idiots will be lucky if they don't get a wayward staff jammed into their stomachs. The Cyclopes security is standing and watching them with their arms crossed. They have lost all interest in insuring the safety of this fight.

Suddenly Brandon stops dancing and ducking. He is not moving and he appears distracted. It looks like he has been frozen somehow. He is staring intently at Dionysus's followers. Among them is Hera, and her laser-beamed eyes are focused on Brandon.

Theodosius strikes at Brandon and only misses because the Cyclops is clumsy. Theodosius is getting tired from the fight. He stops and rests his chin on his upturned staff for a moment while he catches his breath.

"What's wrong with Brandon?" I say to Hermes, "why isn't he moving? Has Hera done something to freeze his feet? I better go down and try to move him or that Cyclops is going to get him."

Hermes puts a strong hand on my arm, "No, don't do that. Hera is laying a trap for you. She wants you to go down there so that you will get in the way and Theodosius will hit you."

I look at Brandon and follow his gaze again. Beside Hera is another person who looks familiar. With a jolt of recognition, I realize this person looks remarkably like Brandon. This must be his lost brother, Liam. I don't know if this is really Liam, or is part of a hypnotic suggestion by Hera, but in any case, Brandon is in trouble because he is stunned and frozen.

The Cyclops takes his staff and aims it like a spear at Brandon's heart. With a mighty thrust, the Cyclops tries to drive the staff into Brandon's chest. The staff hits Brandon and then is deflected by the aegis. The staff bounces back and out of Theodosius's hand. The blow to the chest appears to have unfrozen Brandon and he begins to move again. He zigzags around the arena, out of his opponent's reach. The Cyclops angrily stomps around the arena in search of his staff. As the Cyclops finally locates his staff, the bell rings, signaling the end to the match.

Brandon begins to walk off the arena but the Cyclops is not finished with him. Theodosius swings his staff in the air like a baseball bat and comes at Brandon in a fury. The Cyclops obviously only has a general idea of where Brandon is located and in his rage is having trouble focusing on his target.

The Cyclops brings the staff down hard to where Brandon had been standing and sends the staff crashing through the floor. The ferocity of the strike would have decimated Brandon. The Cyclops is fuming at having missed his opponent. He yanks the staff out of the hole he created and turns around to storm after Brandon.

The Cyclops aims flailing strikes at his retreating opponent. Theodosius growls and flashes his jagged teeth in frustration. The crowd starts chanting "Get him!" "Get the Earthling!"

Brandon is narrowly escaping getting hit, but only because the Cyclops has such bad aim. Theodosius manages to get right behind Brandon and raises his staff high in the air. He is about to inflict a deadly blow, when suddenly there is a high-pitched, blood-curdling scream. The Cyclops stops his staff in mid-air and turns to look for the source of the screaming. Standing at the far side of the arena with a crazed expression is Lamia.

She's not supposed to be here but she must have snuck into the ballroom. Seeing Brandon in trouble, she sprints towards the Cyclops. Her lips are curled back, exposing her teeth in an animal-like grimace. Her eyes are black and her nostrils are flaring. She reaches the battleground and with a running jump, she leaps onto the back of the Cyclops. She scrambles up his back to his head, digging her fingers into him as she goes. She holds onto his head and sinks her teeth into his ear. Lamia tears at the ear while the Cyclops tries to shake her off.

He falls to ground and Lamia continues to bite at him, going to work on his shoulder. In her frenzy, she looks up at the crowds and blood is pouring from her mouth. Theodosius appears to have lost consciousness. The security Cyclopes race to the arena and pounce on Lamia. She is spitting out pieces of Cyclops as they pull her by the legs off of Theodosius. The security Cyclopes each take one leg and start to drag her away. Blood drips from her mouth as Lamia lets out an angry roar. She twists her body to get away from the security but they hold on tight. Then something happens that causes them to drop her legs.

She begins to shake violently. Her body convulses and her legs ripple back and forth like they are made out of jelly. She lets out another roar and her body splits open at her belly button.

A long, scaly tail emerges from her body, like the tail of a snake. Lamia wriggles and rolls in her new body. She is now half snake, half woman. With a slap of her tail, she launches herself through the air across the arena. She lands with a hard thump near the entrance to the ballroom. Without a backward glance she slithers away out the door.

I look for Hera to see if she has been affected by seeing Lamia again but there is no sign of her or Ganymede. They appear to have made a hasty retreat. The ravens in the rafters caw and fly in frantic circles before finding the door to the ballroom and flying away.

The crowd thinks leaving is a good idea too and start to quickly get up from their tables. In their hurry, a panic takes over the crowd and they begin to knock each other over as they try to get out of the ballroom. Hermes whispers to me. "Come on, it's time to go. No one will notice if we take Brandon now. The ships are waiting."

I find Brandon on the side of the arena and take his hand. "Brandon, the ships are ready. We have to go now."

I pull at Brandon's arm but he remains locked in place. "I can't go now," Brandon says. "I need to find Liam. He went over this way."

I consider for a moment if that is a good idea. Hera clearly had a plan to kill us. We have a chance to escape now and we should take it immediately. Before I can open my mouth to say anything, there is a deep rumble under my feet. The chandeliers sway back and forth ominously over our heads.

If one of those were to come down, it would crush us. The floor is shaking and I am afraid I will fall over. I get low to the ground and protect my head with my hands.

"Is this an earthquake?" Brandon shouts over the noise of the rumbling. He has dropped to the floor too, and is crouched right beside me.

Katie and Hermes crouch down on either side of us so that they are flanking us. "It's not an earthquake," Hermes shouts, "this volcano is about to blow. Olympus Mons is the biggest volcano in the galaxy. It's the size of Arizona. When it blows, Earth will be able to see this from space. We have to get out of here, now."

"But if it's a volcano, can't Hephaestus stop it?" I shout. "He's the god of volcanoes."

Hermes shakes his head. "Hephaestus awoke the volcano. He started the eruption but he couldn't help it. He was upset. He told me to take you to safety. He was worried about what Theodosius and the crowd would do to Brandon and you. Has everyone got their feathers? Hold on tight to each other and hold on tight to your feathers. I'm going to get you quickly out of here."

"Wait, I want to get my brother! He's with Dionysus," Brandon shouts.

"No time," Hermes says. "He'll be okay. Dionysus is with him. He'll protect him. Now hold tight because we are going to go fast."

Hermes' feathers have multiplied so that we are in feathery cocoon together. I feel like we are travelling on a high-speed train. Hermes is the conductor and he is taking us on a bullet express out of here. We are going too fast and are too densely packed in feathers for me to see around us as we race out of the ballroom, through the casino, and out the side of the volcano to the surface of Mars. Once outside, there is the briefest hint of sand, wind, and cold hitting my face, but then Katie adds her powers to our protective cocoon. The storm goddess shields us from the harsh environment of Mars as we travel suspended in our feathery casing. Within minutes, we have reached the crater where our ships have been hidden.

The feathers retract and we are left free of the cocoon. The rumbling from the awakened volcano grows stronger and we keep close to the ground to prevent being knocked over. Inside the biodome we are able to breathe easily. The biodome will also facilitate take-off because it mimics Earth's atmosphere.

Athena is already sitting inside of her ship. Our two ships rattle loudly as they sit atop the quaking crater. Thin cracks have appeared on the sides of the crater. Smoke pushes out of the cracks and they widen and grow. Streams of steaming lava are flowing out of cracks and they begin trickling slowly towards our ships. Even before the volcano blows, we will have to fly out of here quickly to avoid our ships being consumed by the molten liquid.

"Brandon, I have room for one person. Come into my ship," Athena shouts over the sound of the growling volcano. Brandon looks at me with a pained expression. He is going to have to leave me. There is not enough room for all of us in one ship with all the fleuranium and it would be ungrateful to decline Athena's invitation. He reaches for my hand and pulls me close to him. The rumbling in our ears has grown too intense for us to hear each other. We squeeze our hands tightly together. We lock eyes and try to communicate.

I want to tell him that *I will help you find your brother. That Hephaestus triggered the volcano because he feared you would get hurt and he knew that would destroy me. That Hephaestus knows I need to hold on to you because you are the best person I know. Because you are family. Because I love you.*

Over the growing noise, I can only mouth "Your brother." His beautiful eyes look intensely at me and I think he knows what I mean. He nods his head yes and puts his arm around my waist. He brings his face close to mine and we press our lips together and kiss goodbye. A wave of warmth moves through me even as the ground is threatening to explode beneath us.

We break apart because we have to hurry and get on board our separate ships. Katie and Hermes have already managed to get inside their ship. I feel panicked as I wonder how I will be able to join them. Katie's amulet is pulsing in my pocket. I reach for it and it acts like a magnet, pulling me into the ship where Katie is already strapped in with Hermes. I am able to slip through the doorway of the ship and then secure myself in my seat.

I look out the window and watch as Brandon makes his careful way over to Athena's ship, pulls open the door, and climbs inside. The metal door clangs shut. Brandon presses his hand against his glass window. He gives me one last look before Athena engages the engines. The bellowing of the ship is eclipsed by the thundering of the volcano.

Hermes engages our engines and my head is thrown back against my seat. I strain my head forward so I can look out once more at Brandon's ship. I look out the window just in time to see his ship take off and pierce the biodome.

We have flown out of the crater and are heading for space when the volcano blows. The sound slams my eardrum painfully. Billows of black smoke shoot up from the surface of Mars and spread out across the planet. The smoke is bracketed by fiery red lava flowing in ever-expanding rivers. Every visible part of the red planet is alive with fire and ash.

The force of the explosion causes our ship to be pushed sideways. Hermes struggles to get the ship back on path. I look at Katie and she is quietly saying chants to herself. Hermes navigates us higher and higher, trying to escape the pull of the volcano.

I look down and see other ships have not been successful at leaving the blast of the volcano and are spiraling into the smoke. I hope that because Athena left before us, she has been able to steer clear of the destruction.

At last our ship is righted and we can fly clear of the forces of the planet. Hermes pulls up a screen on the control panel that shows our immediate vicinity. In our space travels, I have not always enjoyed looking at our view. The universe is wondrous to look at, but the vastness inspires loneliness. Loneliness is right next to despair. It's the small things that bring happiness, not the immense. Brandon holding my hand. My mother tucking notes in my lunch. Hephaestus enjoying my gift bags. Katie helping me with my hair. And in another time, my crush knowing who I am.

I desperately look at the screen on the control panel for a sign of Brandon. There, in the corner, is an object.

"What is that?" I ask Hermes as I point to the screen.

Hermes furrows his brow. "That looks like another ship," he says. Hermes presses a button on the control panel and brings that part of the screen closer. We can see that it is indeed a ship. He brings it closer still and we can see the insignia on the side of the ship. It is an olive tree. Athena's ship has made it.

I lean back exhausted and relieved, but I do not close my eyes. I don't want to fall asleep just yet. I don't want Hades to come visit me in my dreams. Instead, I want to think of Brandon.

I was poised between happiness and despair. Now I can make the journey into deep space seeing the light of the universe instead of the dark.

"See you at home, Brandon," I whisper.

Chapter Eighteen

"Zoe, can you come with me to the back of the ship?" Katie says. "I want to show you what I have packed for you."

I undo my seatbelt and follow Katie. We are close to landing on Earth and I had already secured myself in my seat. At the back of the ship, Katie pulls out a back-pack and unzips it.

"These are the fleuranium cuffs I lent you on Mars," Katie says. "I want you to keep them. Their full powers come into effect in the vicinity of the Earth. They can provide you with protection against attack. The Earth is descending into chaos, and it will get to the stage where people are looting and raiding each other. These have protective properties that will keep you safe." I swallow hard as Katie speaks about the coming chaos of Earth. She reaches into the backpack and pulls out a carved wooden box. She opens it and shows me the jeweled head piece that she let me wear.

"This was made for me by Hephaestus," she says. "You wear it well. It's yours now."

"Katie, thank you," I say, "but I can't take this from you. It's too much."

Katie presses the headpiece into my hand. "I want you to have it," Katie says. "Hephaestus would have given you something if he had the time. Consider it a gift from him, too." I hold the glittering jewel encased in layers of platinum, gold, and fleuranium in my hand. I remember what Hephaestus said about custom-designing things for people. I wonder if by taking this jewelry, I take a little of my two friends with me.

"I have also packed you some clothing," Katie says, "it may be a while before you can get home and pick up your old clothes. Remember to keep your amulet on you. If you ever need me, hold the amulet in your hand and think of me and I will come to you. I am the goddess of storms, and Earth is entering a time of many storms. I am also the goddess of crossroads. If you are ever at a crossroads and don't know what to do, call me and I will come and help you."

I feel confused by what Katie is saying. She sounds like she is saying good-bye.

"Aren't you coming with Hermes and me?" I say.

"No, Zoe," Katie says, "I have to go where I'm needed. We're coming over the Pacific Ocean. I'm going to take a landing pod down there. San Francisco has been decimated by an earthquake and a typhoon. There are many witches there. I have to go help my friends."

I am stunned by this. Of course, Katie would want to help her friends but aren't we beyond helping a few people at a time? Katie is a magical goddess. She could be helping people on a global scale.

I follow Katie to the wing of the ship that houses the landing pods. Katie throws her bag into a pod. She turns to me and gives me a long hug.

"I know you want me to do something bigger than just help my friends," Katie whispers into my ear. "But I can't do that. Earth will not accept that. The gods and goddesses were rejected a long time ago. We're not wanted there."

"But things have changed!" I say. "The earth is falling apart. We need you now!"

Katie looks steadily at me and speaks quietly.

"It doesn't make a difference. The people of Earth will be upset at the latest disaster, then their memory of it will fade and they won't be concerned anymore. They forget and move on and are oblivious to what it all means. Their collective memory is unstable. They long ago lost the memory of what we are to them. They forget we are part of their universe and part of them. Without that memory, they reject us. Most of the Olympians left a long time ago. A few of us have found a small place there, but we cannot have the importance that we once had. I am sorry I can't do more." Katie says this with a catch in her voice. She climbs into the pod and begins to strap herself inside.

"It's okay," Katie says with forced cheeriness, "Hermes will get you and the fleuranium to Colton Chase. Hermes used to deliver the dead to Hades. He can deliver anybody to where they need to go."

I wake up to the sound of waves gently crashing against the beach outside of my window. It's my first morning back on Earth. I'm staying in a little beachside cottage on the island of Nisyros. Hermes deposited me here after we landed last night and then he took off. He's probably having fun looking for cattle he can steal.

I open the window and breathe in the warm ocean air. The breeze blows my hair around and I wish for a rubber band to tie it back. My hair seems to have lost the magic manageability imparted by Katie and has returned to being curly and unruly. I feel the sea-spray upon my face and know my hair will only get curlier as the day goes on.

I go to the fridge and find some fruit and yogurt to eat. I take it out on the front porch to eat while watching sail boats crest the waves. The cottage must be pretty isolated because I don't see any other people around. A riderless horse walks along in the sand. The golden mare looks up at me and blinks her long-lashed eyes as I sit eating my yogurt. I wonder if wild horses are a feature of the island.

Far off the shore I can see a lone swimmer. I watch his steady progress as he comes closer to the beach.

The current looks strong here but the swimmer seems to have no problem making his way through the waves. His arms steadily cut through the water, pulling him forward. With surprising speed, he has reached the shore and he is standing up and wading the rest of the way in. He is tall and golden with shoulder-length, wavy hair. It's Hermes, looking like the Greek god that he is.

He sees me and flashes a smile. He jogs up to the house and finds a stack of towels on the deck. Taking one, he dries himself off, then shakes his wet hair at me so that I get droplets of sea-salt all over me.

"Did you sleep well?" he says, as he helps himself to a strawberry from my plate. He doesn't wait for an answer and instead goes into the house. He comes back with a plate of bread, cheese, and honey before I've had time for another spoonful of my yogurt. He dips a spoon into his bowl of honey.

"You have to try this," he says as he spoons the honey onto my yogurt, "it's the best of the Greek isles."

"Did you sleep here last night?" I say.

"No," Hermes says. "I had some catching up with friends to do. I don't get back here enough."

Hermes claps his hands. "Are you ready to go? I have some people figuring out the whereabouts of Colton Chase. In the meantime, I thought we could take a catamaran out and see some of the islands."

"Aren't we going to wait for Brandon?" I say. I didn't see him last night but I assume Athena is staying with him on another part of the island and will be coming by later.

Hermes takes a couple of rubber bands from his pocket and uses one to tie up his hair. "Brandon is fine. He has done his part in this operation," Hermes says. "Now it's up to you. Be sure to pack a bathing suit. You might want to tie your hair back on the catamaran." Hermes drops the other rubber band beside my plate as he heads back to the beach and jumps in the water.

I wish I knew where Brandon was. Hermes says he's fine but I can't trust anything he says. The god of thieves is down at the dock getting the catamaran ready. I want to question him further, but I know by now that he'll only give me cryptic answers if he doesn't feel like telling me something. If I have to travel the universe with a god, why can't it be with Aletheia, the goddess of truth?

I hope Brandon is okay. Feeling anxious about his whereabouts, I pace around the deck. The tide has gone out and there is an ocean-smoothed plain of sand on the beach below. It looks like the perfect place to practice gymnastics and work off some nervous energy. Since I'm wearing my bathing suit, I decide to go down to the sand and practice cartwheels.

I love the feeling of freedom and power when I tumble. I remember one of my tumbling routines and practice it out on the sand. Even though it's more than a year since I've done this, it comes back to me quickly. I do three tumbling runs and don't fall on my face once.

Down the beach I can see a group of girls walking my way. I don't want to tumble right in front of them. I decide to do one more tumbling run before they reach me.

I stand poised and ready to run at full speed and tumble. I sprint forward and focus on where I am going to land when I hear yelling behind me. I block it out so I don't lose concentration and fall. I do a roundoff, followed by a backhand spring, followed by a back tuck, and then I stick the landing. I throw my arms up in the air like I'm at the Olympics.

"Zoe!" I hear my name being called and I turn around. Standing before me are my old cheer stunt squad Lauren, Paige, Hailey, and Jamie. They must have come up right behind me while I was in the middle of my tumbling run.

"Oh my God, Zoe, I can't believe you're here!" Jamie says. She has a sun-burned face and is wearing her hair in braids. Jamie and the other girls give me a big hug.

We all laugh delightedly as they take turns hugging me. I am so happy to see them all alive and well.

At last I say, "It's so good to see you all! What are you all doing in Greece?"

Paige looks at me with her big eyes and smiles. "We planned to go to Greece last year. Don't you remember? We emailed you about it."

Lauren looks at me and bites her lip. "You probably missed the email," she says, "you had a lot going on then with your mom and everything." The other girls nod their heads and variously say, "I'm sorry, I hope you are okay, that was so sad."

I nod my head and look awkwardly at my feet. I vaguely remember seeing emails from them in my inbox. The messages are still sitting there, unopened. Looking now at their concerned faces, I feel like I've been a bad friend.

"That's right, I remember," I say, "it's so good to see you all."

"We're here to try the thermal springs," Hailey says.

"What are you doing here, Zoe?" Jamie says in a slightly interrogative tone.

I hesitate as I think of a reason I can give them. "I'm here with my cousin," I say. "It's a last-minute trip. He had some travel points that he wanted to use."

Hailey nods her head and says, "That's lucky that you were able to do that. Imagine if you had still been in San Francisco. You could have been caught in the earthquake."

I realize they all would have family and friends who are there. "Have you been in touch with people there?" I say.

“We’ve all talked to our families. They are all okay,” Jamie says. “I think fifty people died. It could have been much worse. All that talk about earthquake preparedness for years really paid off. I mean, there’s a lot of damage but they can rebuild it. We’re here for another two weeks. I’m sure a lot of it will be fixed by the time we get back.” The four of them look at me with pleasant expressions. They are so nonchalant about the natural disaster that has visited their home. I remember what Katie said about the unstable collective memory.

“Don’t you get worried about all the earthquakes, and wild fires, and weird weather that has been happening?” I say.

“I know, right?” Jamie says. “Do you want to get a drink with us? Paige met a dude on Mykonos and took off with him for two days. We want to hear what happened.” Paige blushes and looks away. The other three girls smile and laugh in her direction.

“I would love to go for a drink with you,” I say. “I should let my cousin know. He’s taking me out on that catamaran over there. Let’s go tell him we’re getting a drink and I’ll meet him later.” I decide I am going to take this time to work on my actual human relationships, which I’ve obviously let slide.

“Okay,” says Paige, “I’m sure he’ll understand that the Fire Queens need to catch up.” Fire Queens was the name of our cheer team.

We walk down the beach towards the dock. The damp, ocean-packed sand under my feet is a stark contrast to the dry, cutting sand of Mars. I want to fill my lungs with fresh, healthy Earth air.

“Race you to the dock,” I say and take off running. The four of them immediately start running. I thought I would easily win with my head start but I forgot how competitive they all are. They race off after me and Paige quickly outpaces me. Jamie comes up from the side and tries to grab at my arm. I swerve to avoid her and keep running. She changes tactics and sticks out her foot to trip Hailey. Our little flyer does a face-plant into the sand. I stop and turn around to help Hailey get up.

We continue running but my lead is long gone. Paige has reached the dock first, followed by Jamie, and then Lauren. The three of them each have a hand on a slimy, seaweed-covered wooden post holding up the wharf. Hailey and I jog the final few yards towards the others as they hold out their free hands to us. We give them each a high-five and then reach over to tag the posts.

"That post was gross. Let's take the stairs over there," Lauren says, while pointing to a set of stairs adjacent to the dock. As we climb the stairs and reach the dock, Jamie suddenly clutches my arm.

"Oh my God, why didn't you tell me your cousin is Kristof Nylund?" Ahead of us, Hermes is leaping about the moored catamaran as he organizes boxes.

"He's on YouTube!" Hailey says, "he's so cute."

"I love him!" Jamie says. "Does he have a girlfriend?"

Hermes looks over at us as we reach the boat and breaks into a big smile. He jumps off the deck of the catamaran and onto the dock.

"This is my cousin Kristof," I say. Hermes easily slides into this lie.

"It's nice to meet all of you," he says. "Are you going to come on our catamaran ride? I've packed lots of food and drinks." I start to say no but Jamie gushes, "We'd love to go on your catamaran! Thanks for taking us!" The four of them scramble aboard the boat before I can say anything else.

Hermes sails us out onto the choppy water. We all hold tightly to the railings as the boat bounces up and down and we skim the waves.

He takes us out of the harbor and around to the far side of the island. After a while, he stops the boat and drops anchor. We have travelled a good distance in a short amount of time on the swift-moving catamaran. We are facing an undeveloped part of the island and I don't see any other boats around.

"This is a secret cove I like to go to," Hermes says. "Not many boats go here. There will be lots of fish. Later on, we can take out the snorkels and go snorkeling."

Hermes brings out a cooler full of food and drinks. He makes up a charcuterie plate of meats, olives, cheese, and crackers for us to share. He pours ouzo over ice into two glasses and passes them around. "I hope you don't mind sharing," he says with a wink.

Paige and Jamie sit closest to Hermes. They hang on every word as he tells them about his social media career.

"I can do a livestream of our lunch if you like," Hermes says. Jamie says yes, then leaps across Paige to get closer to Hermes. Hermes turns the phone around to get a shot of all of us. I don't want to be in it and try to duck down but he still gets a shot of me. The four of them happily do the livestream with Hermes. After that is finished, they decide to suntan on the deck and take selfies.

They are having fun, but I'm finding it hard to join in because I'm thinking about Brandon. I wonder if there is a chance his ship didn't make it home. I'm feeling anxious again and decide some more exercise would be a good thing.

"I think I'm going to jump in the water and have a swim," I say.

Hermes looks up from where he's sunning himself on the deck. "Sure, go ahead," he says. "The water is really warm here." Jamie, Lauren, Hailey, and Paige are spread out across the deck, drinking in the sun with their eyes closed. Lauren puts her hand up in a half-hearted wave then pulls her hat down over her eyes.

I'm not a strong swimmer so I put on a life jacket. I go to the end of the boat and jump in the water. The sea is surprisingly warm and not at all what I am used to for ocean water. There is a slight current here and I decide to float in it for a while. I turn on my back in order to keep an eye on the boat as I do a lazy back stroke. The current easily moves me along, but I'm still close to the boat. I close my eyes and enjoy the feeling of floating with the sun on my face. The warmth is relaxing and I feel myself grow calm.

A small wave comes along, splashing my face. I try not to let it bother me and keep my eyes closed. Another wave comes along that pushes me back. I open my eyes and see the water is getting choppy.

Suddenly, the current becomes stronger and I feel like I am being pulled. A powerful force is drawing me backwards. I am being dragged farther and farther away from the boat. The current speeds up and churns beneath me. The water becomes rougher and waves are hitting me harder and faster. I am getting too far away from the boat. Everyone on the boat is sunning themselves and no one is noticing what is happening with me.

I open my mouth to yell and get their attention, but a big wave comes and fills me with water. My head gets pushed down below the rim of the lifejacket. With a kick of my legs and a press of my arms, I force my head back up. I cough and choke on the salty water, gagging as I try to catch my breath. Another wave comes, and I am flipped over like a turtle. Paddling frantically, I quickly right myself but I'm feeling disoriented. I can't see the boat. The waves keep coming and crashing into my eyes. The panic is rising in my throat and I can feel my air passage start to close. I know I need to keep myself together or I'm going to be in real trouble.

I push hard against the water in order to bounce high enough over the swells to see what is going on. I get a quick glimpse above the white caps and see no sign of our boat. The waves must have turned me around. I fight against the current so that I can twist around and see the other way. The surging waves bat at me but I'm able to rotate and see behind me. There's no catamaran in sight, but I see another boat. It's a huge vessel and I realize I am looking at a yacht.

The yacht seems to have seen me too and has noticed I am in distress. They are lowering a dinghy down the side. A man hurriedly climbs down the side of the yacht and drops into the dinghy. I feel relief flow through me as the man paddles the dinghy towards me. He's bent over in determination as he rows hard to get over to me. The choppy waves keep sending salty water into my eyes. It stings and I blink so much I can hardly see.

The man brings the boat alongside me and calls out, "Are you all right? The waves came up quickly. Take my hand."

I grasp the strong forearm he thrusts into the water. With his other arm, he reaches out and takes hold of my life jacket. With one solid pull he plucks me out of the water and into the dinghy.

I land in an undignified heap on the floor of the craft. My hair is in my face because I didn't tie it back like Hermes suggested, and I roughly push it back out of my eyes. The man offers me his hand again to help me to a seat. I take his hand and look up into my rescuer's face. I see the familiar handsome features, the dark eyes, the look of quiet confidence. He looks at me with a concerned expression, his lips parted as he breathes hard after the exertion of saving me.

"Colton," I say his name like a sigh. Feeling startled, my wet hand slips from his and I start to slide back down the damp floor of the dinghy. Colton catches me with his other arm around my waist. He holds me tightly and swings me onto the seat beside him.

"I've got you," he says while breathing hard, "I've got you, Zoe."

Chapter Nineteen

A steward on the yacht brings me a glass of water with lemon in it. I sip it while wrapped in a luxuriously fluffy towel in the main cabin of Colton's yacht. He stares at me with a quiet smile on his face. There's a glint in his dark eyes, which curve upwards into an almond shape. I am overwhelmed by the presence of him. He seems to have an extra vitality in him that leaps out and assails me. Maybe it's because I came close to slipping under the waves to my death, but I feel energized being this close to him. I am aware of the sensation of the towel against my skin, the feel of the salty ocean air entering my lungs, the frantic, adrenaline-charged beating of my heart.

He's taken off his wet shirt and has a towel draped around his shoulders, exposing his tanned chest. Around his neck is a chain necklace with an old-fashioned looking key. I reach for my throat to check to see if my diamond is still there. I feel the solid stone suspended on a gold chain. It's the diamond he gave me in my dream. Somehow that was real and he and I have already shared a night under the stars.

Still, I have to ask. "Do you know me?"

Colton drops his quiet smile and looks concerned. "Yes, Zoe, I know you. You're hard to miss. We ran right into each other last week, don't you remember?"

He's not telling me all I need to know. I am trying to figure out how to phrase the next question without sounding crazy. He gets up from his seat and comes to sit beside me. I am shivering slightly from being pummeled in the water. The warm heat from his nearby body hits me like another wave. It envelopes me and I feel my face flush.

He's sitting close enough to me that I can see the slow rise and fall of his bare chest. I've been this close to him before, but however that happened, he doesn't seem to remember it. I study the lips I kissed and feel my breath quicken at the memory. He continues to look at me and I wonder what he is thinking about. I wonder if some remnant of that shared memory is fighting to get out.

I know I have to talk to him about the fleuranium. If he doesn't remember that night, I will have to lead him into conversation about his work. But the way he is looking at me, I don't think he's interested in talking about work.

"Zoe, that must have been very scary for you in the water," he says, "I'm so glad you are safe. We need to get you warmed up. When you are ready, I can take you back to where you are staying and help you find your friends. But if you have time, I would really like to show you the island."

I tense my legs against the couch I am sitting on because I am afraid I will fall over in shock. I have waited for Colton Chase to ask me on a date for so long. In truth, I didn't think it would ever happen. I put my hand to his diamond again. The diamond is real; he's real; this is real.

"I would like that," I say, as I play with the cut stone between my fingers. The corners of Colton's mouth turn up. I think again about what it was like to kiss him. I flew to the stars that night and I almost took him with me.

Colton's gaze is soft and warm. His quiet smile returns. He says, "There's a beautiful restaurant that overlooks the caldera, the crater at the top of the volcano. It's hard to get to because it's in a remote part of the island. I have a landing pad for my helicopter on the top deck of my yacht. I can get my pilot to fly you back to your place and you can get changed. You can take your time. When you are ready, you can text and I'll send a driver."

The goosebumps on my arms from the cold of the water seem to stand to attention. My throat feels like it is about to close. I can only nod my head and whisper "Okay," by way of reply.

Colton stands and his smile turns broad. He crosses the room and opens a closet full of clothes. He pulls out a light cotton sweater and puts it on. "That's great, Zoe. I have to go to near the caldera now for some business. I can meet you there and we can have dinner. Have you ever been on a helicopter?"

I have been on a spaceship to Mars but I've never been on a helicopter. Brandon comes to mind again as I remember the spaceship. I hope wherever he is, that he is safe. Then I remember what Hephaestus said to me. No one knows anything most of the time. The trick is to accept that the unknown will always be with you. Sit with it, everything will become clear eventually, in its own time. The things that you know for certain, though, those you must hold onto and cherish.

"I've never been on a helicopter," I say, finding my voice. "I would love to have dinner with you."

From up in the air in the helicopter, it's apparent that the whole island is actually an active volcano. Along with towns and seaside villas, there are hot springs and eruptions of steam. Craters dot the countryside, their basins now dry where they were once conduits for rivers of lava during volcanic eruptions. The chief crater is called the caldera. It's a large crater that was created when the top of the volcano exploded during its last eruption.

The helicopter is able to land in a space behind the cottage. While I am inside getting ready for my dinner with Colton, I look out the window and see a wild horse trot into the yard. It looks like the same golden mare I saw earlier. Horses don't usually like loud sounds, and I am surprised it wasn't scared off by the noise of the helicopter. She bends her head down and nibbles at the tall grass that is growing near the cottage. She seems completely comfortable foraging for food close to humans. When I come back later, I am going to look for a store where I can buy some carrots to feed the horse.

By the time I am ready to go it is almost dusk. I put on a long, red strapless gown that Katie packed for me. I text Colton on a phone he lent me and a black car arrives to pick me up almost immediately.

The driver takes us on a road that's near the water so I get a view of the ocean as we drive along. The deep, blue water laps against the pristine white beach. Gradually, the road goes further and further inland, until we begin to ascend the island. We leave the villas and beaches behind and the landscape turns bare. Volcanic rock stretches as far as I can see, the naked expanse only broken up by the occasional heated spring. We are reaching the edge of the caldera.

The driver takes a turn off the winding road towards an outcrop of rocks. Behind the rocks is a large open plain, and at the edge of that is the restaurant. It sits directly above the expansive caldera, which looks like a huge, deep canyon. It would have once been filled with boiling hot lava. The lava flow from this crater built the entire island.

Colton texts me that he will be arriving in a few minutes. I decide to say good-bye to the driver and wait for Colton alone on a bench outside of the restaurant that has a view of the caldera. The vast volcanic canyon stretches for three kilometers.

From this vantage point, I can see the whole of the caldera and the Aegean Sea beyond. The barrenness of the crater contrasts with the lushness of the greenery that borders its perimeter. Serene now, the caldera is a remnant of a time that was both destructive and creative.

A herd of wild horses is slowly traversing a section of the caldera near me. The canyon must offer them a short-cut to the greenery on either side of the caldera. The hundred or so horses do not seem to be in a hurry to get to where they are going. They slowly walk across the caldera, their tails occasionally flicking upwards to strike at a fly. Their bobbing heads punctuate the slow movement of their migration across the mouth of the volcano.

The restaurant hidden behind the boulders is the only piece of civilization I can see up here. It looks newly constructed of glass and wood beam. Some entrepreneur must have had the idea that there is an untapped market of people who want to dine in a restaurant at the end of the world. It doesn't look like they have reached this niche group yet because there are no cars up here.

On the other hand, the road up here was pretty difficult and the best way to arrive here is probably by helicopter. There is enough space here for a chopper to comfortably land. The billionaire crowd are probably attracted to places that only they can easily access.

The setting sun is turning the sky into a patchwork of orange, gold, and purple. I let myself be lulled by the steady progress of the horses down below. If I concentrate, I can hear the sounds of their hoofs as they kick up dirt, carried on the wind across the caldera. The horses saunter along at a rhythmic pace. As I focus on their measured footsteps, I revel in the feeling of being once more a part of the earth.

I allow my gaze to rest on the horizon. It's been a long day and now that I can relax my body feels drained. The nerves in my stomach that were on high alert when I was near Colton are quelled by the tranquility of the scene and my exhaustion. I hope I can stay feeling this relaxed once Colton shows up. I don't want to spill wine on the table or stab him with my butter knife. I don't know how I could end up stabbing him, but I've already hit him in the arm while waiting for frozen yogurt so it could happen.

The sounds from the horses are getting louder. I look down and see that they are running in different directions. They look like they are in a panic. From somewhere in the distance, I hear a faint buzzing sound. The buzzing gets louder and turns into a low roar. The herd of equines kick up clouds of dust as they come together in a large, galloping mass. They run one way across the caldera then suddenly switch directions and run the other way. They are a teeming mass of panicked beasts.

Beyond the horses I can see the source of the roaring: it's a black motorcycle that is thundering down the wall of the caldera. As it nears the horses, the herd splits in half, clearing a path for the motorcycle. Four black horses are too panicked to make a choice in direction and instead run ahead of the motorcycle. The four black stallions charge up the middle of the caldera with the shiny ebony motorcycle close on their heels.

The stallions and the motorcycle are heading in my direction. They are still far away but I can see the straining of the horses in their prolonged gallop. Their mouths are foaming and sweat is covering their backs.

The speeding motorcycle behind them has sparks flying from its wheels. I feel angry at the motorcycle driver for distressing the animals, but then I realize the erratic swarming of the herd is giving him no options for escape.

I stand up from my seat so that I can get a better look at the driver. He's dressed all in black leather and is wearing a bronze etched helmet. As he comes closer, I can see the firm line of his mouth and his square jaw beneath his helmet. The thundering stallions and the revving motorcycle are filling my ears with crashing waves of sound. It's enough to almost prevent me from hearing my own thoughts, but an over powering thought does get through: I've seen this scene before.

My nightmare has come to life. The being who has haunted my dreams on a chariot lead by charging stallions is the being on the motorcycle driving towards me. I know in my heart that this is Hades, the Lord of the Underworld. He has pursued me through the earth and through the sky. I feel overwhelming fear as I realize his relentless invasion of my mind has come to consciousness before me. He is here to seize me and take me deep beneath the earth to his dark domain.

I want to run and hide but I don't know where to go. I turn around to the restaurant and try to open the heavy wooden doors. I push and pull at the door handle but it's locked. I bang my fists hard on the door and no one is answering. I press my face against a window and try to look inside but I can't see anything through the dark tinted glass. There must be a way to seek shelter from my impending doom. I run around to the back of the restaurant. I try to open the back door but it's locked too.

The sun has completely set, and the sky is growing dark. The coming shade of night will soon envelop me. I am now on the wide-open plain behind the restaurant. It is lit only by the moon and the stars. I am desolate and utterly alone, a tiny speck of life in an expanse of emptiness. I am afraid that any minute the black stallions will come galloping around from the other side of the restaurant and trample me. I put my back flat against the restaurant wall and brace myself.

The four black stallions charge out from the right side of the restaurant. They run at full speed into the plain until they almost reach the boulders, then begin to slow into a trot.

After slowing down, they circle back and come to rest a few feet from where I am standing. Their nostrils flare open and close as they seek to catch their breath. Steam is rising from their over-heated bodies and sweat is pouring down their legs.

With a rumble of engine, the motorcycle is propelled around the side of the restaurant. It comes skidding to a halt in front of me. The leather-clad rider jumps off and reaches for the clasp of his helmet. I dig my fingernails into the side of the restaurant wall as I try to disappear into the siding.

I remember those stories where women were attempting to escape being ravaged by a god and were transformed. They became flowers, or trees, or constellations. I believe I could do that right now. I could become a pillar holding up this restaurant for all time. It would be better to be that and to be in the open air than to spend eternity encased in the Underworld.

As I desperately press my palms into the wood, I can feel a splinter making its way into my hand. I pull my hand back for a second in pain, and then immediately press my hand back in place.

The rider leaps forward to try to grab my hand. I evade him, my fingers clawing at the wood. My terrified eyes meet his underneath the helmet. His eyes do not look darkly angry like in my dreams. They look concerned. I know that look. He pulls his helmet off his head and shakes out his hair.

"Colton?" I whisper in bewilderment.

He smiles and reaches for my hand. He takes it and turns it over tenderly in both of his hands.

"Did you get a splinter?" he says, "I'm sorry, I must have scared you. I didn't expect all those horses to be there when I was riding through. They got spooked and I was trying to find a way around them. Let's sit down and I'll get that splinter out of you." He holds my hand and gives me a gentle tug to get me moving. At his touch, a shiver runs through my spine. I hold fast to my station on the wall. He looks at me with a confused expression. He comes closer to me while still holding my hand. He puts his face near to mine and rests his other hand on my shoulder.

"Zoe," he says, "are you okay? What's the matter?"

I snatch my hand from his and my fingers curl into a fist. I hold the fist shaking between us.

"I know who you are," I say under my breath, his face inches from mine. "You've been stalking me. You've been after me for months. You're…" I gulp as I struggle to spit out the name.

He takes a step back and pulls his hands away from me. His concerned expression grows hard, changing the set of his face. His chin tenses and his lower lip juts out. The soft dark eyes turn deep and black. The hint of rejection offered by the withdrawal of his touch has a dark power all its own. I am afraid of him taking me, but at the same time I don't want this man whom I have thought about for so long to disappear altogether.

"I'm Plouton," he says flatly, "but I go by Colton Chase now."

"What? No," I say, "you're Hades! You are the King of the Underworld!"

He sighs and shakes his head. "Zoe, Hades was a god that no one spoke of in ancient Greece. No one wanted to evoke the name of the god associated with death, not even the other gods. Hades had to stay in the Underworld. I never got to go to Olympus or enjoy the splendor of Earth and the sea."

"I was effectively banished because I lost the lottery for domains with my brothers. But I had another name. Plouton, the Lord of Riches. If I was called at all, this was the name that people used. Because the Underworld is filled with riches. Precious metals, diamonds, jewels of every kind, and oil, the black river of wealth that propels the world. I am the most powerful god worshiped today. I am the god of wealth."

He walks over to the side of the restaurant and picks up a bucket that has been stored there. He brings it over to a tap that is near the backdoor and fills it with water. He places the bucket in front of the horses and takes it to each of them by turn to drink. After the last horse has had its fill, he walks over to me again. When I knew him as only Colton Chase he was tall. Now he seems to have grown in size and I feel small and vulnerable as he stands before me. He looks me steadily in the eye.

"I didn't stalk you, Zoe. You've been with me, willingly, for a long time as a shade. Your conscious self just doesn't remember that part of you."

"I don't know what you're talking about," I say. "Shades were the souls of the dead in the Underworld. Are you saying I'm dead?"

He shakes his head and his expression softens. "No, you are very much alive. But, like a lot of things, shades are misunderstood. They are not the dead, exactly. They are the sad and mournful part of the living. When a person gets depressed, a part of them dies. This is their shade. They sink through the Earth and go to the Underworld. When your mother died, you faded away in sadness. In truth, you were more shade than person."

"I haven't ruled the Underworld for a long time but it's still home to me. You caught my eye more than any diamond or sapphire ever could. When I saw that shade of you, so beautiful, the dark with the light, I had to know you. You were like a goddess of rain. A sweet specter in need of care. You stayed by my side in your sadness. I wanted to know the person. I found you on Earth so we could know each other. I fell in love with you. And you fell in love with me too."

I couldn't argue with that. I was obsessively in love with him. But now I wonder how real that love could be when I didn't even know who he was.

"Why didn't you speak to me back then and tell me who you were?" I say.

"You knew I was Colton Chase," he says. "Zoe, I am that person. I am the person who has built companies and has made a great many people rich. You and I lay under the stars together and planned to save the world. That was really Colton and Zoe. We're really going to do that."

My head is spinning and I feel the need to sit down. I spot a bench by the back door of the restaurant. I sit down and put my head in my hands.

"You didn't tell me who you were," I say emphatically. "I didn't know you were Hades or, sorry, Plouton."

Colton kneels on his knees before me and takes my hands in his. I feel the warmth from his hands travel through my palms and fill my whole body. He searches for the splinter in my finger. With a soft stroke of his hand, the splinter is lifted out and the sting in my hand is gone. He takes my hand and brings it to his lips and kisses it. This time his warmth travels from my fingers and fills my chest. My heart is pulsing in my ears.

"Since the gods have fallen, there are many rules we have broken, but there is one that is incontrovertible. There are barriers. You must invite us into your world, and I in turn must invite you into mine."

"When you touched me in the shop, the barriers could fall. You ran away from me before it could go any further."

As we've been talking, a golden mare has trotted onto the plain. She boldly walks past the stallions and sidles up to me. She bows her head down to be patted. I take one hand away from Colton and gingerly give her nose a scratch.

"Maybe she's hungry," I say, "I wonder if we can get something from the kitchen for her."

The golden mare walks several feet away and begins to glow. Her mane and her coat vibrate and become electrified. Light pulses out from her chest and spreads until she is a ball of illumination. The light flashes and explodes and I am momentarily blinded. When my vision comes back, the horse is no longer standing there. Instead, I am looking at a beautiful woman in Grecian dress with hair the color of wheat.

"You are not taking another daughter, Plouton," the woman hisses at Colton.

"That's not my name now," Colton says, as he leaps to his feet. He puts his hand out towards her and a wall of fire shoots up, separating her from us. "It's a different world now and you know it. And she's not your daughter, Demeter."

"She's someone's daughter!" Demeter shouts over the crackling flames, "and her mother can't be here to speak for herself now. You are not going to do to her what you did to Persephone and me!" Demeter's golden eyes turn a dark amber in her anger.

Colton stares at her then looks at me. "This is my ex-mother-in-law," he says. He turns his back to Demeter and addresses me. "She's not a fan, as you might expect. The way Persephone and I started was not right. It forever tainted our relationship that she didn't start by having a choice to go to the Underworld. Things were different then. I lived alone in the Underworld. I didn't understand anything outside of my shadowy realm. But now I've seen the world and I understand people beyond their shades. Zoe, you have a choice of whether you come with me. No one is going to force you."

He waves his hand and the wall of flame disappears. A scorched line of soil is left in its place. He turns to Demeter and says in a low tone, "In the end, I didn't force Persephone either. She chose me."

Demeter's dark amber eyes turn almost black. She steps nearer to the scorched line and says forcefully, "Do not choose him. I know your mother. She is prevented from being here, but in the time I've spent with her, you are all she talks about. Don't leave her for this. Choose your family."

"You know my mother?" I say in surprise.

"Yes," Demeter says with a nod of her head. "She loves you. She loves you as much as I loved my daughter, Kore. When he took my baby, I wandered the Earth crying for her with only Hecate to comfort me. If you leave your mother for him, she'll be in the same pain."

At the mention of Hecate, I remember my amulet. Katie said to use it if I was ever at a crossroads and she would come to me. This seems like a crossroads. I hold the amulet in my hand and think of Katie. Instantly, a translucent image of Katie appears, like a hologram. She stands facing me on the scorched line left by the fire, a shining lantern in each hand. She's dressed as I first saw her, in a hooded cloak that covers her hair.

Katie swings a lantern my way and the flame lights up her exquisite face. She scrutinizes me with keen, intelligent eyes, looking more like a knowing sorceress than the friend who lent me her clothes.

"You have a decision to make, Zoe," Katie says in a clear, strong voice. "May I help you chose your path?"

Chapter Twenty

Katie looks at me and smiles. It's a smile that says, *don't worry, I have all the answers, I'll help you find the right path.* She throws back her hood and shakes out her long, ebony curls. Holding her lanterns in the air beside her head, she turns slowly around. I am guessing she is trying to find her bearings. As her light shines in the face of Demeter, Katie stops briefly and gives her fellow goddess a bow of her head. Katie continues to rotate until she comes to Colton. She looks at him and drops a lantern. She turns quickly back to me.

"What is this?" she says. "I've been here before. Hades, Demeter, a pretty blonde girl, and four sweaty horses?" she turns and takes a step towards Colton. She points at him with a lantern and says, "What are you doing? Are you trying to seize this girl? Did you learn nothing from Persephone?" Katie looks angrier than I have ever seen her.

"Hecate, I am not seizing Zoe. She has a choice. That's why she called you. To help her with her choice," Colton says.

"Did she really choose to come here?" Demeter asks. "Or did you manipulate her into being here?" Demeter looks at me forlornly. The spitting anger that may have abetted her transformation has been replaced by despair. She holds her hand to her heart as if she is in pain.

"There are too many forces lined up to make this happen," Demeter says sadly. "I can't watch this happen again. I'm sorry."

Demeter walks towards the dozen horses milling about the edge of the caldera. Her retreating form becomes diffuse at the edges. A small explosion of light, and she has shed her goddess shape. The circle of horses lifts their heads in unison at the return of their golden mare queen. The horses toss their heads and whinny as she gallops towards them.

Katie looks at Demeter as she is welcomed by the horses. "It's all right, Demeter. I've got this." Katie turns back to Colton. "You used your delivery boy to get her here didn't you? Hermes was working from the beginning to get her here. All that talk about fleuranium and saving the earth was just a way for him to deliver you your package. You weren't going to do anything to help anyone. Neither of you care about that."

I thought it was my idea to go to Mars and get the fleuranium. It had never occurred to me that Hermes had manipulated things to make me think that. I wonder what else he could have engineered. Katie's apparition is shaking and coming in and out of focus. Her anger must be making it hard for her to maintain her presence here. Colton speaks calmly to her.

"It's true that I needed Hermes to help me meet with Zoe. But the choice to stay is hers. The plan to save the earth with fleuranium is real. I would never have come up with the plan if it weren't for Zoe. I need her to see it through. It doesn't work without her. She's my muse." Katie turns away from him with a scowl and looks at me.

"Hermes has been lying. No surprise, he's the god of lies after all." Her flickering form disappears then reappears faintly. She is obviously too upset about the news of Hermes' betrayal to help me.

Katie reaches down to pick up her fallen lantern. She crosses both of her arms across her chest, a lantern in each hand. "I can't stay here. I must go. I will send someone to help you. May you choose wisely." With a shimmer of light, Katie is gone.

I am alone with Colton Chase under the moon and the stars. How different this is from the last time we were together under a night sky.

Colton holds out his hand to me. "End of the world crises tend to accelerate things. Could we take a few steps back and have the dinner we planned?" he says.

I've come this far. I guess there is no reason not to have dinner with the Lord of the Underworld. I take his hand and we begin to walk to the front of the restaurant. I feel the usual flood of warmth I feel when he touches me. Before he can try the door, I say, "I don't think they are open. I tried the door earlier." *When I was running in terror away from you and fearing the earth would open up and swallow me.*

Colton glances at the door and says, “Oh no, that restaurant hasn’t opened yet. They have their grand opening next month. We aren’t eating there. We’re eating here.” He gestures to the empty caldera.

Colton brings his hands together in front of his chest and closes his eyes. He repeats a sentence in a language I don’t recognize over and over and it takes on a rhythmic quality. I realize he’s chanting.

Like a supplicant, he raises his hands pressed together high above his head and he chants into the sky. His hands become a beacon for the moonlight and they shine in iridescent light. I look up at the moon and see its brilliance is increasing. Light projects from the moon like a spotlight onto the caldera. I can see every crack and fissure in the illuminated canyon.

Smoke starts to stream from the breaks in the canyon. The horses up above on the rim of the caldera kick and paw nervously. The caldera fissures expand and more smoke comes billowing out. The horses, including the mare Demeter, gallop away from the caldera towards the plain behind the restaurant. The caldera ruptures split open and flames leap out. Fire runs along the lines of the ruptures, causing them to expand and grow into connected rivers of flame. Within seconds, the caldera has transformed into an inferno.

Colton brings his hands down from the sky and opens his eyes. He stops chanting and spreads his arms wide. The flames dissolve into a hail of ashes. He takes a deep breath and blows a long exhale of air. The ashes swirl into a tornado of cinders that fill the caldera. A mountain of ash is formed. Colton brings his hands together and points them at the mountain. The mountain dissolves in a veil of smoke.

The smoke clears and all at once the caldera is transformed into a glittering city of silver and golden towers. The spiraling roofs are topped with diamonds and emeralds. A crystal bridge is suspended between the edge of the caldera where we are standing and into the caldera itself. Two men are crossing the bridge towards us carrying a small, fully set table above their heads. Another pair of men are behind them, each carrying a tufted, throne-like chair. They set the table and chairs down in front of us.

“I thought we could have dinner with a view of my Underworld home,” Colton says. He pulls out a chair for me and I take a seat in stunned silence.

Waiters with covered platters of food trek across the bridge. One of them carries a bottle of wine. He uncorks it and pours us each a glass.

"To world health," Colton says. I look at my glass and I hesitate. Am I in the Underworld right now, and if I drink, will I have to stay here? Colton seems to understand my hesitation because he says, "I am only showing you what is under the caldera. We're not inside of it. There's no tricks here. I just wanted you to see my home."

The wine-glass is cut-glass crystal. I think the only other time I've seen anything like it is in pictures from royal weddings. I take a sip and feel the heaviness of the glass in my hands.

The server is standing by waiting for my reaction to the wine. "It's good," I say. He smiles and nods and walks over to the edge of the caldera, ready to serve us again.

"I didn't learn about the nymphs of the Underworld," I say. "What type is he?"

Colton takes a sip of wine before answering. "The Underworld nymphs are called Lampades. They were originally torch-bearing nymphs of Hecate. Zeus gifted them to me." I feel the blood drain from my face. I cannot forget that I am with a god who takes what he wants.

"That sounds a lot like slavery," I say. I expect his eyes to turn hard again. What is there to stop him from scooping me up now and carrying me across that crystal bridge? Colton blinks and instead of growing hard, his eyes look softer.

"I know," Colton says, "but that's my brother, that's not me. Once I talked to the Lampades and found out they had no choice to be with me, I refused to take them. I built the city you see here so that they could have a home they would enjoy."

"Then I offered them a place with me. The ones who are here, came here willingly. I also worked it out with Hecate so that she didn't feel I was stealing anyone. She was happy I could offer them a home. Her days as supreme goddess were long gone and her Lampades were sitting idle. She was happy I could offer them something."

Colton is looking at me with dark, warm eyes. I am starting to think that maybe Zeus is the cause of both of our problems. Zeus is the one who offered up Persephone to him like she was a stray dog. Colton was stuck in the dungeon of Earth and didn't know any better. At least he tried to change once he found out the truth.

A server surreptitiously places a salad in front of me and then slips away into the night. I take up my silver-plated salad fork and poke at the nightshade tomatoes. I feel so confused. Colton has been in my nightmares but he's also been in my dreams. A dinner like this under the stars with him was all I wanted.

It's true that Hermes helped me get you here," Colton says, "but it's only because I could see your shade growing stronger. Once your mother deserted you again, I was afraid that your shade would be all that was left.

"I am so glad to see you whole again. Now that you are here, it's all up to you whether you stay with me. My city is open to you." He gestures towards the city of silver and gold beneath us. I look down at the streets paved with diamonds and aquamarines. The soaring, jewel-topped spirals twinkle in the moonlight.

My eyes travel upwards to the sky and I see something. A flying vessel is coming within range of the caldera.

"Is that a helicopter coming to the restaurant?" I say.

Colton puts down his glass and stands up. "No," he says, "I think it's a spaceship."

It gets closer to us and now I can see it is definitely not a helicopter. Hovering above the caldera is a spaceship. It briefly stays stationary, then soars over our heads. It is moving quickly but I have time to glimpse the olive tree insignia on the side of the ship. Athena must have finally returned to Earth with Brandon.

"That's Athena!" I say excitedly, as I jump up from my seat. I run towards the plain at the back of the restaurant, closely followed by Colton.

The small herd of horses grazing on the plain run off into the wilderness as the ship prepares to land. The only horse remaining from the herd is the golden mare Demeter. She trots over to join the four black stallions Colton had watered earlier.

The ship lands, causing a shower of dust to fly up in its wake. Some of the dust lands in my eyes and throat, causing me to cough but I don't care. Brandon is back and he's alive. I smile in anticipation as I wait for the door to open.

Colton looks over at me with knitted brows. I see him looking at me and say, "Athena's got your fleuranium. I didn't know if I was ever going to see that ship again."

The door to the ship slides open. I expect Athena to come bounding out first, but instead Brandon appears at the door. He looks into the dark plain with concentration until his eyes land on me. Our eyes meet and he breaks into a big smile. He jumps down from the ship onto the plain and comes walking swiftly towards me. I clap my hands in excitement and then run towards him.

I reach him and he picks me up in a hug and spins me around. I look up into his beaming face and see his sparkling eyes. His head starts to bend and I feel he is going to kiss me. Remembering Colton right behind us, I pull back so that I can speak.

"Brandon, I'm so happy to see you. I didn't know what had happened to you."

"I'm happy to see you too," Brandon says. He leans into me again in kissing range. I take my hand and place it on his chest to stop him from coming closer.

"You remember Colton Chase?" I say. "Let me introduce you to him." Brandon drops his arms from around my waist and steps back. The smile disappears from his face. He walks over to Colton and shakes his hand. The two of them stand shaking hands and staring at each other for a little too long. I run over to where they are so that I can get between them.

"Brandon helped me get the fleuranium," I say. "It's stored in Athena's ship. You should have got the rest from Hermes."

Colton drops Brandon's hand and stands back staring at him. "Hermes dropped it off with me," Colton says, "We've been waiting for Athena's ship. Thanks for your help, Brandon."

Brandon gives Colton a nod of his head in reply but doesn't say anything. I feel like the hostess at the most awkward cocktail party ever.

"Colton was showing me his home," I say.

"He has a home in Hades. Because… he is the god Hades. But he was called in the ancient world by his other name, Plouton, the god of wealth. Now he goes by Colton Chase. He's going to use his entrepreneur skills to help the planet. That about catches you up, I think."

Brandon's eyes grow large and his hand goes to the battle sword strapped around his waist. He lowers his head and looks intensely at Colton. The two of them are immersed in a testosterone-fueled staring contest.

"This is Hades?" Brandon says. "The god of the Underworld?" Brandon breaks eye contact with Colton and looks at me with a serious expression.

"We are at war with the Underworld. Zoe, you need to come with me right now," Brandon says.

"What do you mean?" I say, "How can we be at war? Where's Athena?"

"I dropped her off in a transport pod over Washington. She wanted to be there so she can attempt to control the airspace and prevent the Cyclopes from returning to Earth. Hera stirred up a revolution with her speech. The Cyclopes have declared war on Earth."

Colton steps forward and gets closer to me. "Zoe, this is ridiculous. There is no war going on. He doesn't know what he is talking about. The Cyclopes are not coming back to Earth."

Brandon steps in front of me and blocks Colton. He holds out his hand in front of him like a shield. "Don't you come any closer to her. Your Cyclopes want to take the Earth. Athena came upon one trying to commandeer her ship. It had dragged an Earthling into the ship and killed him. The Cyclops was feasting on his guts when Athena found them."

Brandon reaches into a leather bag connected to his waist. He pulls out the golden, bejeweled chalice so beloved by Ganymede. Its stem has been twisted and the sides are crushed. Brandon tosses the cup on the ground.

"It murdered Ganymede. Then it tried to attack Athena but she slayed it. It said it was killing in the name of Hera. Athena said the Cyclopes were storming the landing area and breaking into ships and stealing them. They are all heading back here."

Colton picks up the damaged cup and turns it over slowly in his hand. He puts the cup down and looks over at me.

"If this is true, Zoe, you must come with me. I am the only one who can protect you." He holds out his hand to me.

Brandon kicks at the discarded cup.

"Don't trust him, he's one of them!" Brandon says, "The Cyclopes come from the Underworld. Come with me, Zoe. I will take you somewhere safe."

Colton is still holding out his hand to me. "There's nowhere safe he can take you. You need to come with me, Zoe."

While they have been talking, Demeter the mare has quietly trotted up behind Colton. Her eyes look alert and she appears to be listening. She bows her head at me and lowers her back as if to say, "Come away with me. Come with me and I will take you away from all of this."

Demeter is staying close by me because she lost her own daughter. However much millennia have passed, she is still feeling the trauma of the loss of her daughter. I know that pain. I lost my mother.

I look to one side of me and I see Colton. I know that Colton is a gorgeous man I crushed on for a long time. I don't know how I feel about him now. I know that he is the god of the Underworld and wealth. He has a plan to launch a world-saving company, and he says it can't be done without me. That's something I don't understand.

I also don't understand to what extent he employed Hermes and whatever other forces at his disposal to get me here. The earth may be imploding and we may be at war. I don't know what is going to happen to our planet. But I know I have to try to save it.

I look to the other side of me and I see Brandon. He's always had my back. We literally fought back to back against the other preschoolers in a water battle together when we were four. Sometimes I think he is in love with me, but then I remember reading his thoughts and I can't be sure.

There's a lot I didn't see. I didn't see the effect of losing his brother on him. He's lived multiple lives as a hero and I don't know what that means to his life going forward. I love him. He's my family. That I know.

Hephaestus says no one knows anything most of the time. *Everything will become clear with time. The things you know for certain, you hold onto with all your might.* I know Brandon is my family. I choose my family.

"Colton," I say, "I'm going to leave with Brandon. We've been in this life together for a long time. I don't understand anything of what is happening now. I need time to figure it out."

Colton takes a step towards me and then stops himself. There is a momentary flicker of pain in his eyes, then his face turns stony. I see his eyes harden, and at last I can see how they match with those cold spheres that stared out at me from beneath his copper helmet. He is two beings. I wonder if Colton, the man of my dreams, is now locked forever inside the god that haunted my nightmares.

He grows larger as I look at him, and his features grow sharper. He is now Plouton, Lord of the Underworld. His dark sovereignty emanates from him, causing me to take several steps back.

Plouton takes a last, grim look at Brandon and me. There is death in those eyes. He is its intimate friend. He runs his fingers through his black hair and then brings his hand down to form a fist. With his other hand he encloses his fist, as if he is seeking to contain the power within him. Without even putting on his helmet, Plouton mounts his motorcycle. He revs the bike and takes off in a hail of dust, his black hair flowing in the wind. The four black stallions rear up and charge off after him.

The lone mare Demeter trots up beside me. I pat Demeter's head and she shakes her mane at me. Her big, golden eyes close as I softly stroke her velvet cheek. Her eyes open and there is a look of such sadness there. She will forever be a mother bearing the loss of her daughter. She turns from me and slowly trots away.

Brandon holds out his hand and I clasp it tightly. I spent most of the last year floating above the earth and not really being part of it. I have just learned that a piece of me was living beneath the earth as a shade. Holding Brandon's hand, I am grounded and whole. With connection I can do anything. I can save the earth. I can fly to the stars.

We walk together into the waiting ship. After we close the door, I look out the window for any sign of Plouton, but he is gone. I look out over the plain and see the tops of the gold and silver spires in the distance. They break into a thousand, shiny pieces and within seconds they are gone. The Underworld city has disappeared into its home. The caldera has returned to its volcanic slumber. Demeter the Golden mare stands alone on the plain.

I turn to Brandon and he puts his arms around me.

"I love you. I'll take care of you," Brandon whispers.

"I love you, too," I whisper back. "We'll take care of each other." *And all the earth and sky* – comes a thought in my head.

I kiss him and he kisses me back with all the ardor of a lover after a long journey. It's our first kiss born in open love. I don't know where I am going but I know where I am. I am with my family.

THE END

The story continues! Coming Soon: ***Underworld Rising – Book 2 in the Lost Gods Series by Jane Frkovich.***

Get a free story and sign up for the author newsletter, please email janefrkovich@telus.net **or please visit** www.janefrkovich.com**.**

Author Note

Thank you for reading my book. There's a lot more to be said but it's going to take three books to say it. I hope you come back to see how the story ends. I would really appreciate it if you could leave a review for the book on the page where you purchased it. Book reviews are how others find the book. I also want to hear what you think. Authors spend a lot of time by themselves typing away at the keyboard. We spin our stories and they become real to us. Then we send them out into the world and hope they connect with other people. If this connected with you I would love to know that. I promise to read what you have written, as you have read what I wrote. Happy reading and reviewing!

Manufactured by Amazon.ca
Bolton, ON

31952966R00116